A RAFT OF SWORDS

DUNCAN KYLE was born in Bradford, Yorkshire, a few hundred yards from the house where J. B. Priestley grew up.

He started his career as a junior reporter on the *Bradford Telegraph and Argus*, later going on to the *Leicester Mercury* and the *Yorkshire Post*. In the mid-fifties he joined *John Bull* magazine – which later became *Today* – in London and from there he went on to become editorial director at Odhams where he wrote his first novel, *A Cage of Ice*.

It was the success of this book which persuaded him to become a full-time writer and to fulfil his long-held ambition to live deep in the country. He now lives in Suffolk with his wife and three children.

He has written six novels, each more successful than the last: *Black Camelot* is the latest.

DUNCAN KYLE

A Raft of Swords

FONTANA / Collins

First published in the UK in 1974 by William Collins Sons & Co Ltd
First issued in Fontana Books 1975
Second Impression December 1977
Third Impression April 1978
Fourth Impression October 1979
Fifth Impression September 1980

© 1973 by Rupert Crew Ltd

Made and printed in Great Britain by
William Collins Sons & Co Ltd Glasgow

This one for
Angus – our
fiend the
Scottish terror

AUTHOR'S NOTE

Submersibles are manufactured in several countries, including Canada. The *Tyee* submersible I have described bears resemblances to most of them but is not based upon any specific craft. Marine Technology Ltd. is an imaginary company and no resemblance to existing companies in the field of submarine exploration is intended. All characters are imaginary and any resemblances to persons living or dead are coincidental.

BOOK ONE
I

Under the penal code of the Soviet Union, the lending of money at high interest rates for profit is an offence, punishable, if the crime is of sufficient gravity, by death. The seriousness of the penalties does not, however, prevent the existence of loan sharks; it merely makes them extremely careful. Interest rates being, as always, proportionate to risks, they are naturally very high indeed.

On a late evening, in September 1971, an Armenian money-lender waited quietly in an alley off Gorki Prospekt in the Pacific coast city of Vladivostok. Behind him, in deep shadow, his two bodyguards stood ready. At each end of the alley stood a look-out, in case a militia patrol should interrupt the impending transaction. The moneylender was satisfied that his precautions were adequate.

He was not aware, however, of an event which had already made nonsense of his arrangements. His victim, a twenty-four-year-old wireless operator in the Soviet Pacific fleet, had been borrowing money in order to provide additional comforts for his sick mother, and the moneylender's calculation was based first upon the son's unmistakable concern, and second upon the disciplinary effectivenss of his threat to the mother's life in the event of non-payment. The arrangement was now two months old.

What the moneylender did not know was that the sailor's mother had died, suddenly and unexpectedly, two hours earlier. By morning he would have been informed, but morning was far away. The sailor now coming to meet him was no longer the large, gentle young man the moneylender had been dealing with. He was in a black frenzy of grief, angry almost beyond sanity at the brutal unfairness of his mother's death. She was so young; only forty-three. And good. The sailor asked him-self, bitterly and endlessly, why it should happen like this. And

9

to her. Why? He wanted to smash something, anything, to damage the harsh world that had treated him and his mother with this uncaring horror. Or perhaps he should kill himself with the knife in his pocket. Perhaps if he died too. . . .

Because the formalities concerned with her death had kept him at the hospital, the sailor was late for his appointment. He moved quickly, head down, seeing nothing as he walked, his mind numbed with shock and anger.

Had the lookout at the end of the alley seen the sailor's face, he would have signalled with his arm and the bodyguards would have moved closer. But he did not. The moneylender stepped forward, looking ostentatiously at his watch. 'You are late,' he snapped. 'Give it to me quickly.'

The sailor stared at him blankly. 'My mother. She – '

But the moneylender was not interested in sickness reports. Nor, because the alley was dark, could he see the sailor's face. Had he listened, or had he seen, he might have lived. But he was cold and impatient and by nature authoritarian. He gave the boy no chance to tell him what had happened. 'The money. Quick. Or else!'

Tears in his eyes, the sailor hit him with his fist on the side of the head, and the moneylender staggered back, reaching for the pistol inside his furs. He was not quick enough, nor were his bodyguards. As soon as the sailor saw the pistol emerging, he pulled out the knife he had been fingering and stabbed hard, forward and up, into the moneylender's gut.

Then he ran. Because he was young and fit and because his emotions were violent and confused, adrenalin was pumping into his bloodstream. He knocked the lookout effortlessly aside, easily outdistanced the bodyguards, and returned to barracks where he lay in his bunk, weeping quietly until he fell, emotionally exhausted, asleep.

The moneylender lasted four days. For most of that time he was under deep sedation and so unable to speak to the militiamen who waited by his bed. The militia had an excellent idea of what had happened, the Armenian had long been suspected of usury, so the odds were that a customer had stabbed him.

They knew, however, that the Armenian would admit nothing, and for obvious reasons.

Still, when the murderous pain broke through the sedation and the Armenian regained brief consciousness, the militiamen asked who had stabbed him.

Weakly the moneylender shook his head.

The militiaman did not mince words. 'You're dying. Do you want your murderer to go unpunished?'

He waited. The moneylender's eyes had closed and remained closed. Then they opened again. 'The doctor,' he whispered.

His voice was almost inaudible and the doctor bent low to listen. 'Is it . . . true I'm . . . dying?'

The doctor hesitated, then nodded. 'I am sorry. It is true.'

The moneylender lay still, gathering breath and strength to speak. His eyes met the militiaman's and he nodded almost imperceptibly. 'Nikita Ivanov,' he whispered. 'Sailor . . .' He wanted to say more, but could not.

There were two hundred and eighty Ivanovs in the Pacific fleet. Nine bore the forename Nikita, and the patronymic, which would have been useful, was unknown. By the time the militia had decided which man they wanted, Nikita Ivanov's mother had been cremated and her son was three days out at sea. The navy was unsure when he would be back. In the meantime, his captain would be informed and Nikita Ivanov would be placed under arrest on board his ship.

The incident was to have a far-reaching effect upon an adventure that was to bring the Soviet Union to a situation more uncomfortable, internationally, than any event since the Cuban missile crisis.

Several weeks earlier, the Soviet oceanographic research vessel *Acadamecian Vashurin*, owned by the Pacific Oceanography Research Institute, also at Vladivostok, but now, as she frequently was, on Underwater Defence Secretariat secondment, sailed for the island of Sakhalin to make a routine examination of certain long-term experiments under way in the coastal waters. Among the scientists on board was Arkady Mikhailovich Semichastny, a senior research metallurgist from the Leningrad

Institute, under whose direction one of the experiments was being carried out.

Semichastny, a cheerful, fair man of medium height, was originally from Murmansk, the Soviet Union's only major ice-free European port. He had arrived at the Institute via service as a scientific officer in the Soviet Navy. From his father, a harbour pilot, Semichastny had learned a love of the sea, which had only gradually been overtaken by his fascination with the behaviour of metals. Eventually, and happily, the two interests had come together until his principal line of research was into the behaviour of immersed metals. But in these days of specialization, even that was too wide an area, and gradually his attention had focused upon the metallurgy of seabed anchorages. Like many Soviet scientists he was bearded. Unlike many others, he was also gregarious, extroverted and athletic.

As a boy, he had watched the battered British convoys steaming thankfully into Murmansk after their desperate running battles along the Norwegian coast and round North Cape. He had watched them unload tanks, aeroplanes, guns and ammunition for the then hard-pressed Red Army, and though at school the official line was that the imperialists were merely using Russia in their own defence and that the supplies were both inadequate and inferior, Semichastny had actually *seen* the state of the arriving ships, the dragging weariness of their crews, and had developed a lively, if furtive, admiration for them. He had learned English, both at school and at home, because his father spoke it well. As the years passed his admiration inevitably faded and his English rusted from lack of practice, but it returned and improved when, in the mid-sixties, he spent two years attached to the Soviet delegation at the United Nations in New York, where his principal function was to gather intelligence about Western progress in undersea warfare. He was aware of and amused by the reaction his name sometimes evoked among knowledgeable and sophisticated people. Another Semichastny, no relation, had once headed one of the KGB directorates. Often, when he was introduced to somebody new, he would see eyes widen and the quick flicker of fear.

While the *Acadamecian Vashurin* rode comfortably on the low Pacific swell, Semichastny briefed his divers. He often wished he could go down himself, but regulations forbade it and anyway at forty-four he was too old to take up such physically punishing activity. Carefully he described the television pictures he wanted shown, the samples to be brought to the surface. Then he accompanied the divers out on deck and watched the helmets screwed down and the awkward photographic equipment secured on mesh diving trays.

When the two divers disappeared beneath the water, Semichastny entered his laboratory and sat in front of the cathode-ray tube upon which the divers' TV pictures would be projected. Spread in front of him, at the console, were dated pictures of previous observations, going back more than five years. The progress of accretion of marine life was steady; every inspection showed a greater encrustation; but it progressed as expected. Today there would be more, and he wondered what drew marine creatures so forcefully to steel; the process was as inexplicable as the moth's fatal attraction to the lethal flame.

In front of him, the pale, even, flickering grey of the tube changed suddenly as the underwater TV cameras focused upon the experiment. He watched thoughtfully as the camera panned over it, starting at the bottom with the big concrete block which kept the whole thing firm on the ocean bed.

'Stop!' His voice in the laboratory microphone was carried down the speaking line to the divers below. 'Show me that again.'

'Yes, comrade.'

He watched the slow pan again, frowning this time. 'Hold it there.' Then, after a moment, 'I want still pictures of that bend.'

'Yes, comrade.'

He waited until the photographs had been taken, then ordered the inspection to continue. Nowhere else had the same irregularity occurred.

An hour later, with the excellent black-and-white stills in front of him, he wrote a signal which was immediately enciphered and transmitted first to the Soviet Naval Shore Communication Station at Vladivostok, and from there on urgent priority to a staff captain in the office of Admiral of the Fleet Sergei Gorshkov, Commander-in-Chief of the naval forces of the Soviet Union. From there the signal was relayed immediately to Gorshkov himself aboard the old *Sverdlov* class cruiser from which he was observing Black Sea Manoeuvres.

Gorshkov looked at the signal, read it quickly, then again more slowly. It read:

Anchorage irregularities in control experiment Project Sword. Request permission to conclude experiment. Condition blue.

'What's blue today?' Gorshkov demanded of an aide.

'Dangerous, sir.'

'Signal permission. I want a detailed report as soon as possible. In person.'

'Yes, sir.'

'And I want my helicopter. Get it warmed up and have an aircraft meet me at Sevastopol. I'm going to Moscow. Who's the man on Project Sword?'

'Semichastny, sir.'

Gorshkov grunted. 'Bound to be bad news, then.'

Gorshkov wasted no time. In Moscow, a few hours later, when the details had been presented to him again, he studied the giant war map in his basement headquarters, deciding which of the units should be used.

His orders sent, he returned at once to the Black Sea.

II

One hundred fathoms down, the Y (for Yankee) class submarine drifted in a noisy ocean. For several hours a school of whales had sported near by, following and inspecting this vast, silent brother ghosting the cold, concealing current. In his padded chair the captain sat rock still, listening with satisfaction through his headphones to the whistling whales and to the more distant but steady electronic clutter from an uncountable army of shrimps. The captain's hands, arms, feet ached from the effort of immobility; at shortening intervals he experienced an urge to make some kind of violent movement, to shout, to laugh, to sing. Fifty-three hours of silent running had now been accomplished; he did not know how many more lay ahead, so, like the rest of his crew, he fought his impulses and forced himself to concentrate upon each moment rather than the next or the last.

Glancing at the oxygen gauge, he noted that in twenty minutes he must fit a new bottle and found himself looking forward to making the few deft movements involved. The oxygen, he reflected, had been a good idea. The air scrubbers made very little sound, but even very little was too much and the ability to proceed without them had reduced noise levels within the sub to little more than the sound of men breathing. For more than two days and nights no tap had been turned, no lavatory flushed, no cup used. The men sucked water through tubes from plastic containers and ate the processed low-residue pastes which had been developed for space flight.

His eyes flicked round the control room. At their consoles the warrant officers who monitored the inertial guidance system, the sonar and radar mechanisms, the hundreds of gauges which provided information about depth, posture, and air and battery levels, sat staring with forced concentration as the sub slid carefully along the cold tunnel formed by a deep current in a warmer sea. She was making an average six knots, so they had travelled three hundred miles or a little more. With luck they could be clear already, but he was not prepared to allow luck a place among the factors which governed his actions. The Pacific defensive cable networks SOSUS and CAESAR, with their extraordinarily powerful sensors and boosters, were thought to be accurately plotted, but assumptions were not enough; new cables were being laid constantly. One day, he thought wryly, the Earth would be like a ball of string, wrapped in loop after loop of insulated multi-cored copper wire. Only last month, he knew, two cable-laying ships had appeared together, sailing a complex series of deception patterns and then parting, one to race north, the other south, so that the observing sub had had to make a choice and follow one. Where had the other spider laid his web?

The captain realized suddenly that his fingers were tapping lightly on the padded arm of his chair and stopped them, pursing his lips in anger at his body's disobedience. He glanced again at the little line of warrant officers, each of whom met his eye and gave a small shake of the head. Apart from the whales and the shrimp, the submarine was alone. A hundred or so miles more and the current would begin its eastward swing; then he would be round the corner, not necessarily out of electronic surveillance reach, but giving little indication of the direction of his approach. It was even possible that this particular cold layer was unknown to the opposition; it was, after all, comparatively narrow in both depth and width, and fairly newly discovered. If, at the end of another hundred and fifty miles, another day and night of silence, there were no indications of observation, then the chance might be taken. He looked forward to giving the order to descend to one-eighty, and raising speed to forty knots. He found the words forming in his mouth, almost uttered, and then controlled himself savagely. It was time to change the oxygen bottle, to give his disobedient body a task.

Eleven hours later, the sonar warrant officer picked up his pen, wrote four words rapidly on a sheet of paper and passed it to the captain. The captain looked at the man's face, knowing already from its expression the nature of the message. Then he lowered his eyes to read the confirmation: WARSHIP TWELVE THOUSAND CLOSING. He turned the paper towards the sonar man and pointed interrogatively at the word WARSHIP. The man nodded, in no doubt about the information given to him by his instruments and interpreted by his experience.

Now the silence changed character. What had been before, an ache of boredom was now all tension. The sonar warrant officer lifted his hands, fingers spread. Ten. A minute passed and his thumb folded. Nine. The little finger. Eight. Seven. The captain's eyes closed tightly in mourning for his mission. One part of his mind told another that the sub might not have been spotted, that the warship might pass by without noticing. But in his heart he knew.

Three. Two. On the control deck the little group of men sat staring at their instruments as the minutes slid by. One. Sadly the sonar technician turned and shook his head. A minute later he wrote again and passed the slip to the captain. Two words: STATIONARY OVERHEAD.

The submarine went through several prescribed procedures designed to shake off pursuit; its pursuer remained obstinately above. A few hours later another warship arrived and the captain knew there was no point to further manoeuvring. He ordered the ballast tanks blown and took the sub up through the gloom into the light, opened the hatch on top of the sail and watched bitterly as the two submarine-hunting destroyers circled him delightedly, like terrier puppies round a hedgehog. Then he ordered the radio operator to transmit the code word for failure. This failure was not the first.

III

In spite of the efforts of the small army of headscarved women who had scraped energetically at the cobblestones of Red Square since five o'clock, a large part of the road surface was still, at seven, covered in a thin layer of snow that was turning rapidly into slush under the wheels of cars and lorries. More than ever, people stood well back as the curtain-windowed Zis limousines sluiced through the slush towards the Kremlin gate, flinging the black, icy mess aside.

In one of the cars, gnawing nervously on his lower lip, sat Arkady Mikhailovich Semichastny. The reasons for his nervousness were two: first, the level of the meeting he was to attend; secondly, the knowledge that when he faced the meeting, he would be unable to give facts and figures, chapter and verse. He would be able to offer suppositions, extrapolations, conclusions and that was all. They would expect more, and he had no more to offer.

For Semichastny the day had begun early. At four he had been picked up at his tiny flat in the academic housing block at the Leningrad Institute. He had checked quickly that his briefcase held the necessary documents (he had also checked it three times the previous evening). Then, at the airport he had supervised the loading of a long, glass-fibre box into the military transport jet which then flew him to Sheremetyevo Airport, Moscow. Now the ordeal, which even minutes ago had seemed unreal, was coming visibly closer. Through the windscreen he could see the dark red of Lenin's mausoleum, the grey Kremlin walls, the brilliant Red Star high in the sky above them. Semichastny was not ambitious; he was interested neither in power nor the company of the great; a few minutes away lay a terrifying weight of both. He wished the day were over. Had he known what lay ahead, he would have wished it even more fervently.

Others of the black limousines that hurried across the early-morning misery of the Square carried senior officials from ministries and departments. For most, the day was beginning unusually early and for some it would be wasted. But each represented an area of the state's resources and not until after certain decisions had been made would it become clear which of the resources would be needed. Until that moment, they would wait and listen.

As Semichastny's fibreglass box was unloaded from the boot of the car and carried carefully inside, the Minister for Foreign Affairs of the Union of Soviet Socialist Republics, Andrei Gromyko, stood at his office window, five floors above. When the rest of those attending the meeting had taken their places, he would be informed. Meanwhile he sipped a glass of lemon tea and watched as the the box was unloaded and the other cars disgorged their passengers.

There was a knock on his door and his private secretary stepped into the room. 'They are all there, Comrade Minister. It's seven-thirteen.'

'Admiral Gorshkov?'

'Is preceding you. He is on his way now.'

Gromyko nodded, took a final sip of tea, and walked briskly out of the office. He glanced at the lift, thought of the couple of hours he would now spend seated, and decided to walk down the stairs. He entered the committee room a few seconds before seven-fifteen a.m., walked to his place in the middle of the table, seated himself and looked round. The table was a long oval; every face was visible from the Foreign Minister's chair. Several faces he knew, one or two he did not. From behind his chair, his private secretary handed him a sheet of paper with a seating plan showing the name, department and function of each man. The Foreign Minister read it through slowly and in silence, glancing up, as he absorbed each name, to identify the individual. When he had finished, he handed the plan back to his private secretary. He would no longer need it. Admiral of the Fleet Sergei Gorshkov sat on his right. Beyond Gorshkov, and in order round the table, were Lieutenant-General K. B. Kirilin, deputy director of the *Glavnoye Razvedyvatelnoye Upravlenie*, General Staff Intelligence of the Red Army (known as GRU and one of the Soviet Union's two principal intelligence arms); Lieutenant-General J. V. Khlin of Air Force Intelligence, a department whose functions were principally strategic; Professor A. M. Marasov, controller of the design laboratory at Baikonur; Academician N. S. Pinchuk, head of Advanced Physics at the Central Scientific and Research Institute; Rodion Shenko, principal of the North American department of the Ministry of Foreign Affairs; Vice-Admiral S. V. Tolstikov, Controller of Oceanographic Research; A. M. Semichastny of the Leningrad Institute; and finally, on the Foreign Minister's left, Lieutenant-General Ivan Zarubin, head of the main arm of Russian espionage and counter-espionage abroad, the First Chief Directorate of the *Komitat Gosudarst-vennoi Bezopastnosti* (KGB). In chairs away from the table, sat various aides, briefcases round their feet, ready at a moment's notice to supply information not instantly available in their superiors' heads.

Andrei Gromyko spoke, as always, quietly. 'Good morning. I have called you here today, comrades, to examine and discuss a matter which may be of no immediate importance.' Around the table there appeared a few frowns and puzzled glances. 'You will therefore wonder why this meeting has been called so urgently and so early in the morning. The reason is simply this: though the matter *may*, as I said, be of no immediate importance, it is possible that it may be of the most urgent and vital importance to the long-term position of the Soviet Union in international affairs.'

The faces watching him were still and attentive. Gromyko did not waste words. 'To explain this, it is necessary to digress for a moment into a brief review of the development of our national capacity for offence and defence. Admiral Gorshkov.'

Gorshkov, a heavy man in his early sixties, whose long, down-curving nose somehow suggested his brilliance, remained seated, as had Gromyko. The others, if and when required to speak, would stand. His voice was low and somewhat gravelly, his sentences deceptively simple. 'The Americans developed their Polaris programme very quickly,' he began. 'They employed in its design and building a planning technique, then new, called critical path analysis, with which you are all now familiar. The result was that the Polaris rocket went from design to deployment in one and a half years.' He paused. 'Until that moment, we had had a considerable lead in rocketry. We have now caught them up again, possibly surpassed the Americans. But the Soviet Union, comrades, did not build its counterpart to Polaris in eighteen months. There was a gap. A very long gap. And, while it lasted, we were vulnerable in a way we did not like. So, until we could create our own force of nuclear submarines equipped with rockets which could be fired from beneath the surface, it was necessary to develop an effective if temporary counter. This weapon was a product of two separate streams of research: one for the short-range, so-called cruise missile, which remains a valuable naval weapon, the other for the underwater launching techniques pioneered in the Polaris programme. This new weapon, which finally came into production in 1964, was a short-range missile with a nuclear warhead, capable of being fired at pre-selected targets. It was fired, comrades, by radio signal, from launching ramps in strategic locations in comparatively shallow water.'

Gorshkov looked round, aware that to several of those present this was hardly news. 'The system was given the code-name Sword. As our force of rocket-launching submarines came into service, Sword became obsolescent. However, the undersea platforms and the Sword missile itself proved to have remarkable durability. Long immersion had very little effect; our control experiments demonstrated its continued effectiveness. So, although some installations were ultimately removed for a variety of reasons, others were left in position.

'One such Sword installation, comrades, is now our problem.'

Gromyko nodded. 'This year the Soviet Union was among the signatories of an international agreement under which, with certain provisos, the major powers agreed to co-operate in the peaceful development of the oceans.' Lips twitched among his audience. 'I know. But we are signatories. The treaty specified localized conferences on future development co-operation in several areas, one of which, and by far the largest, is the Pacific Ocean. I shall shortly be attending the Pacific conference, in Vancouver, a city on the West Coast of Canada.' He turned, nodding to his secretary, and a moment later curtains parted to reveal a screen at one end of the conference room. On it, back projected, was a map of the North-Western United States and Western Canada. The secretary crossed to the map and pointed with a forefinger to a small circle upon which was a representation of a rocket.

'You see, comrades,' Gromyko went on, 'that the installation is off the northern tip of Vancouver Island. There are six Sword missiles, each programmed to a specific target. The targets are: the Royal Canadian Navy headquarters at Esquimault at the southern end of Vancouver Island; the city of Vancouver itself; three important manufacturing centres of the air and aerospace industries, the Boeing plants at Seattle, Everett and Blaine; and the port of Seattle itself. The missiles have a range of up to four hundred miles. All the targets are within it. Any questions?'

Silence.

Beneath the table, Semichastny's palms were sweating. Any time now they'd be after him like a pack of wolves. If he didn't know, *why* didn't he know? How dared he come here so ill-informed! His eyes flicked from Gromyko to Gorshkov, to the terrifying KGB man Zarubin. Wishing he were a million miles away, he none the less forced himself to concentrate as Gorshkov again took up the exposition.

'When the missiles were first placed in position,' Gorshkov was saying, 'it was a comparatively simple matter. They could be, and often were, carried in merchant vessels. The ship merely stopped one dark night and lowered the complete installation into the water at a previously chosen and suitable site. Divers supervised its positioning. Sometimes a submarine acted as a work-horse for the correct positioning of heavy concrete retaining blocks. There were a few minor problems, but nothing very difficult.

'This,' he went on, 'was because access itself was not difficult. A submarine could approach most areas of the ocean with relative ease. That situation has now changed. Map please.'

Another slide was back-projected on to the screen, this time showing all of the North American and part of the South American continents. The most striking thing on the map was the presence, on both Atlantic and Pacific oceans, of a thing that looked a little like a spider's web. 'These,' Gorshkov said, 'are the underwater listening systems known by the code names SOSUS and CAESAR. They consist of lines of super-sensitive acoustic receivers which pick up the sounds made by submarines. The receivers are fixed to cables for the transmission of information to a central computer, which can instantly identify a vessel's "signature"; in other words, identify the distinctive sounds made by a particular vessel. Any questions?'

'As I understand it,' (the speaker was Air Force General Khlin) 'it is possible to locate and destroy cables.'

'Some, yes. Not all,' Gorshkov said. 'The cable systems are double, treble, even quadruple banked. Furthermore they are not easy to find. We destroy, they renew. So it proceeds. But, comrades, there is more. Currently under construction is a defensive system infinitely more sophisticated, named the Suspended Array System. In essence it consists of a vast, triangular frame, its three legs some ten miles apart, believe it or not, which will rest on the Atlantic and Pacific abyssal plains. They make use of the curious oceanic phenomenon which you, Admiral Tolstikov and you Comrade Semichastny, know well: that sound travels great distances through the cold lower layers of the ocean. Ultra-acute hydrophones, strung along the structures of the Suspended Array System, will be able to detect submarine noise throughout the entire Atlantic and most of the Pacific.' Gorshkov stopped speaking and for a moment or two there was silence.

Then Gromyko spoke again. 'We are still able to position submarines close to the North American coast. But now they know about them. The submarines are shadowed. Comrade Semichastny, open your box.'

Feeling both foolish and vulnerable, Semichastny rose and unfastened the catches of the fibreglass box which lay on a trestle behind his chair. 'Comrade Minister, you wish me to describe – ?'

'Of course.'

'Very well. The firing ramp is anchored – no, secured is a better word – to the ocean bottom as follows. Four large concrete blocks, each weighing roughly five tons, are laid in a square. It is unlikely they would move, but still possible. So each block is held in position by four conventional Danforth-type anchors. In twenty-three locations the system has worked perfectly over a period of years.'

Zarubin, The KGB chief, said, 'Don't boast. The facts alone.'

Semichastny swallowed. 'The firing ramp is fastened to the concrete blocks by chains, the advantage of this procedure lying in the flexibility of chain, which can give under pressure, but will return to its normal form once the pressure is removed. The chains were specially designed to facilitate this process. In addition, comrades, they received a coating of a durable plastic containing antifouling chemicals. So the pull of the four chains remained balanced and the build-up of encrustation of marine life was inhibited. This is understood?' He glanced from man to man, found they were all watching him impassively, and decided to take their silence as assent.

'We have maintained control experiments in various underwater locations since the first siting of Sword installations. In each case we have sought to match the general sea conditions to those prevailing on the Sword locations. I discovered recently that, in an experiment off the coast of the island of Sakhalin, whose waters closely resemble those of Vancouver Island, one chain has become so encrusted with marine life that it has begun to kink. In other words, it is twisted and can no longer straighten. Ultimately, it will snap, at which point, comrades, the launching ramp will become dangerously unstable.'

Zarubin asked the awkward question. 'How soon?'

Arkady Semichastny swallowed. 'It is impossible to say with accuracy, comrade.'

'What,' Zarubin pursued, 'is the precise condition of the chains off Vancouver Island?'

'I don't know. Probably similar.'

'When were they last inspected?'

'Four months ago.'

'And?'

'They were sound. So, at that time, were the chains of the Sakhalin experiment.'

'It seems to me,' Zarubin said coldly, 'that we are being asked to accept as dangerous fact a situation which is pure conjecture.'

'As I said at the beginning.' Gromyko spoke quietly. 'You will remember, General Zarubin, indeed all of you will remember, two past incidents which have a bearing here. First, consider the stupid action of the Pentagon in sending its spy planes over the Soviet Union at the time of the 1960 Summit Conference. The plane was shot down and Nikita Sergeyevich Khruschev felt himself compelled to abandon the conference in anger. In doing so he allowed the Americans to escape in part the consequence of their action.'

'Escape?' Zarubin questioned. 'The reverse is true. The

world became aware in the most dramatic way of American provocation.'

'Indeed they did. The world also began to suspect that the Soviet Union was rash, intemperate, and unsophisticated. After all, there was nothing new except wreckage. We knew about the spy planes already. Nikita Sergeyevich Khrushchev's celebrated outburst threw away a magnificent opportunity to exert powerful international pressure both at the Paris Summit and later. But, worse than that, it compelled us to have diplomatic sulks for years afterward. We had no flexibility. We had been so publicly angry that the anger could not be forgotten, by ourselves or anybody else. For years we were anchored by one leg to the memory of that incident. Our initiatives were slowed; opportunities were lost. We did not *use* the incident well.'

'If you say so, Comrade Minister.' Zarubin's voice was almost theatrically quiet and there was a tiny emphasis on the *you*. Semichastny felt his heart thud as he looked from one man to the other, horrified by these dangerous tides of dislike, of contempt, that could so easily flood over every man in the room.

Gromyko's mouth tightened in brief anger, but his voice remained gentle. 'The second case concerns the sending of missiles to Cuba. It is my belief that for the American, Kennedy, the rashness we exhibited in Paris was the key to that affair. He did not believe in our ultimate strength of purpose nor, at that moment, comrades, did we. The result was the heaviest reverse we have ever sustained in international affairs. That reverse, and the universal knowledge of it, changed our face for ever. The Soviet Union was no longer inexorable. Our forward impetus was halted. When Kennedy punched our nose we retired from the fight. We were unwilling for war and everybody knew it. Since then, as you know, we have pursued changed targets. We seek peace and co-operation. We no longer rattle rockets. We subvert, yes; harder than before. But we are everybody's friend as we wait and work. That is the legacy of Paris and Cuba.

'In the light of all this, comrades,' – Gromyko was ostensibly addressing them all, but the words were aimed clearly at Zarubin – 'what would be the effect internationally if Soviet missiles, armed, nuclear missiles, were discovered in another nation's territorial waters?'

'Unfortunate, but hardly surprising,' said Zarubin.

'Unfortunate, certainly.'

'But no more. We are strong enough to be self-sufficient.'

'Then let me put it this way. I have no wish, and the First Secretary and the Prime Minister agree, to be standing on Canadian soil, talking about international co-operation and trust, while armed nuclear missiles are bounding about in the water nearby.'

Zarubin bowed his head slightly. 'With respect, Comrade Minister, you would be well out of range. I assume there is no possibility of an actual firing.'

'There is *always* such a possibility,' Gromyko said softly. 'It may be great or small, but it is there. And even if an explosion did not occur, I should stand well within the range of the world's calumny. Who would trust the Soviet Union again? For years to come? Let us consider *not* the worst eventuality – explosion – but the next in magnitude. Suppose that the rockets were damaged and large quantities of radio-active material released. Radiation would first be detected, then it would be traced. The remains of the rockets would be found. If the guidance systems were found, they would be examined. The world would know the targets of the rockets.'

'Both sides have rockets permanently directed towards all the major strategic targets,' Zarubin said.

'The world would also know,' Gromyko went on, 'that the Soviet Union was prepared to risk radio-active contamination of centres of population in time of peace. That we talk peace while positioning rockets within the boundaries of a nation like Canada.'

'Boldness rarely fails,' Zarubin said.

'Unlike harvests,' Gromyko rejoined sharply. 'May I remind you that our wheat harvest this year was poor and that to feed our people we must buy from other countries? From one of two countries that have wheat to export? Preferably Canada.

If not Canada, the United States. The wheat is vital The days when starvation was tolerated in our country have gone, General Zarubin. It has been our achievement to banish hunger. Bellies are full everywhere. Except,' he added in a deliberately pointed afterthought, 'in the Lubianka.'

Still standing beside his box, Semichastny waited for the icy little argument to end, afraid that he might somehow be caught in between. He was alone and exposed, the only man on his feet.

But Admiral Gorshkov intervened. 'We must get them out,' he said. 'It is as simple as that.'

'Indeed it is.' Gromyko was smooth again, unruffled, one of the two or three men in Russia who, Semichastny thought, need not fear the KGB. Or was even *he* free of fear? He saw how Zarubin stared in cold silence at the Foreign Minister, but Gromyko refocused briskly on the rockets. 'Given the impossibility of approaching the site by ship or submarine, other methods must be employed. I summoned you here, comrades, in order that each of you, and each of your departments, should understand the situation, and be ready to offer any assistance that may be necessary. A number of things are clear. The operation is technical; it must be clandestine and it must be successful. Here is what I intend: a small committee consisting of you, Admiral Tolstikov; you, Comrade Semichastny. Professor Marasov or, more likely, one of his specialists who was involved in Project Sword. You, General Zarubin, or one of your North American specialists, and Comrade Shenko of my ministry. In three days, I want a plan. The plan must work. The rest of you will offer instant and total assistance in any of the committee's requirements. And you, Admiral Tolstikov, will chair the committee. Thank you, comrades.'

Gromyko rose, walked round the table and looked into Semichastny's box. The metallurgist rose quickly and stood rigidly beside it.

'This,' Gromyko said, 'is the offending chain?' His thin smile, etching deeper the already heavy lines of his face, was intended to put the other man at ease.

'Yes, Comrade Minister.'

The two-metre section of steel chain lay in a few inches of sea water. Though the water had been changed regularly, death had crept among the barnacles and limpets since the chain had been removed.

'It stinks,' Gromyko said quietly. 'The box and the whole situation.'

'Yes, Minister.'

Gromyko nodded. 'It is curious, is it not, how often events depend on one link in a chain?'

Zarubin had approached. He glanced at the chain, then at Semichastny. 'It appears,' he said, 'to be wringing its own neck.'

'That is true.'

'Let us be sure,' Gromyko said quietly, 'that it is the only neck to be wrung.'

The men not nominated for the committee departed quickly after a brief, almost silent breakfast. Professor Marasov took advantage of the Foreign Minister's suggestion that he appoint a deputy, and departed too. Zarubin, who could have done the same, predictably did not; he chose to have his cake and eat it. When the committee sat at 10 a.m. under Vice-Admiral Tolstikov's chairmanship, both Zarubin and his appointee, a KGB colonel named Belyaev, were present. Belyaev had at one time been at the embassy in Canada. The committee was now six strong, instead of five. Two of the six members were KGB.

'I see no need for a formal agenda, comrades,' Admiral Tolstikov said. 'I suggest we first establish the technical limitations upon any action we may take, before discussing the nature of the action. Is that agreed?'

Heads nodded.

'Very well. First the rocket itself. Will you describe it please, Doctor Bers?'

Bers, Professor Marasov's deputy from Baikonur, nodded. 'Compared with space missiles, which, as you know, are of relatively flimsy construction, the Sword missile is almost robust. The propellant tank helps to support the casing, which is of aluminium alloy. It is approximately six metres in length, with a diameter of sixty-five centimetres. Its weight is one and a half tons. Its warhead is stable in normal circumstances.'

'Restrictions in handling?' Tolstikov asked.

'The Sword missile is encased in a cylinder of thin, stainless steel, effectively a vacuum. Upon firing it bursts through the end of the cylinder. The integrity of the cylinder should be maintained.'

'And if it isn't?'

'Under certain circumstances, the fuel could become unstable.'

'It would explode?'

'The fuel only. The warhead should not. However, if the warhead were damaged in an explosion, accidental fusion could occur. Even without that, a substantial quantity of radioactive material would be released.' Doctor Bers paused. 'An explosion of the rocket fuel would certainly kill everybody within a short radius. Those farther away would inevitably be fatally contaminated by the radioactivity.'

Tolstikov said, 'And, of course, a detectable increase in radioactivity would result?'

'That is so.'

'So special tools are needed for handling?'

'Not necessarily,' Bers said. 'Ideally yes, but not necessarily. There are points upon the cylinder's surface to which handling lines may be attached.'

Colonel Belyaev asked, 'Could divers do it?'

Bers hesitated. 'In perfect conditions, perhaps. I would not recommend it.'

'Very well.'

'Let me say this,' Bers said. 'Two things are to be avoided. One I have described: damage to the casing. The other is any excessive shaking or rocking of the missile.'

'Such as might occur at sea?' Tolstikov asked.

'In a *rough* sea,' Bers said. 'I am sure you will see that to expose the rocket fuel to a rough sea would be like putting it in a cocktail shaker. The fuel would become progressively more unstable. However, in calmer waters there would be no problem. It would be wise,' he added, 'for the missiles to be delivered as soon as possible into the hands of competent rocket technicians with proper facilities.'

'You don't want much,' Zarubin said coldly.

'I'm sorry, General. I am being asked to describe the parameters.'

'How many attempts,' Zarubin pursued, 'have been made to approach by submarine?'

'Six,' Admiral Tolstikov said. 'The last of them along a newly discovered cold current and in a silent-running submarine. On every occasion, the submarine was located and shadowed. Quite apart from the fact that the Sword installation lies within Canadian territorial waters, there is the need to carry out the operation in total secrecy.'

The nature of the problem was now delineated and, it seemed, virtually insoluble. It was discussed for the rest of the day in an atmosphere of increasing depression. Political considerations demanded a perfect operation; a perfect operation demanded facilities not available in the location; the six rockets were large, cumbersome and could hardly be more ostentatious; total secrecy was required. The factors formed an unbreakable circle, each cancelling out one or more of the others.

Arkady Semichastny did not smoke. In this he was alone among them. So, at the end of the long day, he took his aching head for a walk through the cold night air of the Park of Culture and Rest. He walked for a long time, his head gradually clearing. It was after eleven o'clock when he returned to his hotel. He ordered a glass of tea; it was too late to eat and he was not, in any case, hungry. Then he bought a copy of *Krokodil* because he knew his mind needed distraction if he was to get any sleep at all.

Curiously, the paper gave him an idea which was to keep him awake almost throughout the night.

IV

The cold light of morning did not gild Semichastny's idea. For a while, despite the long hours of thought he had given it, Semichastny was inclined to scrap it. It was, after all, rather fanciful; it depended upon one or two factors that might be incapable of resolution. While he bathed, he thought it through again and decided that though his plan might sound extravagantly fanciful, that was because it was intended to deal with a mad situation. Also, if certain components of the plan ceased to be problematical and were, in fact, capable of realization, then the plan had an excellent chance of success.

When, at eight o'clock, the meeting was reconvened, he waited for other solutions to emerge, but none of the other members had produced one. At last, he said, 'Comrade Chairman, I believe I have an idea. It is not yet a plan.'

Tolstikov, Zarubin, Bers, Belyaev and Shenko listened carefully. When Semichastny had finished speaking, Tolstikov said, 'Thank you, comrade,' and turned to Dr Bers. 'Does this meet your requirements for the handling of the missiles ?'

'Indeed it does. It is difficult to imagine a better form of protection than Comrade Semichastny suggests.'

'In that case,' Tolstikov began –

General Zarubin interrupted him. 'It depends, as ever, upon the KGB.'

'I was about to say that,' Admiral Tolstikov said mildly. 'But can it be done ?'

'That appears to depend once again,' Zarubin said coldly, 'upon whether Comrade Semichastny has his facts right. I shall investigate.'

'And report within the period laid down by the Minister,' said Tolstikov. He restrained a sigh. Everything seemed always dependent upon the KGB. Control passed with endless inevitability into their hands.

Zarubin knew precisely what the Admiral was thinking. He

said, 'If the plan cannot succeed, it seems you people should be ready with another.'

'*We* should be ready,' Bers said.

Zarubin smiled. 'I'm talking about your own areas of expertise. I doubt whether you would seriously call mine in question.'

'It is essential,' Vice-Admiral Tolstikov said to Admiral Gorshkov later in the morning, 'that the KGB should not control this operation.'

'Why?'

'Because in doing so they gain a toehold in whole areas of naval and scientific activity.'

Gorshkov smiled grimly. 'Also you do not like Zarubin?'

'Perhaps. That is not the point.'

'I agree with you. But supposing that the plan turns out to be workable? Who *is* to control it?'

'I suggest myself. After all, I shall be present in Vancouver for the Pacific conference preparations. I hold naval rank. This is a navy matter.'

Gorshkov grinned at the portly oceanographer. 'I don't see you, Sergei, as an espionage agent.'

'Nor do I. But I *shall* be available. I shall also have direct and legitimate contact with Moscow.'

'That still leaves First Chief Directorate, KGB, Zarubin and his people running the operation on the ground. In the water, I should say.'

'They must be there,' Tolstikov argued. 'But they don't know enough.'

'You'd be surprised what they know.'

'About these requirements. About the sea, the oceanographic problems. We do not know what we shall encounter. We need a non-KGB man to control the operating group.'

'Who then?'

Tolstikov told him.

Gorshkov chewed thoughtfully at his upper lip. 'He is not a man of action.' Then he thought a bit more. 'You have a point, Tolstikov. I'll think it over. Send me his records. Zarubin can supply men of action.'

In his second-floor office in the headquarters building of the KGB in Dzerzhinsky Square, Moscow, almost next door to the Lubianka Prison in Dzerzhinsky Street, Lieutenant-General Ivan Zarubin was dictating signals to KGB Chiefs of Station in the United States, Canada and West Germany. They contained demands for information on the availability of a variety of exotic products of modern technology and the people required to operate them.

Both the West German and United States officers were able to answer by return and their answers were not helpful. In the United States, the two machines whose names Zarubin had found in his files were experimental prototypes built for the United States Navy and permanently engaged on highly classified work. The back-up facilities necessary for the operation of the German product were such as to rule it out of consideration.

Head of Station, Ottawa, passed the instruction to his Victoria-based operative by means of an open telephone line from an Ottawa hotel. He disliked doing so, but in view of the urgency of Zarubin's personal demand he had no alternative. Furthermore, since Vancouver is nine hours behind Moscow time and four behind Ottawa, he felt it prudent to wait until later in the day when the telephone lines were busier and there was less chance of encountering an idle operator who might listen.

The agent promptly set off on the ferry from Victoria to Vancouver, and on arrival three hours later, went to the offices of the *Vancouver Sun*, principal evening newspaper of the Province of British Columbia.

In the shiny entrance hall, with its modern sculptures, a commissionaire asked his business and directed him to the newspaper's library ('morgue' was the word he used), where the agent, posing as an American magazine writer, asked to look at certain files of cuttings.

He was invited to enter the work area, instead of standing at the counter, and the envelopes containing the cuttings were brought to him by a pleasantly helpful girl.

'If you wish,' she said, 'we can copy them for you. There's a 'small charge, of course, but then you can take them away.'

'Thank you.' During an hour of careful reading, the agent selected several cuttings from the files; he then had them copied and handed over three dollars. He left the building, took a taxi to the bus station, and used a public telephone to call a small and specialized Vancouver company. Posing as a reporter on the business section of the *Vancouver Sun* he asked generally how things were going and then, more specifically, what things were happening and when a photographer, if a picture were required, would be able to take photographs ? Finally, he asked whether his friend worked there still. The 'friend' was a name he had found in the newspaper cuttings. He was told that the answer was no; that his 'friend' had returned, regrettably, whence he came.

'Thanks,' the agent said, meaning it. Even now he was often surprised by the easy availability of valuable information.

'Not at all,' said the friendly Canadian voice. 'Give us a good write-up, huh ?'

The agent caught a bus to Sea Island Airport and was in time to join the Air Canada Hawaii to Montreal flight when it staged at Vancouver. Time-zone changes over three thousand miles made it late evening by the time he arrived in Ottawa, where he made a phone call. In his taxi from airport to the Parliament building, he stuffed the cuttings, plus the additional notes he had made, down the side of the back seat cushion. At the point where the taxi stopped another man was waiting.

'Finished with the cab, bud ?'

'Sure,' the agent said. 'Glad to help.'

He spent half an hour pretending to rubberneck, then went to the cinema and finally to a hotel where he spent the night, preparatory to returning to Vancouver the following morning.

The man who had taken the taxi told the driver to take him to another hotel, alighted there, walked through the hotel lobby and out of the restaurant entrance. From there he walked to the Soviet Embassy Building.

Zarubin had given orders that he was to be awakened the moment the report came through from Head of Station,

Ottawa. So he was, at three-thirty a.m. He had to wait angrily for half an hour while the computer-generated cipher was translated. When the result was brought to him, he sent for maps, then for naval charts, studied them for a while, then dictated detailed memoranda to Head of Station, London, and Head of Station, Rome, and ordered them sent on the highest priority over the diplomatic wire. His own sleep had been interrupted; he would pass on the courtesy to two Heads of Station.

At the eight-thirty meeting, he was able to report that the necessary facilities *appeared* to be in existence and that he was already taking action to make them *available*.

'I would be grateful if, in future, you would clear all such action with me first,' Vice-Admiral Tolstikov said mildly.

'Don't get above yourself, Admiral,' Zarubin said. 'This is KGB business.'

'Of course.' Tolstikov smiled. 'Please don't misunderstand, General Zarubin. It is simply that as co-ordinator of the recovery operation, it is necessary that I should know.'

Zarubin's eyebrows rose. 'Co-ordinator?'

'I don't pretend to understand it either. But that is the wish, it seems, both of the Foreign Minister and Admiral of the Fleet Gorshkov. Perhaps you will be kind enough to inform us of the detailed arrangements you have made so far?'

Zarubin controlled his anger and complied. Two could play at that game and the Minister of State Security carried influence comparable with Gromyko's. He was to discover later that day that Andrei Gromyko, ranging delicately ahead, already had the highest backing. Later still, Zarubin was to make even greater demands upon his self-control, when he learned the name of the expedition leader.

At three-thirty p.m. that same afternoon, the telephone rang in a picturesque stud-and-plasterwork Elizabethan cottage near the small market town of Sudbury, Suffolk, in the south-eastern part of England. It rang several times before it was answered, because the telephone was on the floor of the untidy north-facing room Henry Baxter used as a studio, and had been completely covered in the course of the morning by sheets torn off Baxter's sketch-pad and tossed aside.

When he had located the instrument Henry Baxter crouched bent-kneed beside it and picked up the receiver.

'Hello.'

'Mister Baxter?' The girl's voice was unfamiliar and had a slight foreign accent. 'One moment please.'

He hung on, irritably, annoyed as always by people who used their secretaries to save their own time and to hell with other people's.

'Mr Baxter?' A man's voice this time, also unfamiliar, also with a foreign accent.

'This is Henry Baxter.'

'My name is Giuseppe Marinelli of Marinelli-Milano. You know of my company?'

'Yes, I do.' Baxter was suddenly excited. Marinelli-Milano were one of the big Italian magazine printing and publishing concerns. They were modern and very design conscious. 'I admire your work.'

'As I admire yours, Mr Baxter.'

'Thank you.'

'As a matter of fact,' Marinelli said, 'I would like you, if you are not too busy, to do some work for me.'

'I imagine I'll be delighted. But I wouldn't have thought my stuff was for you.' Henry Baxter was a commercial artist, specializing in paintings to illustrate romantic stories in the better women's magazines.

'On the contrary. We need precisely what you do. However, it is urgent and we would need to discuss it at some length.'

'By all means,' Baxter said. 'Where do we meet?'

'There is the difficulty. You see, I am in Rome now. Tonight I fly to Mallorca for a business meeting. Mr Baxter, could you come to Mallorca?'

'What, tonight?'

'It would be most helpful. Also profitable for both of us. Your fares, your hotel bill, will of course be . . .'

'I don't see why not,' Baxter said, calculating quickly. He

36

had two commissions in hand, not due to be completed for fourteen days. 'For how long?'

'A day or two. Bring your wife if you wish.'

'You are serious, Mr Marinelli?'

'Of course. I want you to work for me. I want you happy.'

'All right,' Baxter said. 'How do we get there?'

'I will arrange for your tickets to be at the London BEA terminal. You fly to Mallorca and go to the Hotel Son Vida, near Palma. I look forward, Mr Baxter. The flight is at eight-thirty.'

For Henry Baxter, and even more for his wife, the next few hours were hectic. Jane Baxter protested at the rush. She had not had her hair done; her clothes weren't ready; it wasn't fair to drag people off as suddenly as this. All the same, she enjoyed it. They left their car in the railway station car park at Colchester and went to London by train.

'I don't believe there will *be* any tickets,' Jane Baxter said a little breathlessly as their taxi approached the BEA terminal in Cromwell Road.

'Marinelli is real, I assure you,' Henry said. 'What I wonder is – how he got on to *me*!'

'Because you're clever, darling.' Jane laughed. 'Do you suppose we could stay a bit longer than a day or two?'

There were reservations for Mr and Mrs Henry Baxter on the eight-thirty departure for Palma, Mallorca, and soon they stepped off the Trident jet into the still pleasantly warm Mediterranean evening, and took a taxi to the ancient castle which had become the Hotel Son Vida. An elegant and clearly expensive room had been booked for them, a room with a long, magnificent view across the mountain-side, the city and the sea beyond. There was only one snag: a message from Signor Marinelli. He apologized profusely; he had been delayed and would not arrive for thirty-six hours. He assured them the wait would be worth while.

Jane Baxter spun happily in the middle of the room. 'Do you know,' she said. 'I don't mind if he *never* arrives.'

Which was useful. But not for the Baxter family.

The telephone rang the same day in the home of Nicos Coulouris, a Greek shipbroker who operated his business from Lebanon. His apartment in Beirut was in one of the high white blocks overlooking the bay where even the lowest rentals were huge, and rose steadily towards penthouse summits. The interior of the apartment was remarkably plain. Such items of furniture as Coulouris had were expensive, but they were few. To his occasional visitors, the appearance of the apartment was surprising; in Beirut people of his wealth tended to live in onstentatious rather than quiet luxury. Coulouris had uncarpeted, though polished, floors, and plain white walls.

Coulouris explained it, when he had to, by saying that he felt a need for simplicity in some part of his life. Perhaps, he would add, because his family had a long-standing monastic tradition. It was, in fact, a deliberate hair shirt, a visual and permanent reminder to himself of his Marxism, a daily demonstration of a deeply-held belief in the corrupting effect of possessions.

He had been a Communist since boyhood, a Party member from the age of twenty-two. His membership had originally been clandestine through necessity; it remained so deliberately. Even during the war, when Coulouris fought as a partisan in German-occupied Greece, he had not fought as a Communist guerilla but with the right-wing, army-oriented patriots. Before the war, on instructions, he had entered the office of a Greek shipping line in the port of Piraeus. After it, he had returned to shipping, become a broker, and prospered.

Much of his prosperity came from his representation of Soviet shipping interests. When Russian or East German-built ships were sold to Middle-Eastern countries, Coulouris was frequently the broker. For more than twenty years, since his move from Piraeus to freewheeling Lebanon, he had arranged the movement of cargoes of cotton and of gun cotton, of tanks for water storage and tanks for battlefields. Business like this could not be conducted in secret; Coulouris had always covered it by expressing surprise. 'Why do I represent the Russians?' he would ask. 'Because they want me to. Though why they pick a right-winger like me, I can't imagine.' His rarely expressed political views were always carefully right-wing. The result was that Coulouris was a mystery in Beirut; not a big mystery, or an important mystery, but a bit of a mystery, and widely admired for it.

He met the KGB Head of Station, Beirut, on the beach, in his shirt-sleeves, and together they strolled quietly in the sunshine, picking their way between the colourful beach umbrellas and the browning sun-bathers.

'Don't imagine,' Coulouris said warningly, 'that my representation of Soviet interests is not well known over there. This is an international business.'

'So are you,' said Head of Station. 'I sometimes think the Soviet connection is too great, but everybody knows you serve Greek, American, Italian and Arab interests too.'

'Not in North America; at least, not much. In America they look at me a bit sideways.'

'Frankly, so do I, sometimes. Without justice, I admit. You're an anachronism.'

'No,' Coulouris said. 'I am the scout locust. I just *seem* to be an anachronism.'

'I know. I am told the oil industry uses the machine we require.'

'Not yet.' Coulouris circumnavigated a pair of bikini-clad girls. 'The Canadian company would like to sell to the international oil companies.'

'So they would welcome you.'

'They would indeed. But they might suspect. And later . . .'

Head of Station, Beirut, spoke carefully. It had already been decided in Moscow that when Coulouris's usefulness was balanced against the importance of the Canadian venture, Canada won. At sixty-five, Coulouris had a limited future and must be aware of it. All the same, this was not the moment to rub in the fact.

'We can arrange a covering purchase order at some future date,' he said. 'You will in no sense be implicated. This company must, after all, have many visitors.'

Coulouris shrugged. 'If that's the way you want it.'

'It is,' the KGB man said. 'And I'm sure you have friends in Vancouver.'

'I have acquaintances who believe they are friends,' Coulouris said. 'I can talk about timber shipments with them.'

'Perfect. Now, it's a hot day.' Head of Station, Beirut, was perspiring freely. He came from Northern Russia and found the Mediterranean heat trying. 'How about a nice cool beer?'

'For me, fruit juice. I never touch alcohol.'

'*Chacun a son goût*. But let's get out of the sun, eh?'

Coulouris followed the KGB man across the warm sand towards one of the bars that lined the beach front. He was frowning. He sometimes thought the new generation of Russian Communists was beginning to look almost American.

Head of Station, Beirut, was new. He had spent less than a month in Lebanon, and since his cover was an active position in the agricultural machinery export section of the Trade Delegation, he had not yet been positively identified as KGB Head of Station. All the same, he was suspected, and was under discreet observation by several Western agents and freelance intelligence operators in the city. A meeting between an export official and a shipbroker was perhaps innocuous. If the export official was, as suspected, KGB Head of Station, it was worth reporting. In the event, it was reported routinely by an Arab representative of the French SDECE, and by a German who, oddly enough, worked for DI6, formerly known as MI6, the British intelligence department responsible for espionage and counter-espionage abroad. The French report occasioned no interest in Paris. In London, the airmail letter addressed to a Post Office box number in Parliament Street was filed, and only later remembered.

V

On the morning following the arrival of Henry and Jane Baxter at their hotel in Mallorca, Henry's brother, John Baxter, heard the doorbell ring at his flat in the South London suburb of Blackheath. It was eight a.m. when he went to answer it, still in pyjamas and dressing-gown. Outside stood a man wearing dungarees and carrying a concertina-type tool-box.

'Are your electrics all right?' the man said.

'As far as I know. I didn't call for help.'

'No, I know. It was them downstairs. Something's wrong with the wiring in this bloody block. Can I check?'

John Baxter opened the door wider. 'Come in. Help yourself.'

The electrician went from room to room, flicking the light switches on and off. 'Seems okay. I'll just try the power circuit.'

'You start early,' Baxter said. 'Like a cup of tea?'

'Thanks, guv.'

The tea was freshly made. Baxter filled a beaker, heard the electrician in the bedroom, and took it to him.

The man glanced up and grimaced. 'It's this one here, guv. Directly above, you see. There must be a bloody junction-box under here and somebody's made a cock-up of the wiring.'

Baxter handed him the beaker. 'Mine seems all right.'

The electrician nodded in the direction of the wall. 'Call themselves electricians! I wouldn't let some of them string up my bloody sweet peas. It's a floorboard job, this. Sorry guv.'

Baxter grinned. 'What's been happening down below.'

'What hasn't! Bloody toaster plays God Save the Queen. I tell you, some of these bleeders'd botch up eating their own breakfast. Thanks for the tea.'

'Will you be long?'

'Hope not. You in a hurry, guv?'

'Not for half an hour.'

'Plenty. Leave it to me.' The electrician was already folding back the carpet. 'Don't worry. I'll leave it like a new pin.'

Baxter watched idly for a moment, then remembered he had neither showered nor shaved. Was the man trustworthy? He seemed so. 'I have to get ready. Will you be all right?'

'Okay, guv.' The electrician was busily prising up a short floorboard.

The electrician heard the shower switched on and listened to the steady hiss of the water, while pretending to look beneath the floor. While the water hissed like that, it was falling directly into the bath; when Baxter stepped into it, the sound would change. He was wise to wait, for Baxter did, in fact, leave the bathroom for a moment to glance quickly round the bedroom door. Satisfied that the electrician was still working, he stepped into the shower.

The electrician opened his tool-box to expose a large manilla envelope in the bottom, then he took a pair of tweezers from one of the side racks, and placed the envelope beneath the floorboards. Two other items followed it. All were pushed carefully to one side, out of sight. Then, for the sake of appearances, the electrician pulled up the junction-box and took his time stripping the plastic insulation from a wire before re-connecting it. He was tightening the screw as the shower was switched off and Baxter returned.

'Okay, guv. Just done. Too bloody idle to tighten a screw, some of 'em.'

As Baxter dressed, floorboard and carpet were deftly and neatly replaced, the tool-box closed. By the time he was tying his tie, the workman was ready to go.

'Thanks, guv. Sorry to trouble.'

'No trouble,' Baxter said, closing the door.

He was wrong. It was trouble of the deadliest conceivable kind.

In the committee-room within the Kremlin wall, Vice-Admiral Tolstikov sat waiting. The meeting time was still half an hour away, but he had asked Arkady Semichastny to arrive early. Semichastny had received the instruction with mixed feelings. He was aware that his plan had been given general approval, though Zarubin's approval must be assumed since it had not been expressed. There was therefore a credit mark to his name to weigh against the trouble with the chain, which was his department's albatross and therefore in part his own. Over the last few days, Semichastny had been pleasantly surprised to find his thought and organizational capacities had not disgraced him among these high-ranking men. He had been surprised, too, by something else: the ever-present and universal tension, often amounting to menace, all around him.

Semichastny was not by nature a coward. Physically he was hard and he relaxed in energetic and mildly hazardous ways, skiing and rock climbing. But neither was he political; the byways and pressures of power-centres were foreign to him, and he was, by nature, unsuited to them. When he was climbing, he knew that death was the penalty for carelessness, and could face the knowledge cheerfully. The fear engendered in him by the obvious cross-currents among his superiors was something far more terrifying. He had told himself from the beginning that he must at all costs avoid becoming the man in the middle, and the summons from Tolstikov might well be a piece of ally-making. He approached the committee-room with a lively apprehension.

'Sit down, sit down, comrade.' To Semichastny, the admiral's bonhomie was anything but reassuring.

'Good morning, sir,' he said.

'I wanted you here early,' Tolstikov said, 'because there is something I wish to discuss with you.'

'I see.'

'Yes.' Admiral Tolstikov looked at him thoughtfully. Semichastny was not going to like this. He said, 'On the question of the people we actually *send* to Canada. We have solved, more or less, the other problems. Now it is a matter of choosing people and I would value your opinion. Particularly in view of your experience in North America.'

'I was only in New York,' Semichastny said. 'At the United Nations.'

'That's what I mean. What would you say were the requirements. What kind of men?'

Semichastny blinked. Something lay behind the question, but he didn't know what. 'Well, I suppose English-speakers.'

'Of course. And?'

'Some knowledge of the sea, perhaps. Though I suppose it's not strictly necessary for every man. Familiarity with the American scene is probably important too.'

'Go on,' Admiral Tolstikov said encouragingly. 'This is most useful.'

'Let me see. Well, obviously a thorough briefing on the

43

technical aspects will be necessary. Physical fitness, too. And the ability to improvise well in case anything goes wrong.'

'Excellent!'

'I feel I have merely stated the obvious.'

Tolstikov beamed at him. 'Not at all. You have given me a very accurate description. Of yourself.'

Semichastny's scalp crawled. For a moment he gaped at the admiral. Then he recovered enough to shake his head.

'It's often like that,' the admiral went on smoothly. 'We don't recognize things until they're pointed out to us.'

At last Semichastny managed to speak. 'I'm the wrong man!'

Admiral Tolstikov frowned deliberately. 'Both Minister Gromyko and Admiral of the Fleet Gorshkov agree with me. Your record has been closely examined. You were an efficient service officer. You have all the requisite qualities and background. You know America.'

'Vancouver,' Semichastny said soberly, 'is more than three thousand miles from New York. It is in another country. Surely this is work for the KGB.'

'They are involved, naturally,' the admiral said. 'As you already know, Colonel Belyaev has served in Canada. He will be your second in command.'

'But – ' Semichastny began.

'No buts,' Admiral Tolstikov said briskly. 'It is an order. You have a considerable opportunity to serve the motherland.'

The municipality of Burnaby, British Columbia, lies a few miles inland from Vancouver, but is effectively a part of the metropolitan Vancouver area. It was there, in the early sixties, that a new university was built on a superb elevated site over-looking the river. The university, like the river, was named after Simon Fraser, the Scots explorer who opened up the wild province more than a century ago. The prospects for the new university seemed, and perhaps remain, excellent. It is very modern, magnificently equipped and a delight to the eye. Like many modern universities, however, Simon Fraser has attracted more than might be expected of the youthful disaffected; within it are large groups of Trotskyites, Maoists, anarchists, orthodox Marxists and revolutionaries of every shade. Among them was a law student named Joe Kotcheff.

Kotcheff had originally taken his degree in sociology. Later he had applied for, and been awarded, one of several scholarships made available for Canadian students at Moscow University, where for two years he had studied the Soviet legal system. Returning to Canada, by now under Russian instructions, he had begun the study of law with the intention of practising at the British Columbia bar. It has long been the policy of the Soviet espionage system, that one or two gifted lawyers should be available in every important Western centre, and Kotcheff, able and dedicated, was scheduled for a long career in the Soviet service.

His instructions came to him in a long, innocent letter from a fictional aunt in Toronto. The code was simple and effective. By writing down every seventh character, Kotcheff put together detailed instructions for the task he was to undertake. He was also given instructions on how to make contact. He memorized the message, then burned both the letter and the translation slip. He then went to the library of the Law Society in Vancouver and began to work through several years' Law Reports. Having found several suitable cases, he went to the court building and checked the cases again in the files of submitted papers. The task took him all of one day. At the end of it he went to a bookshop on Theatre Row and placed a folded sheet of paper on which five names and addresses were listed, inside a paper-back copy of Jack Kerouac's *The Dharma Bums*. He then bought a copy of *Newsweek* and went out of the shop without looking back. When he had gone, an apparently casual browser in the shop took the Kerouac book from its shelf, paid for it, and left.

Outside in the street, the browser went directly to a public telephone box, extracted the sheet of paper, and dialled the first telephone number on the list. A woman's voice answered. The agent asked politely if he could speak to her husband.

When the man came on the line, the agent asked, 'Have you still got your boat?'

'Who is this?'

'You won't know my name. I may have a business proposition for you.'

'No. I sold the boat.'

'A pity. And your licence?'

'Say, who is this?'

'If you have your licence . . .'

'Well, I haven't. They took it away and they won't give it back. I'm in lumber now.'

'Thank you.' The agent hung up and moved to the next name on the list. This time the conversation was more productive.

He met Ed Bonney an hour or so later in the quiet, dark, downstairs bar of the Sylvia Hotel on English Bay. The two men shook hands and sat quietly for a little while, each sizing up the other, while drinks were brought.

Then the agent said, 'Show me your licence, please.' He took the proffered certificate and looked at the date carefully to be sure that it was both current and genuine.

'It's okay,' Ed Bonney said. 'I won on appeal. They had to give it back.'

'Yes.' The agent looked at him again. Bonney was a big, dark man, awkward in his dark suit, with a heavy black stubble on a square, hard face. His shoulders and thighs were thick with muscle, which bad tailoring merely emphasized.

'As I told you,' the agent said, 'I may have a business proposition.'

'What kind?'

'Profitable.'

Bonney grunted. He said, 'Profitable means trouble. Is it crooked?'

'That,' said the agent, 'depends on your outlook. But broadly, though the answer is no, I should not wish you to be caught.'

'Sorry,' Bonney said. 'No dice.' He began to rise. The agent used his forefinger to write a figure on the tablecloth. Bonney watched carefully, then resumed his seat.

'Fifteen?'

'That's right. A little more than a week's work. There will also be a normal charter fee for your boat.'

Bonney nodded. 'Drugs.'

'Not drugs.'

'No? I've been approached before. Less money than that, but big money all the same.'

The agent said, 'You would be doing your normal work, nothing more. You would make a pick-up higher up the coast, come down through the Inside Passage in the normal way. The only difference is that either out there – ' he pointed towards the dark water of English Bay – 'either out there, or in the main harbour in Burrard Inlet, you will make a delivery.'

'Salvage regulations are dead tight. I can only deliver at listed points.'

'There is nothing in the regulations,' the agent said, 'to stop you simply abandoning . . . whatever it is . . . and sailing away.'

'That's all?'

'At a precise position.'

Bonney thought for a moment. 'How will you pay?'

'Seven thousand five hundred before you sail. The rest on completion. In cash.'

'You said whatever it is. What is it?'

'There is no reason,' the agent said, 'why you, or anybody else, should know.'

'Who are you?'

'No need to know that either. You will have no need to contact me. When the time comes I shall let you know and half the money will be paid.'

'Let me get this straight,' Bonney said. 'I make a pickup. Sail down through the Inside Passage, then dump. That's all?'

'Precisely that.'

'It's too easy,' Bonney said. 'What are the risks?'

The agent said carefully, 'There should be none.'

'And if there's trouble?'

'All of us,' the agent said, 'are taking careful precautions to avoid trouble.'

'But if I'm caught?'

'You should not be caught. Your skill and your knowledge

47

of these waters should rule that out. I expect you to ensure that you are not caught.'

Ed Bonney finished his Scotch. 'I'll think about it.'

'Until tomorrow. I shall telephone at eight o'clock.'

'Mornings I leave at seven.'

'Six-thirty, then.'

The agent watched Bonney walk away. He was certain that the answer would be yes. Bonney's conviction, discovered by Kotcheff in the law library, had been for a brutal, local form of piracy. Violence had been used. The appeal had been won on a point of law, but Bonney's guilt and ruthlessness were not in doubt.

What the agent now needed was another Bonney. He finished his drink, left the bar, and went to a drug store at the bottom of Denman Street, from which he telephoned the third name on his list. There was no reply. Both numbers four and five, like number one, had been unable to recover their licences, which made them useless. That left number three.

Next morning, after telephoning Bonney and hearing his acceptance, the agent again telephoned the third number on his list. He had to telephone several times, but finally he reached the man. Later they met and everything was satis-factorily concluded.

By evening the agent had fulfilled his task. He was able to report that two tugboats, with experienced, ruthless and essentially criminal skippers, had been successfully hired.

From their room in the Hotel Son Vida, overlooking Palma, the yacht would have been visible if Henry and Jane Baxter had been inspecting Palma Bay through binoculars. In fact they were in sun-bathing chairs, on the tree-shaded terrace by the swimming pool, when the page found them. Behind the page walked a dark-haired youth in striped tee-shirt, faded jeans and rope-soled shoes.

'Mr Baxter?' The youth's English was heavily accented.

'Yes.'

'A message, from Signor Marinelli.'

'Ah! Good!' Baxter sat up. 'Is he here?'

'There.' The boy pointed towards the bay. 'He has a leg . . . he fell. He send me. You come, please? I have car.'

'Whereabouts down there?'

'On a yacht,' the boy said. 'He apologize, but . . .'

Baxter shrugged. 'Okay. Why not?'

Jane stretched comfortably. 'I'll wait here, I think. It's so nice by the pool.'

'Signor Marinelli ask for the signora to come too, please. Lunch on yacht is arranged.'

'Oh, dear. I was so comfortable.' Jane sighed regretfully.

'Up you get!' Henry Baxter said. 'Lunch on the yacht he said and lunch on the yacht it is.' He turned to the youth. 'We'll change. Won't be long.'

'Signor.'

While the Baxters climbed the oak staircase to their first-floor room, the youth went to the hotel cashier's desk and asked for their bill. When it was presented to him, he paid it in cash taken from a large roll of one-thousand peseta notes.

He then peeled off two more notes and said in excellent Spanish, 'Mr and Mrs Baxter are leaving today. Will you have the maid pack their bags, please.'

'Yes, sir. Will they be returning?'

'No. I will collect the bags later.'

As Henry and Jane Baxter came downstairs again, they were mildly surprised that the desk clerk should give them a smiling bow of farewell. They did not, however, know what it meant, and merely smiled back.

'They're so courteous,' Jane said. 'Do I look all right?'

'Splendid,' Henry grinned. 'You look as though you always lunch on yachts.'

The dark-haired youth accompanied them in the taxi to the harbour, where a small outboard dinghy was tied up. After delivering them to the white sixty-foot cruiser that lay moored in the bay, he turned the boat round and returned to the hotel to collect the bags.

By the time he came back, Henry Baxter was already puzzled. Signor Marinelli had not yet appeared. It was again explained politely that Marinelli had slipped and fallen and hurt his leg, that the leg was painful and a doctor was below with him. Though puzzled, Henry Baxter was not yet concerned. He was sitting with Jane in the covered well at the cruiser's stern, looking out at the harbour, when he saw the outboard dinghy approaching.

'I expect that's to take the doctor ashore,' Jane said.

'Expect so.'

Henry watched idly as the boat approached. Then he saw the dark-haired youth handing suitcases up to the deck.

'They're *ours*,' Jane said suddenly.

Henry had realized it in the same moment. He said, 'What the hell's going on!'

'I don't understand,' Jane said. 'Did they say – '

'They bloody well didn't! I'm going to find out.'

Then two things happened. First came the starting roar of the cruiser's two powerful diesels, and while Henry and Jane Baxter were still looking at each other with incredulity, a man opened the door of the saloon. They turned and saw that he had a gun in his hand. 'You will come inside, please.'

'Look, what the hell – ?'

'Inside.' The muzzle of the gun moved threateningly.

Helplessly, disbelievingly, Jane and Henry Baxter obeyed.

VI

Nicos Coulouris arrived in Vancouver aboard an Air Canada DC8 Trans-Polar flight from London. He had boarded the aircraft in the damp gloom of a drizzling autumn day, and it was into an almost identical wet stillness that he stepped when it landed more than seven thousand miles away. At Sea Island airport he was met by a Canadian who would have described himself as a friend. James Scott's friends were almost all men in the same business, which was the moving of ships and cargoes across the face of the earth.

By this time, several Russian agents were already at work in Vancouver, but they were operating on a 'need to know' basis, and none needed to know of the arrival of Coulouris; nor did he know of their existence, though he would have expected it.

Coulouris rode into Vancouver in James Scott's Lincoln, checked into the room that had been booked for him at the luxurious Bayshore Inn, and went to dinner with Scott at a German restaurant in what is known in the city as Robson-strasse. For a long time they simply talked about shipping while they grappled with huge platefuls of pork and potatoes and drank Rhine wine. Afterwards, over coffee, Coulouris began to talk about off-shore oil drilling in the Persian Gulf and the problems of maintenance of the sea-bed oil installations. He told Scott that an oil company with which he was involved had recently been considering the purchase of a German sub-mersible.

Scott, as Coulouris had previously taken the trouble to dis-cover, had an interest in Marine Technology Limited, one of two Vancouver-based organizations working on the develop-ment of small submarines for underwater industrial and defence use. He said, 'Why German?'

Coulouris shrugged. 'Why not? Unfortunately the vessel's performance is not yet adequate.'

'For the Gulf?'

'Oh, it's all right for the Gulf. But there isn't a year's work for it there. They'd charter it out when they didn't need it.'

'You've heard about ours?'

'No,' Coulouris lied. 'Tell me.'

'It's called the *Tyee* submersible,' Scott said. 'Built here. Submerges to about three thousand feet. Forty-eight hours' oxygen, twenty miles' range. Takes two men, three in a squeeze.'

'What can it do?'

'Everything from torpedo-recovery to tightening nuts and bolts. There are two exterior arms, operated from inside the sub. It's quite a performer.'

'Price?'

'Not so fast, Nicos. With your connections, I'm not so sure –'

Coulouris said, 'It is on the strategic list? Then I'm not interested.'

'As a matter of fact, it's not. All the same, like I said, you have some connections people here don't like.'

'The Russians?' Coulouris waved a hand dismissively. 'They are not the worst. Let me tell you I have connections *I* do not like, either. The Arabs, for example. But I wear many hats, old friend, and tonight I am wearing the Arab fez. It's business.'

'With you Greeks it's always business.'

'Not always. Anyway, we have talked enough business for tonight. I'm tired.'

Scott rang him at ten o'clock next morning at the Bayshore Inn. Previously he had called in at the Marine Technology Ltd. building on the harbourside. 'Nicos? You know the sub we were talking about?'

'I'm so tired I can't remember anything we talked about. This jet travel. At my age . . .'

'The sub, Nicos. The little submersible. *Tyee.* You remember?'

'Faintly.'

'Like to see it?'

'I don't think so. You said – '

'I know what I said. Take a look, all the same.'

'Very well. A little later. Will it be working?'

'No. Not here in Vancouver, anyway. But I expect we could arrange . . .'

'Don't bother, James.'

'No bother. There's another one, up the coast. Doing recovery work in Jervis Inlet. You could see that.'

'We'll see. We'll see.'

Coulouris was smiling as he hung up the telephone. If there was one thing as predictable as tomorrow's dawn, it was salesmanship.

That same afternoon he visited Marine Technology Ltd. and allowed himself to be persuaded to inspect the *Tyee* sub. He climbed inside, listened to the stereo system designed to keep the crew happy, sniffed the oxygen, and listened to the soft hum of the air purifying equipment.

Then he sat and watched a film made to demonstrate the submersible's performance. When he left, he took with him a small parcel of literature including performance figures and reports upon the tasks *Tyee* had carried out, and the film. These he promptly air-freighted to Ottawa where they were collected and delivered by an obscure route to KGB Head of Station, Ottawa.

Next day, with Scott and an eager, anxious executive of Marine Technology Ltd., Coulouris was flown up the British Columbia coast in a small seaplane which landed on the water of the long, deep, mountainous fiord called Jervis Inlet. There the small, bright orange *Tyee* sub was working at a depth of a thousand feet, trying to raise a tugboat which had sunk, months earlier, in a storm. Coulouris was given a special demonstration of launching techniques. He asked a great many perceptive, if casual, questions, all of which were answered with precision because a half-million dollar sale was conceivably in prospect. Unknown to James Scott and the Martec executive, their answers were being recorded on a small tape machine in Coulouris's pocket, via a lapel microphone. At the end of the day the tape was also sent to Ottawa, where it was transcribed and then sent onward to Moscow via the diplomatic bag. The answer to one of Coulouris's questions was of special interest to Arkady Semichastny in Moscow. It was a very casual question.

COULOURIS: This operation for example. How long will it take?

SCOTT: Looks like weeks. Agree, George?

GEORGE: (other name unknown): Five. Maybe six.

For several days, Semichastny and his KGB second-in-command, Colonel Pavel Belyaev, had been busy. The relationship between the two men was chill and formal, but they were working effectively together for the excellent reason that they had been instructed to work effectively together. Inevitably, most of the organizational responsibility had fallen upon Belyaev. Semichastny, as the author of the plan, and leader of the expedition, had the approval and backing of two of the half-dozen most powerful men in the Soviet Union. As the days went on, he refined and polished his conception of the operation, demanding of Belyaev the implementation of detail. The KGB man and his superior, Lieutenant-General Zarubin, resented the second place they had been obliged to take; nonetheless, the vast resources of the Committee for State Security were being deployed without reserve.

The two men had met as frequently as Semichastny's travels would allow. When, as had happened, the oceanographer had been in a distant part of the country, he had remained in contact by telephone and teleprinter. A six-seater, twin-engine Tupolev passenger jet had been placed at his exclusive disposal, and in it he had made a visit first to the harsh, semi-arctic country flanking the banks of the Pechora River, which empties itself into the Arctic Ocean five hundred miles east of the North Cape. The Pechora, navigable for almost five hundred miles back towards its source in the foothills of the Ural Mountains, bore certain vital resemblances to British Columbia and to the Inside Passage between Vancouver Island and the mainland. There Arkady Semichastny learned a good deal. From the Pechora he flew to Vladivostok, on the Pacific coast, and caused some confusion among the bureaucrats of the Ministry of Trade by helping himself to several items already marked for export to Japan. Had he not been armed with written instructions from the Ministry of Foreign Affairs guaranteeing his requirements absolute priority, he could not have achieved his objective. As it was, he had only to snap his fingers and work crews were produced to do his bidding. It was not until he demanded that a fast cargo-vessel of twenty-two thousand tons, which happened to be discharging cargo at the time, be despatched urgently on a round voyage of more than ten thousand miles, with her holds empty and a cargo of less than a hundred tons lashed to her deck, that he struck real resistance. Even this was overcome with the arrival from Moscow of a crisp teleprinted message from the Trade Minister himself.

He gave orders to the cargo vessel's master in person. The orders included replacement of some of the ship's crew by naval personnel, detailed instructions about his rendezvous and, in particular, about a course which would take the ship north towards the Aleutians before it began a long, south-eastward swing paralleling the coastline of the North American continent. Arrival was to be timed so that the ship appeared off the northern tip of Vancouver Island in the darkness. When the cargo had been off-loaded, the ship was to turn immediately and begin a return voyage to Vladivostok.

He left the selection of naval personnel to Pacific Fleet HQ, and returned in his twin-jet Tupolev to Moscow. In the appointment of the crew, Fleet HQ turned naturally to the reserve pool of men in the Vladivostok naval barracks, and among the men chosen was a wireless operator named Nikita Ivanov. Three days after the cargo ship sailed, a radio message addressed to the captain was received from the militia in Vladivostok. The message said that Nikita Ivanov was suspected of murder in Vladivostok and requested that the captain hold him confined, under close arrest, until the ship returned to port.

As it happened, the message was received during the 6 a.m. to 2 p.m. duty shift by Ivanov himself. He had been half expecting it, but it was a severe shock all the same. The penalty for murder was death and Nikita Ivanov knew the circumstances of the moneylender's death would not be regarded as extenuating. Therefore, in a few weeks, he would be convicted and executed. He tapped out his acknowledgment of the message, but did not enter it into the radio log. A few minutes later he transmitted a further message, signed in the captain's name, reporting that orders had been carried out. Naturally enough, he did not log that message either. From that moment on, he began to rack his brains for some method of escaping from the ship. However high the risks might be, he knew he would have to accept them, for the risks could be weighed only against the certainty of death.

On the day following the successful planting of a large envelope and other items beneath the floorboards of John Baxter's South London flat, Colonel Belyaev put in motion the second stage of an operation. He did so in a signal to KGB Head of Station, Hamburg. The signal consisted merely of a code word, but it triggered action on written and detailed instructions sent two days earlier to allow Hamburg Station time to arrange their ploy.

Like police organizations throughout the world, Hamburg police are notified when local doctors are going away, either on holiday or for any other reason. Any member of the public, needing to consult his physician, will be supplied with the information that Dr A is standing in for Dr B until the former returns from his skiing or his conference. It was easy for KGB Hamburg to discover the name of an absentee doctor.

In London, John Baxter was surprised to be pursued into the underground car park beneath the Plaid-Cromwell Shipping Corporation's black glass office building, by a secretary. He was about to get into his car.

'Mr Baxter! Mr Baxter!'

He swung round, quickly. The girl was running.

'Oh, I *am* glad I've caught you!' The girl laid a hand flat on her ample chest; she was badly out of breath.

'What's the matter?' Her expression was enough to identify her as the carrier of bad news.

'You'd better come upstairs. That's what he says.' *He*, Baxter knew, was the girl's boss, managing director of the Plaid-Cromwell subsidiary for whom Baxter worked.

Baxter closed the car door and followed her tapping heels back into the building. In the lift he asked again what the problem was, but the girl simply said, 'He wants to tell you himself.' She continued to look at him with sympathy.

When he reached the managing director's office, he found Lavering wearing the same grave, sympathetic expression. 'What is it?' he demanded. 'What's the bad news?'

Lavering handed him a cable. 'Your brother.'

Baxter's heart lurched. He read the cable quickly 'Regret inform you Henry and Jane Baxter seriously injured car crash Hamburg. Please telephone Dr Kleinmann, Hamburg 70-61579.'

'Mind if I use your phone?'

'Help yourself. I'll clear out. I looked up the international dialling code for you.'

'Thanks.' Baxter reached urgently for the phone and began

to spin the dial. As he did so, he realized that the fact that the cable had reached him at Plaid-Cromwell was, of itself, a hopeful sign. His brother knew where he worked; no Hamburg doctor could know, therefore Henry was at least conscious. Or perhaps Jane. One of them, anyway.

He listened to the clicks of the circuit routing, then to the ringing of the telephone. At last a man's voice said something in German.

'Doctor Kleinmann, please.'

'Kleinmann. Ein moment, bitte.'

A click, then a man's voice said, 'Kleinmann.'

'I'm John Baxter. I had a cable from you.'

'Baxter? Ah, yes. The news is not good, I am sorry.'

'How is he? How are they?'

There was a brief pause, then Kleinmann said, 'Herr Baxter, could you come to Hamburg?'

Baxter felt his stomach tighten. 'As bad as that?'

'The injuries are very serious. We are, of course, doing all we can. However . . .'

'You mean,' Baxter asked levelly, 'that they may die?'

'It is a possibility. They receive intensive treatment here. I am sorry.'

Baxter began to ask why on earth they were in Hamburg, but realized the doctor would not know. He said, 'I'll come over tonight if there's a flight. Which hospital?'

'Alster General, Herr Baxter.'

'I'm on my way.'

He put the phone down and reached for the telephone directory. A moment later he was talking to BEA. Yes, there was a direct evening flight to Hamburg and a seat was available.

He left his car where it was and took a taxi to the air terminal. He was wearing a light mackintosh and carrying a little overnight case he kept habitually at his office. Unexpected trips were no novelty to Baxter.

While he waited, and during the flight, he had plenty of time to think, but he could find no reason why Henry and Jane might have crossed the North Sea. It was not, after all, the holiday season, and Hamburg was not a holiday city. Nor, so far as he knew, did Henry work for German magazines. Henry's illustrations were of a very English character, and though Baxter knew very little of German publishing, he couldn't imagine a market there for Henry's paintings.

He was also mildly surprised that Henry had not told him of the trip. Usually Henry, or more likely Jane, would telephone and say, 'We're off again. Italy this time!' Or Spain, or Switzerland. They took an annual holiday abroad and that was all. John Baxter felt suddenly sick at the realization that he might never speak to either of them again.

The BEA Trident nosed cautiously down through the Hanseatic murk that hung over West Germany's second city, landed on the damply gleaming runway, and taxied towards the terminal building. As John Baxter left the heated interior of the plane and stepped into the razor-edged Hamburg wind he shuddered; it seemed to him to carry the chill of death. In the terminal building he showed his passport and was passed quickly through. As he did so, a loudspeaker was announcing in English: 'Will John Baxter, BEA passenger from London, please report to the information desk. Will John Baxter . . .'

He glanced round, located the illuminated sign and strode quickly towards it.

'Mein Herr?' The girl smiled at him.

'I'm John Baxter.'

She smiled again and indicated with her hand a man who had been waiting nearby. As she did so, the man moved towards him, hand outstretched. 'Herr Baxter? Doctor Kleinmann.'

Baxter shook hands. 'What news?'

'It is good you came so quickly,' Kleinmann said. 'I have a car outside. Come.'

Baxter hurried after him to the waiting Mercedes. A driver sat in front and Kleinmann opened the rear door to allow the Englishman to enter. As the car pulled away, Baxter said, 'Is there no improvement then?'

'I would not hope for too much.' Something in Kleinmann's

tone made Baxter glance at him inquiringly, but the doctor was looking straight ahead.

Baxter sat still containing his misery as the car drove smoothly into the city. The Alster, he knew, was the stretch of water in the middle of Hamburg. and he was a little surprised when, after driving for some minutes through the brightly-lit city, the lights became fewer in number and the surroundings more industrial. Suddenly, through the window he glimpsed ships and cranes and the dark waters of the river.

'Is it far?'

'Not far now.'

A few minutes later, the car stopped on the dockside beside a ship whose black-painted sides were scarred here and there with rust trails.

'We are here now,' Kleinmann said.

Baxter gaped. 'Where's the hospital?'

Kleinmann did not look at him. He said, 'You will step out of the car and walk up the gangplank.'

'What!' Baxter glanced round. The driver of the Mercedes had turned in his seat and was now, Baxter realized dazedly, pointing an automatic pistol at him. An eight-inch silencer gleamed blue. 'What the hell?'

'You will walk up the gangplank. You will be covered all the way, from the moment you leave the car, by a rifleman on board the ship.'

'I don't know who you're after,' Baxter said desperately, 'but you've got the wrong bloke.'

'Do as I say,' Kleinmann said. 'I warn you, we will not hesitate to shoot.'

Astonished and bewildered, John Baxter began to obey. He climbed out of the car and stood briefly on the roadway looking at the deserted gangplank, then up at the ship, finally back to Kleinmann in the car.

'You cannot see him,' Kleinmann said. 'But he is there. You are, at this moment, being watched along the sights of a rifle.

The silencer on the end of the driver's pistol twitched towards the gangway. Helplessly Baxter walked towards it, still carrying his overnight case.

Kleinmann's voice followed him softly from the car: 'I repeat, we shall not hesitate.'

As John Baxter slowly climbed the gangplank, he was not to know that both Kleinmann and the hidden rifleman would hesitate a long time before firing; indeed they would not dare to fire at all, because Baxter was an irreplaceable component in the plan under which his captors were acting.

Fifty yards away a dockyard policeman watched a solitary figure, carrying a case, climb the gangway. He did not take much notice, but, as it happened, the man's face was briefly illumined by a cargo light. The policeman noticed how forlorn he looked. Later he was to remember, but that night he merely glanced at the hammer and sickle on the ship's flag, and shuddered. The policeman had fought in Russia. He was pleased to think he would never touch its awful soil again.

While it is impossible to know with any precision, Western intelligence experts have estimated that between eight and ten per cent of Russia's gross national product is ploughed back ultimately into the maintenance of security. This figure does not, of course, include defence expenditure. Whatever the figure, there can be no doubt that the Soviet Union spends more per capita and probably more overall on security and intelligence work than any other nation on earth. One result of this is the lavishness of the facilities available.

All Western counter-espionage agencies have long known of the existence, for example, of special training camps, founded by the Committee of State Security and administered by its First Chief Directorate. One of these is New Woodville, a village built during the later stages of the 1939-45 war to duplicate exactly life in an American town. New Woodville has no Russian name; nor has it Russian money, Russian goods or Russian habits. It has a small supermarket and a drug store, both built after careful study of American retail marketing techniques. The cars in its streets are Fords, Chryslers, Buicks and Ramblers. The TV programmes piped to the colour TV sets in the carefully-copied suburban houses are recorded from NBC and CBS. In the kitchens are Frigidaires, in the bathrooms Remington and Norelco razors, Pepsodent and Colgate toothpaste and Elizabeth Arden and Revlon cosmetics. In the basements of the houses, male KGB operatives in training or on refresher courses, tinker with Black and Decker drills, or build plywood dinghies while the women sew mini-dresses from McCall patterns on swing-needle Singer sewing machines and practise conversation about hairdressers, gynae-cologists, life insurance, and the price of IBM stock.

The schoolhouse was modelled upon an original in the state of Maryland: white-boarded and built in a careful approxima-tion of fake Colonial architecture. It is scheduled for replace-ment as uncharacteristic, but while Arkady Semichastny and Colonel Belyaev were in New Woodville the schoolhouse was still fulfilling an educational function, as a school for spies.

Belyaev had given the school several days to select and test suitable candidates for the Sword missile recovery expedition. Now, resentfully, and only after receiving specific permission from the State Security Committee itself, he had brought the non-KGB man Semichastny into this sacred KGB sanctum. He had demanded candidates aged between twenty-eight and thirty-five, and he required six of them. Other stipulations governed appearance: they must be of assorted physical shapes and sizes; skills: all must be expert in the use of small arms and be capable aqualung divers; characteristics: none must be subject to seasickness. Belyaev had also instructed New Woodville's 'mayor' that the operatives, from whom the six would be chosen, must be given a rapid and detailed course of instruction in the problems concerning the raising of the Sword missile. He had *not* asked for operatives speaking faultlessly-accented English, because there was no need to do so. At New Woodville only English was spoken and intensive courses in regional accents were standard.

Twelve men and two women sat in a lecture room in the wooden schoolhouse when the 'mayor' took Semichastny and Belyaev in to meet them.

'You can dismiss the women,' Belyaev said curtly.

'It's a women's country.' The 'mayor' smiled easily.

'But not a women's operation.' Belyaev surveyed the assembled men as the two women rose and left.

'OK,' the 'mayor' said. 'Where d'you want to begin?' He handed Belyaev and Semichastny a list of names.

Semichastny looked at him. 'English names?'

'We don't use any others. One or two, as you'll see, are of European origin: Italian and German, but the forenames are all English.'

Semichastny grinned. 'Alphabetical order, then. We'll start with William Adams, then Michael Bagley, and so on.'

'Sure,' the 'mayor' said amiably. 'If you'd follow me, gentlemen.'

The two men interviewed William Adams in a separate room. Adams was thirty, bearded like an Old Testament prophet, and wore beads and bell-bottomed, unpressed trousers. His record gave his birthplace as Novosibirsk, but nobody could have guessed it, for he spoke in a strong, slow, mid-western drawl. His record showed he was supposed to have studied English literature at the University of California at Berkeley, and that his 'class' in that giant university included three other men named William Adams.

'Where were you born?' Semichastny asked.

'Wichita. Wichita, Kansas, man. Not Wichita Falls, Texas.'

Semichastny and Belyaev grilled him, with help from the 'mayor', for half an hour. At the end, Semichastny said in amazement, 'He seems faultless.'

'He *is* faultless,' the 'mayor' said. 'He can recite world-series records from Babe Ruth on down, tell you which pop singers have topped the charts in the last ten years, how to get at the alternator on a '64 Fairlane and give you a damned good critique on the poetic development of Ezra Pound's *Cantos*. He could be tripped up in only one way. If he had to name friends, he could do so. But if he were expertly confronted by them, he would probably be lost, even with the beard.'

Belyaev's cold glance contained a gleam of pride. 'Enough?'

'Let's see the next,' Semichastny said.

Standards naturally varied; even so they remained astonishingly high. Each operative had a long and carefully constructed background story and had been drilled in it. Their appearances, attitudes, supposed political allegiances, were all apparently authentic.

Selection proved difficult, not because there were too few suitable candidates but because there were too many, but in the end they had their six. Their names were William Adams, Michael Bagley, Joseph Field, Alexander Hallows, Francis McRae and Peter Stretton. Neither Semichastny nor Belyaev knew their true names. All were duly equipped with passports: three American, one British and two Canadian. Where appropriate, their documents included appropriate visas and work permits, executed with meticulous perfection in the KGB Document Laboratory at Dzerzhinsky Square.

'It's all very scientific,' Semichastny told Colonel Belyaev approvingly as the little Tupolev jet winged towards Sheremetyevo Airport, Moscow, that evening.

Belyaev nodded. 'Scientific, yes. But on what basis, comrade, did you make your selection?'

'Fitness for the job.'

'In your own view?'

'Yes.'

'Science goes so far, you see, comrade. After that it is people, and people are difficult.'

'I don't see much difficulty with the ones we've got.'

Belyaev smiled grimly. 'There is none,' he said. 'Not now.'

VII

The defections in the nineteen fifties of Guy Burgess and Donald Maclean, followed by the later defection of their master, Kim Philby, finally broke the long-held and deeply-rooted belief of the Britsh security services that the upper and upper-middle classes were secure. It was a belief that had weathered the earlier, war-time treachery of a Cabinet Minister's son, John Amery, and it might have continued longer but for the Keeler/Ward/Profumo scandal which hastened the downfall of a predominantly Etonian Conservative government. The next British Premier, Harold Wilson, was determined that no security scandals would undermine his administration, and in 1964 he appointed a long-nosed MP with an inquiring and subtle mind to examine the security services on his behalf. George Wigg, MP (later Lord Wigg), examined and reported, and in due course a certain amount of blue blood was drained from the upper echelons of DI6 (sometimes known as Special Intelligence Service).

The man who took charge of the Russian section of DI6 was, like the then Prime Minister Wilson, a Yorkshireman, a grammar school boy and a graduate of Oxford University. There the resemblance ended. Tommy Gawthorpe was a miner's son, six feet two in height and beefy, and he retained the harshness of his unfashionable provincial accent. He looked like the former rugby player he was, black-jowled, grizzled and hard.

On an October morning, in his office on the fifth floor of a building in Parliament Street, he was looking down a list of reported movements when the name of Nicos Coulouris caught his eye. 'Arrived Middle East Airlines from Beirut, departed Air Canada for Edmonton/Vancouver/Victoria' he read.

Gawthorpe pressed a button. 'Coulouris,' he said to the assistant who answered his ring. 'We had something else about him the other day.'

The young man, whose name was David Norton, did not remember, but was wise enough not to say so. 'I'll get it, sir.'

He returned moments later with the Beirut report which had been received seventy-two hours earlier, and Gawthorpe read it slowly, twice. 'First,' he said, 'he's seen talking to KGB Head of Station, Beirut. Then he's off to Canada. Why?'

'We don't know the man *is* HOS Beirut, sir.'

'We suspect though. Why Canada? Get me Coulouris's file.'

He examined the file slowly. There was no doubt about Coulouris's involvement with the Russians, nor in twenty years had there been any effort at concealment. Gawthorpe drummed his thick fingers on his desk. 'I smell something.'

His assistant, nodded but did not speak. He could smell

nothing, and Gawthorpe did not appreciate answers like can-you and what's-that-sir.

'Get on to Vancouver. See if we can find out what he's up to.'

'Right, sir.' The assistant made to retrieve the file, but Gawthorpe placed a heavy hand on the card folder.

'Leave it.'

For a little while after David Norton had gone, Gawthorpe lay back in his chair and stared, without seeing it, at the elaborate plasterwork of his ceiling. Finally, frustrated, he buzzed again. 'Tell me about Vancouver.'

'Biggest city in Western Canada, sir. Principally a timber town and a port. Terminus of the Canadian Pacific Railway. A small amount of shipbuilding. Big Chinese population. That's about it.'

'It isn't, you know. There's something else if I could only lay my mind on it. Something I've read somewhere.'

The assistant said, 'The conference on co-operation for the peaceful development of the Pacific takes place there soon.'

Gawthorpe's large, even teeth showed briefly, but it was not a smile. 'I know. It wasn't that I was thinking about, either. There's something else.'

The assistant left him and went to work on the Vancouver files. Two hours of reading produced very little. Canadian grain for Russia was often loaded at Vancouver; the Royal Canadian Mounted Police regarded the port as the principal point of entry for drugs; large numbers of Vietnam draft-dodgers had crossed the border from the United States and settled there. He typed his notes out and presented them to Gawthorpe who read them, noted the contents in his mind, and continued with other work. From time to time, however, Gawthorpe's brain returned to the Coulouris/Vancouver question, sucking at it irritably as though it were a dental cavity.

The Russian cargo ship carrying John Baxter sailed within two hours of his arrival aboard. It moved down the Elbe, passed through the Kiel Canal, and on the tide the following morning entered the Polish port of Szczecin. There John Baxter was taken from the ship to an airfield and flown to Moscow. As he climbed from the aircraft, he happened to glance up at a jet passing low overhead; it was, ironically, a BEA Trident bound for London.

A car was waiting, and Baxter entered it. Even now, more than twelve hours later, he did not know why he had been taken prisoner. Nor did he know where he was. No one had spoken to him, no information had been given. He took what consolation he could from a belief that he had been enticed to Germany solely in order to be taken on to Russia, which must presumably mean that Henry and Jane had not been injured in a car crash. Even that, however, was an assumption; there was no way to be certain of it.

From Moscow Airport, Baxter was driven into the city in a car with curtained windows. When he got out of it, he was in the courtyard of what was clearly a prison. The room he finally entered had painted brick walls, a table and two chairs. He was, by this time, in a state of profound depression, which deepened over the two hours he remained alone in the room.

Three men finally entered. Two were armed, uniformed guards; the third man, wearing civilian clothes, sat down at the table and opened a file he was carrying.

Baxter said angrily, 'I am a British citizen. I demand to know – '

'Be quiet.'

'I *demand* – '

'Silence. Or you will be beaten.' The man across the table lit a cigarette and looked at Baxter. 'I shall now inform you of the arrangements we have made concerning you. To begin with, it is possible that you may eventually be allowed to return to Britain. That depends entirely upon the extent of your co-operation with us. I advise you to consider everything you do and say with that fact in mind.'

Baxter shrugged helplessly. 'I have the right to see the British consul.'

'Don't be absurd. You have no rights. Even survival beyond a specified period will be a reward, not a right. You will answer now the questions I ask. First, your name is John Faulds Baxter?'

Baxter nodded.

'Answer please.'

'That's my name.'

'Yes will do. Your age is thirty-six?'

'Yes.'

'You are an engineer?'

'Yes.'

'Specializing in mechanical handling?'

'That's right.'

'Describe your work to me.'

This, Baxter had realized hours earlier, was the only conceivable explanation for what had happened. Ludicrous, but conceivable. He said, 'I am employed by Plaid-Cromwell shipping.'

'What as?'

'In mechanical handling.'

His interrogator stubbed out the cigarette and said, 'To reinforce what I told you about co-operation, I will tell you that you are in an establishment of the Committee of State Security of the Soviet Union, which you may know as the KGB. We hold, quite literally, powers of life and death. Answer me now.'

Baxter said wearily, 'I am the pilot of an underwater work submersible. You, probably, will call it a miniature submarine.'

'Owned by?'

'By Plaid-Cromwell. You must know this. It's hardly difficult to find out. Newspapers and TV have – '

'Built by?'

'By Martec. Marine Technology Ltd.'

'Where?'

'Vancouver, British Columbia.'

Belyaev felt himself relax. There had been no bungling. They had the right man. He continued to stare coldly at Baxter.

'You worked there?'

'Yes, for a year.'

'And now?'

Baxter said, 'Plaid-Cromwell bought a *Tyee* submersible and are the licensed operators in Europe. There's nothing secret about it.'

'What do you do now?'

'What's required. Undersea cables, recovery work, pipelines.'

'And for the British Admiralty?'

Baxter closed his eyes, thinking furiously. He'd done a good deal of torpedo recovery work on the firing ranges in Loch Long and in Raasay Sound, off the Isle of Skye. On the other hand, there was remarkably little new technology in torpedoes. The details were certainly secret, but hardly critical. He said, 'I imagine you know well enough.'

'Tell me.'

'Torpedo recovery in deep water.'

Belyaev closed his file. 'We have a task we require you to perform. I will explain it to you.'

For twenty minutes, then, Belyaev set out the detail of the operation. Baxter listened with growing incredulity. At the end he said, 'I agree it is possible. But you see, don't you, that once I'm on Canadian soil, you won't see my heels for dust.'

Belyaev smiled. 'You underrate us. At the moment you are supposedly in Germany visiting an injured brother. There is nothing to prevent your return. Nothing, that is, in Britain. However, there are arrangements. You may remember, for example, that an electrician called at your flat in . . .' Belyaev consulted the file briefly '. . . in Vanbrugh Park, not long ago.'

Baxter's stomach contracted.

'You will remember that floorboards were raised. What you do not know is that certain items were placed beneath them: torpedo drawings, reports of searches, locations and performances. And a miniature camera, of course. Some microfilm. That kind of thing. If your British security people knew about that . . . hm?'

'It's not top-secret stuff,' Baxter said hopelessly.

'No? I think it is, though whether it is worth the classification is another matter. A single anonymous phone call. You see?'

Baxter saw very clearly. He said, 'And if I co-operate?'

'This material can easily be removed. No one need know.'

'It doesn't fit,' Baxter said savagely. 'From your point of view, I already know too much. You daren't release me.'

Privately Belyaev agreed, but he said, 'Once the Sword missiles are recovered it no longer matters. There would be no evidence; the Sword is itself obsolescent and unimportant; your story would appear at best unlikely. If you told it too vehemently, it might even appear to be fantasy. However, for the time being we have taken two other precautions. Your brother and his wife are under restraint, shall we say, on a Soviet naval vessel in the Mediterranean. And if, ultimately, we really feel we cannot return you to Britain, a trail has been laid: the documents, the flight to Germany, your voluntary boarding of a Soviet ship in Hamburg. Difficult to follow perhaps, but far from impossible. You would then appear to be a defector, would you not?'

Two days earlier, in Ottawa, the Ambassador of the Soviet Union had requested a brief interview with the Canadian Foreign Affairs Minister.

'Ask him why.'

'He says it's personal, sir. But good and urgent.'

'Personal?' The Foreign Minister laughed. 'What the hell have they got on me? Okay, fix it.'

Soviet Ambassador Semonov entered the office in the Foreign Ministry that afternoon wearing a comfortable, relaxed air. He accepted tea and a cigarette and glanced round. 'I'm sorry to put it like this, but I should prefer our discussion to be in private.'

'As you wish.' The Canadian had a tape machine running.

When the room was cleared, the Ambassador said, 'You have met Minister Gromyko?'

'At the UN. Several times.'

'Yes.' Semonov sipped his tea. 'I am sorry to tell you he has been unwell in recent weeks.'

'Then I hope,' said the Canadian Foreign Minister, formally, 'that you will extend to him our wishes for a speedy recovery.'

'Thank you. It is not serious. However, he is most anxious to attend the Pacific conference. It is, as you know, a subject upon which he has expended much time and thought.'

'I'd be sorry if he couldn't. Will his illness prevent it?'

'Not really. The problem is one of transport. I should like to emphasize that Minister Gromyko is most sensitive about the illness. He would like it to remain confidential.'

'Of course. Go on.'

'He has had an infection of the inner ear, which has affected his sense of balance.'

The Foreign Affairs Minister nodded sympathetically, suppressing his own quick thought about Soviet sense of balance.

'The result,' Ambassador Semonov went on, 'is that he is forbidden by his doctors to fly. Pressure upon the ear is to be avoided.'

'So how does he want to come?'

'By sea.'

'But won't that affect his ear? Movement and so on?'

'Apparently not.'

'Well, I don't see why he shouldn't come by sea. It seems a small courtesy. What ship will he use?'

The Ambassador placed his cup on the tea table as he spoke. In doing so, he was able to avoid looking into the Minister's eyes. 'A cruiser,' he said. He straightened again and added quickly, 'Another advantage, of course, is that we can offer to other delegations appropriate Russian hospitality. So much better than a hired hotel.'

The Canadian Foreign Minister smiled. 'I shall, of course, have to consult the Department of Defence and receive the approval of the Government.'

'I understand. Thank you for receiving me.'

After the Ambassador had gone, the Foreign Minister discussed the proposal by telephone with his colleagues, who felt that the opportunity to examine a Soviet cruiser at close range was not to be missed. In arriving at Vancouver, the ship would pass quite close to the Royal Canadian Navy base at Esquimault on the southern end of Vancouver Island, but was unlikely in passage to see anything important.

Semichastny and Belyaev received a summons to the central Government building within the Kremlin wall the day following John Baxter's arrival in Moscow. When they entered his office, Gromyko was standing, as he often did, by the window which looked out over Red Square. As the two men stood to attention on the red carpet, Gromyko turned. 'Comrades, I understand your preparations are complete.'

'Yes, Comrade Minister.' Semichastny said.

'And the Englishman?'

'Has no alternative but to co-operate.'

Belyaev said, 'He understands that.'

'Good.' Gromyko sat down at his desk. 'When do you leave?'

'We await only the final confirmation.'

Gromyko looked from one man to the other. He may have been smiling; as always it was hard to tell. He said, 'You have it. The Canadian Government is pleased to welcome a cruiser of the Soviet Navy. A mooring will be provided in English Bay, Vancouver.'

'English Bay,' Semichastny said, 'is perfect. Quite perfect.'

'I sail tomorrow on board the *Suvarov*.' Gromyko rose, walked round the desk and shook hands with both men. 'At all costs, secrecy,' he said.

They nodded.

'Go, then. Remember this also. You have sentenced me to waste two long periods at sea. I do not like the sea.'

It was still impossible to determine whether or not Andrei Gromyko was smiling. They about-turned quickly and left the room.

Less than two hours later a party of nine men entered an Ilyushin jet transport at a military airfield south of Moscow. They were beginning a long and complex journey that would, nonetheless, bring them to Vancouver within forty-eight hours. The first stage of the trip was simple; they went from one military airport to another, this time outside the Hungarian capital, Budapest. There they entered two Volkswagen microbuses which contained sleeping bags, spirit stoves and a quantity of damp clothing for purposes of authenticity. Hungarian entry visas and date stamps had been entered in the West German passports provided for them by the KGB Documents Laboratory.

There was no trouble at the border post on the main crossing between Hungary and Austria, nor, after a few hours' driving, was there any problem in entering West Germany. They were Germans returning from a perfectly legitimate holiday at Lake Balaton. Only one member of the party might have given them away and he, immediately before leaving Hungary, had been shown a photograph of his brother and sister-in-law on the deck of a warship, surrounded by armed Russian sailors.

In Munich the two microbuses were returned to the car-hire company from which they came and each of the two separate parties rendezvoused with a KGB contact who collected the German passports and supplied them with replacements. The six agents from New Woodville then caught the train for Frankfurt and caught a Lufthansa Boeing for London. Later, in an Air Canada DC8, they would fly to Edmonton, Alberta, and travel by train through the scenic delights of the Rocky Mountains to Vancouver.

That was the best, simplest and least clandestine way of making the journey. Belyaev had decided, however, and Semichastny had agreed, that John Baxter must not travel via London for the obvious reason that somebody might recognize him. Accordingly the three men travelled via Lisbon to Mexico City and from there on a charter flight to Edmonton. They, too, passed the final hours of the journey in a luxurious Canadian-Pacific Railways observation coach, admiring the Rocky Mountains. Baxter stared yearningly at the huge peaks and valleys, wishing there were some way of escaping to them, but could see no conceivable way of escape that offered any prospect of survival for Henry and Jane Baxter.

Returning from a lunch date on the Tuesday four days after Baxter's departure for Germany, the managing director of the company he worked for, Kenneth Lavering, was a little resentful that he had heard nothing. He sympathized with Baxter, and hoped the news that had greeted him on arrival was not as bad as seemed likely. All the same, Baxter should have let him know what was happening.

'Any word yet?' Lavering asked his secretary.

'About Mr Baxter? No, sir.'

Lavering went into his own office and began work. An hour later, with Baxter's continued silence still nagging at him, he buzzed for his secretary. 'That telegram. Do you remember what hospital it was?'

She stared at him blankly. 'No, Mr Lavering. There was just the message.'

Lavering said, 'There was also a telephone number. Ask the Post Office if we can have another copy.'

He worked on until she returned. 'They say they can only send a copy to the addressee.'

'I hope you told them Plaid-Cromwell Shipping *was* the addressee.'

'Mr Baxter, I mean,' the girl said. 'I don't exactly sound like Mr Baxter.'

'No. All right.' Lavering nodded, dismissing her, and reached for his private telephone. He was about to dial when it occurred to him that he should wait a while in case, by a fluke, he should speak to the same operator as his secretary, so he left it half an hour before telephoning.

'My name is Baxter, Plaid-Cromwell Shipping,' Lavering told the cable supervisor. 'Cable address PLACRO London. A cable was sent to me here on Friday, from Hamburg, and I seem to have lost it. Could you repeat the message?'

'Yes, sir. I'll call you back.'

Lavering gave her numbers for both the company and his own extension and told his secretary to inform the switchboard that any calls for John Baxter were to be referred to him. Ten minutes later the cables supervisor was on the line. Lavering wrote down the cable message and the telephone number, thanked her, said he was aware there would be an additional charge, and hung up. He then dialled the code for Germany followed by the Hamburg number and waited.

He listened for more than a minute as the number rang, then broke the connection and dialled again in case the first call had been misrouted. Again there was no reply. It was odd, he thought, that a hospital should fail to reply. 'Teutonic *inefficiency*,' he muttered to himself as he replaced the receiver. He then instructed his secretary to dial the number every five minutes for the rest of the afternoon and returned to the papers on his desk. At five-fifteen she reported that there was still no reply.

Kenneth Lavering was a persistent man and disliked failure. After his secretary had left, he telephoned the international operator, explained his problem, and asked if he could be connected with the Hamburg exchange. There was a short delay. It wasn't usual. At last, however, he got through.

The Hamburg operator took the number and checked. 'It is certainly the home of Dr Kleinmann,' she said.

'*Home!*' Lavering said. 'It's not a hospital?'

'No, sir.'

'Look,' Lavering said. 'I'm not familiar with German systems. Would you *expect* a reply from a doctor's home?'

'Yes, sir. Unless he is away.'

'Surely they'd have *someone* to answer?'

'I mean away from home, sir. If you wait, I will check.'

He waited two minutes. By that time he was beginning to suspect he had been disconnected, but then the operator returned. 'Dr Kleinmann is on holiday, sir.'

'Holiday? Do you know for how long?'

'Two weeks. Until Samst – until Saturday.'

'Would Hamburg police know of any road accidents in the area?'

'Yes, sir.'

'Put me through.'

The operator could not do that, but she gave him the number and he telephoned the police in Hamburg. Once again Kenneth Lavering had to hold on for some time, but eventually he heard the answer to his question. Hamburg police had no record of a serious car accident involving British visitors named

Baxter. They also told him that Dr Kleinmann was a general practitioner in private practice.

Baffled and angry, Kenneth Lavering replaced the receiver. As an experienced executive he was familiar enough with the phoney accident or illness which was the commonest of all excuses for absenteeism. But John Baxter was a keen and conscientious man, senior enough in any case to be given a couple of days off if he wanted them. He could also remember the anxiety on Baxter's face. No, he decided, it wasn't an elaborate fiddle.

Then another thought struck him. Baxter *had* got through on the telephone. He, Lavering, hadn't actually been present, but afterwards Baxter had given him the gist of what the doctor said. Yet Dr Kleinmann was on holiday!

He lit a cigarette, thoughtfully. It was now after six o'clock. He knew exactly the action he should take; it was action he was, in fact, *required* to take. Baxter was a signatory of the Official Secrets Act and had recently been engaged on work with a high security classification, and the rules were absolutely clear: 'The unexplained absence of persons bound under the Act shall be reported forthwith.' Did this count as 'unexplained absence'? There was, after all, the best of reasons why Baxter should have gone. On the other hand, the detail was strange enough to be worrying. Lavering poured himself a whisky and sipped it undiluted, uncomfortably aware that his reasons for not reporting Baxter's absence were mildly discreditable. Lavering wanted to watch a football match on television that night, and a phone call to the police would mean long hours of questions and waiting about. After which, almost inevitably, John Baxter would appear next morning in the office with good, sound reasons for everything.

The hell with it, Lavering finally decided. If no news had been received by mid-morning the next day, he *would* report it. He drank the last of the whisky, locked his office, and went home to Leatherhead.

VIII

In the course of the same afternoon, Thomas Gawthorpe, head of the Russian section of DI6, received two messages. The first, from Vancouver, British Columbia, reported that Nicos Coulouris, the Greek shipowner from Beirut, had booked a first-class seat on Air Canada for a flight from Vancouver that evening, to London.

He looked at it angrily. Whatever Coulouris may have been doing was now over and the chances of identifying his contacts over there now lost.

'He's been up to something, the bugger,' Gawthorpe muttered to himself. 'But what?' He reached for a pad and wrote on it: 'TG to Van, enciphered. Report even rumoured contacts Coulouris urgentest.' Then he rang for his assistant and instructed that the message be sent without delay.

An hour and a half later, while he was in a meeting with Government computer data retrieval experts, working on the interminable and insoluble problem of refining cross-references and improving correlation, his assistant interrupted him with a single sheet of paper, a yellow inter-office secret memorandum from the Admiralty Department of the Ministry of Defence.

'What's this?' Gawthorpe asked.

'I'm sorry, sir. I thought you'd want to see it at once.'

'Excuse me, gentlemen, please.' Gawthorpe nodded to the computer men and took the slip of yellow paper. When he had read it, he stared at it, thoughtfully, for more than a minute, then he rose. 'I'm sorry, we'll have to go over all this later.' He then returned to his own office.

'Tell me,' he demanded of his assistant, 'why Gromyko's going to waste heaven knows how long on some uncomfortable cruiser!'

'Reasons of health, according to the Canadians.'

'Balls!'

'It's perfectly possible, sir,' his assistant protested. 'He's no spring chicken.'

'He's no fool either. And these Russian ships aren't cruise liners. They're modern, but they're uncomfortable. Are they going to park one for inspection? Why? Gromyko's no more aboard for health reasons than I'd take a cruise on a coal barge. I want a meeting and I want naval security in on it. Right?'

'Immediately, sir.'

Gawthorpe had some difficulty in convincing the meeting of the sense of his suspicions. The two unconnected incidents remained unconnected and Gawthorpe stared at the naval commander who pointed out reasonably enough that there was a long tradition of using naval vessels as conference headquarters. 'Wilson did it, after all, on *Tiger*. Even Bulganin and Khrushchev used a cruiser when they came to Britain in the 'fifties.'

'The fact remains,' Gawthorpe said, 'that something's going on over there, and I want to know what it is.'

The meeting broke up with nothing achieved except a stubborn increase in Gawthorpe's determination.

A little before seven o'clock that evening Admiral Sir Darren Hogg was about to pour himself a glass of Madeira when the telephone rang in his flat in St John's Wood. He replaced bottle and glass on the silver tray which had been presented to him on his transfer from C-in-C Mediterranean to the Admiralty, and went into his study to answer it. He lifted the receiver. 'Yes?'

'Are you free for half an hour?' a voice asked.

'I am.'

'Then I'm coming over.'

Admiral Hogg replaced the receiver and returned to pour his Madeira. He sipped at it while he read the closing market prices in the *Evening Standard*. He did not allow himself to be intrigued. In a little while he would know why his caller was coming over; until then, he calculated the position of his stock portfolio, using a silver propelling pencil and the margin of the newspaper.

When the doorbell rang, he answered it himself. His daily woman had left at five, leaving a cold meal ready, and half a bottle of claret breathing to one side of the fireplace.

Gawthorpe came in, as he thought, gently. He liked what he knew of the austere Hogg and to enter energetically would be to create a wrong ambience. Hogg was, by nature, a quiet, precise man and it was sensible to indulge his tastes, especially when a favour was required.

The admiral smiled quietly, partly in greeting, partly in acknowledgment of Gawthorpe's deliberate gentleness. It occurred to him that a time bomb ticking in a corner was also deliberate and quiet, concealing its energy, and that Gawthorpe was not unlike the bomb. He said, 'Will you take a glass of Madeira?'

'Thanks.'

'Or would you prefer a little whisky?'

Gawthorpe looked at him appreciatively. 'I think perhaps I would.'

'I rather thought you might. Soda? Apollinaris?'

'Whisky and Polly,' Gawthorpe said. 'I haven't had one in years.'

'It becomes increasingly difficult to come by,' Hogg said. He led Gawthorpe towards the fire, gesturing to a chair, and when Gawthorpe was seated, sat himself. He then waited. He had met Gawthorpe many years earlier, when, as Director of Naval Intelligence, he had called in D16 to tighten security in the underwater warfare research station at Portland after the Portland spy case, and the two men, though not friends, had come to work together with a considerable degree of mutual understanding.

'They're up to something.'

'Are they, indeed? *They* being our friends?'

'The fourth ally,' Gawthorpe said. 'I don't know what it is.'

'So you are irritated.'

'I have no *reason*,' Gawthorpe confessed, the memory of the afternoon's meeting fresh in his mind, 'to be so certain. Or very little. I just know.'

'You sniff the wind. Very sensible. What do you smell?'

'Let me put it this way. I have two facts. As follows: one, the KGB Head of Station in Beirut is seen talking to a shipbroker who does Russian business, whereupon the shipbroker takes himself a little trip. Secondly, a Russian cruiser will arrive in a few days in the same place.'

'Which is?'

'Vancouver. Maybe there is a third. The Pacific Conference on peaceful development is happening there too. I just feel it links up.'

'On the other hand,' the Admiral said, 'you've been right before.'

'And wrong.'

'Certainly. But not through lethargy. I rather imagine I know what it is you want.'

Gawthorpe grinned. 'I shouldn't be surprised.'

Admiral Hogg looked steadily back at him. 'I take it our American friends are becoming less liberal in the exchange of information?'

'A good deal less. They don't see why they should exchange a bucketful for a cupful. I don't blame them.'

'Which brings us,' the Admiral said, 'to my American brother-in-law?'

'You won't see much of him these days, I don't suppose.'

'Unhappily not. California is a long way away. However, I'm spared the excessive company of his wife.'

Gawthorpe said directly, 'Could you stand it? Just for a day or two?'

Admiral Hogg smiled. 'We do worse things for England. Though not much, I think. What is it you wish to know?'

'It sounds daft, doesn't it? I just want to know if there's been any monkey business. Unexplained nonsense, you know.'

'Very well,' Admiral Hogg glanced at his fingernails. 'I am, of course, retired.'

'From which two things flow. First, your brother-in-law may be more reluctant to talk. I know that. Secondly, don't worry about the cost.'

'Thank you. When do I leave?'

Grinning, Gawthorpe glanced at his watch.

'So soon? And the explanation for this surprising trip? For my sister-in-law, you understand.'

Gawthorpe said, 'There's a British actor/producer, in Hollywood. A friend of ours. He's thinking of making a film about Sir Francis Drake and he needs technical advice.'

Admiral Sir Darren Hogg smiled. 'I first went to sea in the *Iron Duke*, not the *Golden Hind*.'

As Hogg escorted his visitor to the door, Gawthorpe said, 'It's the late flight. I'm sorry. A car will pick you up. Eight-thirty. The driver will have your tickets and some dollars.'

'Thank you.'

'Thank *you*.' Gawthorpe shook hands. 'I'm very grateful.'

'So am I. I shall enjoy California. Oh, by the way.'

'Yes?'

'You ought really to find out what sort of cruiser the Russians are bringing into Vancouver.'

The expenditure of ten dollars a head was enough to give the party led by Arkady Semichastny and Pavel Belyaev the perfect reason for a prolonged, almost leisurely survey of Jervis Inlet. In the sporting goods department of the Hudson's Bay Company's big department store in Vancouver, licences to fish for all British Columbia sporting fish, including all five species of salmon, but excluding steelhead trout, were obtained, after which two cabin cruisers, one four-berth, the other six, were hired from a company in Vancouver for a period of two weeks. The hire company clerk looked at Belyaev's cash with some suspicion. 'Yes,' he said grudgingly, 'we do rent on a deposit basis, but we sure prefer a credit card.'

'No problem,' Belyaev said. He produced the plastic, oblong card of the Diner's Club. The account would ultimately go to an address in Montreal, where it would be settled by the KGB. As he signed the docket, the clerk asked, 'Do both boats go on this?'

Belyaev laughed and Semichastny realized he had not seen him laugh before. 'Not a chance. They pay for their own boat.'

Semichastny produced the Carte Blanche. As with the

Diner's Club card, the bill, when later presented, would be settled immediately.

Within an hour the two boats, with hired fishing tackle aboard, were heading out of Burrard Inlet beneath the vast span of the Lion's Gate Bridge, which guarded the entrance to Vancouver's superb harbour. They were not hurrying. On the way they intended to reconnoitre the various shelter points on the coast in case, during the movement of the Sword missiles down the Inside Passage, the weather became rough. So the two boats proceeded in line astern round Point Atkinson and turned into Howe Sound, the next fiord to the north. Later in the day, they visited Trail Bay on the Sechelt Peninsula, farther to the north. They spent the night at anchor at Garden Bay Marine Park, and proceeded at first light next morning into Jervis Inlet where, under the pretence of trolling for salmon, they watched the launching of the *Tyee* submersible from its barge. Some Polaroid photographs of the operation were also quietly taken and the operation was studied and discussed as it proceeded.

'What is the procedure now?' Semichastny asked John Baxter as the barge-crane lifted *Tyee* from the water.

'They'll connect up the battery charge lines and run the donkey engine,' Baxter said. He said it reluctantly, as he did everything reluctantly now. He was well aware of his own importance in the recovery of the Sword missiles and was frequently tempted to jump over the side and let the Russians get on with it as best they could. But he didn't. In the impossible equation he faced, he could find no moral justification for the sacrifice of two innocent lives. Had it been wartime, yes. Had there been a threat to a lot of other innocent lives, possibly. But, so far as he could tell, the Russians were removing the missiles for reasons which threatened nobody but themselves. So far as he could tell. Baxter was uncomfortably aware that he knew remarkably little and might be wrong.

Belyaev was watching *Tyee* through night glasses. 'How long will it take to recharge the batteries?'

'Six hours perhaps. It depends on how much juice they've used.'

'And when is the oxygen cylinder replaced?'

'Standard operating procedure is replacement on surfacing, check before diving. Did the man who hooked up the wires go inside?'

'Yes.'

'He'd only do that to check the oxygen.'

'Very well. Lookouts at night?'

'Variable,' Baxter said. 'In busy waters, everybody's careful.'

'Here, less so?'

'Here? There'll be a man on watch, but I expect he'll stay below most of the time.'

'Then tomorrow,' Belyaev said, 'is as good a time as any. We watch for one more day.'

'I suppose so,' Baxter said quietly. His heart was suddenly thumping. Perhaps it was his closeness to *Tyee*, the sight of the tugboat's lights across the water, that had given him the idea. There might, he thought tensely, be a remote chance, the faintest possibility, of reversing the situation. He was thinking rapidly. The chance would come later, if at all. But, if he was clever, it ought to come.

As darkness fell, the fishermen in the two cabin cruisers reeled in their lines and the boats headed for Saltery Bay on the north side of Jervis Inlet, where they dropped anchor for the night roughly half a mile from *Tyee*.

On the flight deck of a BOAC VC10 which had just taken off from Tokyo and was banking to give the passengers a view of Fujiyama, the young navigator said, 'I don't really understand what we're looking *for*, skip.'

'Just Russian warships.'

'There'll be plenty in the Sea of Japan,' the navigator said.

The captain was patient. He was fifty and greying and had flown in Coastal Command during the war. 'Single warships. In particular a solo cruiser on any kind of easterly course.'

'What I don't understand,' the co-pilot chimed in, 'is how you tell a cruiser from a destroyer. Or – what are those other things – frigates?'

'It gets harder,' the captain said. 'Once upon a time, corvettes were tiny, frigates bigger, destroyers bigger still, and then came cruisers, battle cruisers and battleships. It was easy. Now everything seems to be somewhere between four and ten thousand tons.'

The co-pilot was twenty-six years old, born as the war was ending. He also enjoyed an easy relationship with the captain. He said, 'In those days, I suppose you could always count the masts.'

'Shut up and look,' the captain retorted in mock anger. 'It's a serious request. We comply.'

'Yes, sir.'

The BOAC crew saw nothing. Nor did three Vulcan bombers homeward bound from Australia, and also obeying orders to keep a lookout. But later that day a British destroyer on her way from Hawaii to the Japanese island of Hokkaido noticed a Russian cruiser that looked almost top heavy, bustling past her heading east. He radioed position and course and the cruiser was spotted again, the following day, by another British V-bomber crew sent to find her.

KGB Head of Station, Hamburg, was in his Volkswagen, on the autobahn to Bremerhaven with a minor task to fulfil. His orders governing the collection of John Baxter had been very detailed, and now that Baxter was safely wherever he was (the agent did not know where) there remained instructions to be carried out.

In Bremerhaven he drove round the suburbs until he found what he wanted, a suburban post office. Having done so, he reached behind him and took a novel from the back seat and began to read. The novel was by Aleksandr Solzhenitsyn, and Head of Station, Hamburg, was not only greatly enjoying it, he could see no reason why it should not be published at home.

Just before the post office closed for the night, he went in and wrote, in English, on a cable form. He waited while the girl counted the words and calculated the charge, then he paid, returned to his Volkswagen, and drove back to Hamburg.

The cable was waiting on Kenneth Lavering's desk next morning. It read: 'Condition of both still critical. Am assuming seven days' leave okay – Baxter.' Lavering was glad he had not reported Baxter's absence the evening before. The matter had been on his mind all evening, spoiling his enjoyment of the football match. Now, he felt justified. Plaid-Cromwell's *Tyee* submersible was undergoing renewal of some wiring and would not be in action for more than two weeks. Baxter's seven-day leave was reasonable, justified, and in any case could hardly have been denied.

IX

It was curious, Admiral Sir Darren Hogg reflected, how well the habits instilled in a lifetime with the Royal Navy were suited to air travel. If all the pampered executives who complained about jet fatigue had spent their formative years on the on-off-on-off watch-keeping system, and had developed the sleep habits it demanded, they could cope easily with the speed of modern long-distance travel. Shortly after take-off from Heathrow, the admiral asked the steward for a cognac. For half an hour after that he sat quietly, the balloon glass cupped in his hands, occasionally sniffing the bouquet, occasionally sipping the spirit. Finally, when it was done, he put the glass to one side, tilted back his first-class seat, and went to sleep. His own built-in alarm would awaken him four hours later.

The plane was two hours from Montreal when he awoke. He ordered bacon and eggs and coffee, ate, and read *Time* magazine until the plane landed. As the Montreal passengers disembarked, he went with them into the transit area and put through a telephone call to San Diego, California. He then returned to the aircraft.

As it flew on to Chicago, he continued reading. At Chicago, he went through immigration, changed to a United Airlines flight, and slept for two hours to Los Angeles. On the brief hop from Los Angeles to San Diego he ate scrambled eggs. He had slept six hours out of fourteen and was ready either to sleep or to talk, depending on Chuck Whitmore's inclinations.

Knowing Chuck, there would probably be talk, and the early hours and whisky were Hogg's allies.

A black Lincoln, with an admiral's pennant hooded on its bonnet, was waiting for him at the airport, and its driver, a petty officer, knew better than to talk without first being addressed. Hogg arrived at the home of his brother-in-law, Admiral Charles W. (Chuck) Whitmore, United States Navy, at one o'clock in the morning.

As the two men shook hands, Hogg asked, 'How's Dolly?'

'Apologetic.' The corner of Chuck Whitmore's mouth moved wryly. 'She was dog-tired. Said to say hallo for her. She'll see you in the morning.'

'It will be nice,' Hogg said, 'to see her again. It's nearly three years.' This was a polite fiction and both men knew it. Dolly Whitmore and Darren Hogg had the same natural affinity as an Aberdeen terrier and a tabby cat. The two men had married sisters, forty years before. Hogg's wife, Eleanor, had been the quiet, studious one; Dolly, the extrovert, wanted to dance all night and play tennis and golf all day. Both men knew that Hogg had made the more fortunate choice, and their long friendship, dating from Chuck Whitmore's appointment in the early thirties as a junior naval attaché in London, had been conducted at one remove from Dolly, who would have wrecked it if she could.

'You'll be tired,' Chuck said. 'Want to go straight to bed?'

'Not particularly. 'Do you?'

'Nope. I took a snooze earlier. Come on in the den and we'll murder some Scotch.'

In the panelled room, with its leather armchairs, its books, its pool table and its framed photographs, Chuck Whitmore handed Hogg a bottle still wrapped in tissue.

Hogg smiled. 'What is it?'

'Glen Morangie. Just for you, sonny.'

'I can remember when we thought Johnnie Walker Red Label was a luxury.'

'So can I. Sometimes I wish it still was. What the hell's all this about a movie?'

'I'm not sure, myself,' Hogg replied. 'Friend of a friend

85

wants some technical advice. You know how things happen in Britain. It will be a pleasant change.'

Whitmore said gently, 'Retirement's hell, right?'

'How long have you to go?'

'Year and a half. Can't say I look at it with much enthusiasm.'

'I've had six years. One feels a little ineffectual. Out of touch. I suppose there are compensations.'

'Such as?'

Hogg laughed quietly. 'I wish I knew.' He stood, walked over to a rack on the wall, and picked up a small leather case. 'How long since you used these?' He had given them to Chuck thirty years earlier.

'The billiards balls? Years, I guess.'

'Then come along. Three hundred and one up. For one dollar. Let's see if the world's second best navy can still beat what remains of the third.'

Admiral Whitmore slipped off his jacket. 'I'm not sure that's so funny.'

Hogg nodded. 'It's not funny at all. But I'm afraid it's true.'

It was not difficult to keep the conversation to naval matters. They moved round the table in easy companionship, refilling their glasses occasionally, relaxing in the quiet, comfortable room to the soft click of the ivory balls. Hogg was careful not to probe deeply; he steered well clear of current strategic problems, knowing Whitmore would be surprised and hurt if he overstepped the understood boundaries. He relied partly on the malt whisky, but far more on the long years of trust, and was prepared to wait for the occasional titbit.

At three-fifteen in the morning, with the score at two games each and the decider under way, they were discussing submarines. Hogg said, 'I'm told there was a Yankee-class nuclear sub in Loch Morar three months ago. They're getting very impertinent.'

'You should have forced the bastard to surface,' Whitmore said. 'We have, a few times.'

'It was spotted coming out, not going in.' Hogg tried for, and missed, a cannon off a cushion. 'Damn!'

'Wait till your cable network's complete. You'll hear them

flushing the heads at fifty miles.' Smoothly, Whitmore flicked his ball off the red into a centre pocket.

'It really is as good as that?'

'The SOSUS/CAESAR network is tops, Darren. In the beginning the Russians ripped a cable up here and there and there were holes they could get through. Now it's double and triple-banked. We've laid those lines like blue-assed spiders.'

'So nothing gets past? *Nothing*?'

Chuck Whitmore chalked his cue and blew away the excessive dust thoughtfully. 'Can't say *nothing*. You never do know that.'

'All the same, you seem confident.'

'Do I? I reckon I might. They've been trying all kinds of approaches in all kinds of places and we keep sitting on them.'

'Do you? How things have changed, Chuck. I've done some long sea searches. So have you. But you still have an awful lot of water to watch.'

'We got a lot of wire, too.'

'Yes.' Hogg potted the red neatly. 'But the Pacific's a big ocean. Not bad, eh?'

'Bet you a dollar you can't do it again. We're watching them from the Mexican coast to Alaska, Darren. They bump the wire. The bell goes and a couple of destroyers just go sit on 'em.'

Hogg missed and paid up. 'Consistently?'

'Oh, sure. About three months ago, they were bumping the wires off Norfolk, Virginia. We watched the whole way. They're always trying somewheres. Few weeks ago they were nosing round the north west and Seattle.'

'Seattle? You mean they actually entered Puget Sound?'

Chuck Whitmore laughed. 'No chance, Darren. Five times, six maybe, they ran towards the coast from deep water. Nukes every time. The last one even came in running silent but we got him.'

Hogg played his next two shots in silence. Americans always tended to speak in strictly American terms, but Seattle was virtually the north-western extremity of the United States; beyond Seattle lay British Columbia. As casually as he could, he asked, 'What do you think they were doing?'

Whitmore shrugged and bent over his cue. 'Surveying, probably. They never stop mapping the ocean bed.' He played his shot, missed, and straightened. 'One of my guys reckons they've got a competition on.'

'What kind of competition?'

'Oh, you know. Kind of thing the sub guys do. Hero of the Soviet Union for the first guy round the island.'

'Which island would that be?'

'Vancouver island. They nose in towards Queen Charlotte Strait.'

Hogg said, 'That's preposterous, surely. There is not enough water for a sub in the Inside Passage.'

'Sure there's not. But that's what they seemed to be trying. Then they stopped just like that. Next week, it'll be Panama or the Bering Strait.'

The cargo vessel ploughed rapidly north-eastward; radio operator first class Nikita Ivanov stood at the stern and watched the wake streaming white behind her. It had been like this for many days now, the steady thump of the engines, the wake streaming behind, the enormous, empty ocean. The cargo ship was *not* heading just north to Kamchatka or somewhere near the Aleutians, it had already come too far. They were crossing the Pacific; he was now in no doubt about it. Standing there, Ivanov glanced up from time to time at the radio cabin in an action that had become a reflex. Literally any second of any day, a fatal signal could arrive: some demand for interrogation of the prisoner, a routine inquiry about personnel now that one radio operator was supposed to be imprisoned. Since that first signal, which he had acknowledged and left unlogged, there had been no further radio traffic concerning him. He tried to take comfort from that fact, and from the one additional factor in his favour: his own presence in the radio room for eight hours out of every twenty-four, so that the odds against his receiving any transmission about himself were two to one. All the same, he had spent the whole voyage in a debilitating state of suspense. His nerves were on edge, he slept badly, food had almost to be forced down his throat.

Watching the racing, bubbling wake, he watched, too, the sharks which had stuck close to the ship for several days now, two of them, scavenging on the ship's waste and apparently prepared to follow for ever. Their black fins were less than forty metres from him now, and he shuddered as he watched their effortless speed. If the time came, if the opportunity were ever to offer itself, Ivanov knew that he would have to enter the water. At the first sight of land within swimming range, he would have to go over the side, sharks or no sharks.

He watched for a while, and then resumed his programme of physical exercise. For days now he had been doing several hours of calisthenics, trying to toughen his body for the ordeal that might, if he were lucky, lie ahead. His shipmates laughed at him, of course, but he'd concocted a story about a girl who thought he was too fat, and carried on.

Purposefully, he began to run round the after deck, jerking one knee up to his abdomen with each step, feeling the strain on abdominal and back muscles. In an hour, his duty period would begin and if it was like the rest of them on this trip it would be quiet; there had been remarkably little radio traffic. So he would sit in the radio room, endlessly squeezing two small, hard rubber balls, and toughening himself with muscular tension exercises.

Running, he came close to the rail, saw the fin of one of the sharks, and shivered again.

At one o'clock in the morning, four frogmen slipped silently into the waters of the inlet from one of the two white cabin cruisers. They wore wetsuits and had on their backs cylinders of compressed air sufficient for nearly two hours.

They swam silently forward towards the lights of the tugboat half a mile away; four men in two pairs, the two leading swimmers pulling behind them an inflated plastic bag containing a variety of tools. The bag, weighed down by the heavy metal, floated low.

The tugboat lay at anchor bow-on to the slight ebb from

the long inlet, and behind her at a distance of some fifty yards, a sixty-foot barge rode at the end of a towline.

The swimmers moved gently along the slight current until they came abeam of the tug where their leader stopped, slipped back his rubber helmet, disconnected his breathing equipment and trod water, watching and listening. Apart from the movement of the water, there was no sound. His eyes told him that the only light on the tugboat's starboard side came from the saloon amidships. He restored his hood and mouthpiece and swam on. The four men surfaced beneath the overhanging stern of the flat-topped barge.

A few minutes later, having completed his inspection of the barge's bottom, the leader tapped the shoulder of another swimmer and pointed to the deck, four feet above.

John Baxter nodded, bobbed until his hands could reach the deck, then waited until he felt the boost from below which enabled him to climb on to the flat deck. There was a splash, of course, and he could hear the water dripping from his suit and breathing apparatus on to the wooden deck boards, but loud though the noises seemed to him, neither was loud enough to alert the tugboat's watchkeeper.

He slipped off his flippers and the air cylinder pack and crept forward the four feet to where *Tyee II* stood. The little submersible, twenty feet long, ten wide, ten high, made a strange, futuristic shape in the pale moonlight. Her fibreglass hull was bright orange, the forward observation ports seemed, as always, to stare at him like three cataracted eyes. Above the ports, the telechiric arm, with its wrist, elbow and shoulder joints, looked somehow like a huge, waiting dentist's drill. He stared at *Tyee II* resentfully. If ever there was a perfect escape mechanism, this was surely it. She could descend to three thousand feet and move silently on her electric motors at five knots; she could hide so efficiently that *nobody* could find her. Yet he, who wanted above all to escape, dared not use her for that purpose; could only obey the orders he was given and carry out the job assigned to him. Until, he thought grimly, his opportunity came.

There was a swishing behind him and a soft thud and

another frogman joined him on the tug's deck. Baxter wondered why they bothered to supervise him. He was helpless. They knew it and he knew it; and two men used more oxygen than one, though that was not for the moment important and came into his calculation merely as a matter of habit.

Reaching up, Baxter grasped the hand ring above him, then put his foot into the foothold and heaved himself upward towards the submersible's sail. The little sail, conning tower in the old parlance, housed the hatch which was the only means of entering or leaving *Tyee II*. When he was standing on the hull, he paused for a moment, crouching, to see whether all remained calm, then he reached over to unfasten the hatch clips and swing the cover up on its hinge. A moment later, with a practised wriggle, he was in the forward crew sphere, standing looking upward to the little circle of night sky framed in the open hatch above. Suddenly a dark figure was silhouetted in the hatch and his Russian guard was climbing awkwardly down beside him.

Baxter stood on the footrail and closed the hatch but did not secure it. Nor did he switch on the lights. Instead, with a pencil torch, he did a swift check on the instruments, ensuring that oxygen and battery were at operational levels. Then he turned to his companion. 'Okay.'

'Right.' The Russian bent to flash his torch twice quickly out of the centre of the three observation ports, then rose and pointed to the pilot's couch.

Obediently Baxter lay face down on the foam-rubber mattress. The control buttons and levers were grouped neatly on his right. To his left the little TV camera was mounted so that it could be swivelled downward to point out the centre port. Glancing across, he watched the Russian lie down on the observer's couch on the other side of the crew cabin.

It was all so familiar, yet so unreal. During his three years with *Tyee* submersibles, he'd been through the movements a thousand times; by now they were easy, familiar and natural. As he stared through the little porthole of reinforced glass, he half-thought he might awaken from a dream and find it was *not* all happening. Yet the stillness, the absence of movement on the deck outside, the failure of a reassuring voice to come through the underwater telephone, all confirmed the reality to him.

Ordinarily, now, he would be waiting for the crane to lift *Tyee II*; for the deck boards to move below him, for the brief swing out over the water and the lowering. Now he could hear nothing except their own breathing, see nothing except a few square feet of the barge's deck. He lay waiting, wondering whether the watchkeeper would notice any change of movement, would go on deck to check the sub and barge. Baxter hoped he wouldn't because, if he did, the tugboat's crew would die.

He lay still, staring forward, for a good ten minutes before he saw the first, gleaming skin of water sliding across the deck boards towards him. It had worked, then! The frogmen had succeeded either in opening the cocks or drilling holes in the barge's bottom, and the barge was now sinking beneath them.

Baxter rose quickly and climbed up to tighten the compression ring of the hatch cover, then returned to the couch. By now the deck boards were invisible and the water surface was moving up towards him. In a minute or two the ports would be covered; this was the most dangerous moment of the operation for the sinking barge would exert a different pull on the towline, and the watchkeeper, if he were alert, might quickly sense it. Baxter watched the water line move smoothly up the glass. Remarkably, the barge was going down almost level, hardly tilting at all. Soon he would apply gentle forward power to the twin three-horse-power electric motors and operate the pump to shift oil ballast and *Tyee II* would slide smoothly beneath the surface.

But the time was not yet. For the moment, *Tyee II*'s tobogganlike skids rested on the deck and the sub's ten-ton weight had not been taken by the water. He waited until he felt the first free movement and then operated the oil pump, decreasing the sub's buoyancy until he felt the skid again touch the deck boards. Keeping his eyes on his watch, he allowed a full minute to elapse. Now the engines should be submerged. Ten per cent of forward power and he felt her inch forward; a few more feet and the dive could begin.

'Now,' he said, and moved the two levers.

'All right?' the Russian asked. Baxter almost laughed at the anxiety on the other man's face. It was an absurd situation. The Russian in charge of this part of the operation had no knowledge of it, no command. Yet he *was* in command and Baxter, the expert, was totally subordinate.

'It's okay,' he said, glancing at the depth gauge. 'Thirty feet. We'll move out to the middle and go deep.'

A squirt of power on the starboard engine turned *Tyee II* and he watched the gyro compass until the turn was completed. Then, at three knots and increasing her depth by a hundred feet a minute, *Tyee II* moved towards deep water.

In the middle of the Inlet, where the bottom lay more than a thousand feet below the surface, *Tyee II* was down to seven hundred and fifty feet. Baxter controlled her to that depth, brought her round again on the compass, and headed out of the Inlet. The two sets of communications equipment, the underwater telephone and the range and bearing signal transmitter, were shut down. With the stream to assist, the sub was soon more than two miles from the spot where the barge had sunk.

He turned to look at the Russian and was pleased to see he was sweating. He said, 'Crack your skull like a walnut, that pressure outside.' The Russian winced, but it wasn't much of a triumph. Nobody would find *Tyee II* now and he remained helpless to do anything more valuable than a trifling verbal needling.

Gawthorpe received three pieces of information during the day. The first, from Admiral Sir Darren Hogg in San Diego, California, had been telephoned by the admiral to the film producer in Los Angeles who was a 'friend' of DI6. Admiral Hogg reported five or six detected attempts by Russian submarines to approach the coast of British Columbia at Queen Charlotte Strait. Purpose unknown. Gawthorpe read it with great interest and mounting frustration. He took no satisfaction from apparent confirmation of his suspicions that *something* was up. The question was *what*? He was nowhere near answering it.

The second message came from a British destroyer bound for Hakodate on the Japanese island of Hokkaido. It had been picked up first in Singapore and forwarded via the normal merchant service radio channels and schedules to London. In it, the captain reported sighting a Soviet cruiser making all speed on a course a little north of east. The ship, the report said, was so loaded with radar that she appeared top-heavy and Gawthorpe had no need to ask, though he did so, to what class she belonged.

The naval commander who had earlier declined to take much interest in Gawthorpe's suspicions, came to his office with a portfolio of photographs. On top were pictures of ships of the outdated Sverdlovsk class of heavy cruisers, which both men looked at briefly and put aside. They were far more interested in the next group of pictures, which showed a long, slender vessel of 6,000 tons. Towering high above the decks was the surveillance radar code-named Top Sail in the West. Forward of it was the missile control radar, a surface-to-surface missile launcher, and, farther forward still, the launcher for SAM missiles.

'If ever a ship looked top-heavy,' said the commander from naval security, 'this is it.'

Gawthorpe nodded. 'But surely Gorshkov wouldn't let a *Kresta II* class cruiser go into a Western port.'

'They're due to be replaced,' said the commander.

'Not until the eighties, they're not. And how many of the bloody monsters can they have sitting around anyway?'

'There are two of them – and two more under construction. This must be either *Valerian IV* or the *Suvarov*.'

When the commander had gone, Gawthorpe rang for David Norton. 'It's a *Kresta II* cruiser they're sending to Vancouver.'

His assistant whistled. 'They're leaving her there?'

'On a mooring. For several days.'

'Well, it proves one thing, sir.'

'I know it does,' Gawthorpe said. 'It proves that, whatever

94

this bloody operation is, it matters. Because that ship's solid with equipment. Russian naval ships aren't built for comfort, but these *Kresta II*'s have so much equipment crammed aboard the crew must sleep in the bilges. It's no holiday trip for Comrade Gromyko, that's for sure.'

His third piece of information came, to Gawthorpe's intense irritation, from the London *Evening Standard*. It was a four-line paragraph on the back page, sandwiched in among the racing results and a story about London's proposed new ring road. The story was datelined Vancouver and it read: 'A two-man submarine sank today in deep water in a fiord on the coast of Canada. No crew were aboard.' Gawthorpe read it on his way home as his train left London Bridge station. 'Midget submarines.' he thought. 'That was what I couldn't remember about Vancouver!' At the next stop, East Croydon, he alighted from the train and telephoned his office. Then he caught the next train back to London, where he went directly to an office on the floor above his own where the civil service knight, who controlled DI6 and was traditionally known only as 'C' in the intelligence service, was waiting for him, having been delicately levered out of the bar of his club, the Reform, by Gawthorpe's assistant.

'C' listened intently, then he said, 'This is not a system job. It's for an individual. We need precisely the right man.'

Gawthorpe thought for a moment. 'Burgess, perhaps, but he's in Hongkong on – '

'I know what he's on,' 'C' said. 'And don't take him off it. Who else?'

'Calder. He's also spent time in Canada, which helps.'

'I don't believe,' 'C' said ruminatively, 'that we want to inform the Canadians. Not, at any rate, at this moment.'

'Very good. But I'll send Calder, quick!'

'Yes,' 'C' said. 'Quick indeed!'

BOOK TWO

X

An hour later, James Calder emerged from his briefing in Gawthorpe's office. He was slightly numbed by the size of the assignment he had been given. He had been playing squash at the Foreign Office club when the summons came. He instantly apologized to his surprised opponent, left the court, showered in two minutes, dressed in three more, and took a taxi to Parliament Street.

Gawthorpe nodded a brief greeting. 'Sit down, Calder, and listen.' He then gave James Calder, in detail, such information as he had. While he was doing so, he was interrupted. 'C' came unannounced into the room.

'I have just spoken,' 'C' said, 'to the Secretary of State for Foreign Affairs. There is one instruction from him. The Pacific Conference must in no way be compromised.'

Gawthorpe said, 'Does that mean we call off?' His voice grated a little.

'He did not say that.'

'Right. Understood. It's another handicap, Calder, but you'll have to grin and bear it. He's thinking of Krushchev in Paris, I expect, when the U2 was shot down.'

'I take it,' Calder said, 'that he'll be going to Vancouver himself.'

'Yes, he will,' 'C' said. 'From your point of view, it could be useful. There will be a Foreign Office delegation with him and they will serve as a point of contact, if necessary, of decision-making, for you. He means what he says.'

'I expect he does,' Gawthorpe said.

When 'C' had gone, Gawthorpe continued with his briefing. At the end, he produced two sheets of computer print-out. 'In Vancouver,' he said, 'we have this slight advantage: there are a great many British immigrants. Some have become Canadian citizens and we can't do anything there. But there are others, who are still British, and some of them are ex-service, still on the reserve list. From them you can *demand* co-operation if necessary. Right?'

Calder nodded, taking the list and glancing down it. There were about thirty names, most prefixed with a service rank. For each name there was an address and a telephone number. In most cases the occupation was also listed. He was still occasionally surprised by the department's efficiency with detail and thought momentarily of the surprise some of these people might feel at the sudden appearance in their lives of an agent demanding help.

Calder said, 'Okay. They might be useful. So may the striped-trousers in the Foreign Secretary's entourage. But I need a contact.'

'You have one. Her name – '

'A woman?'

'Her name, I was about to say,' Gawthorpe went on, 'is Elizabeth Donald; at least that's her name as far as you're concerned. She is a voice on a telephone. If you have information to pass, or require assistance, or if we have news for you, use this number in Vancouver.'

'Okay.'

'You'll fly out tonight and get cracking on – '

The telephone full-pointed Gawthorpe's sentence for him. He listened for a moment, then hung up. Calder noticed the angry pressure at the corners of his mouth. He waited for the head of the Russian department to speak.

'That was Commander Bowen,' Gawthorpe said evenly. 'Naval Security. Apparently we have one of these little subs over here.'

Calder nodded, wondering why Gawthorpe hadn't known.

'You mean *you* knew, too?'

'Yes,' Calder said.

'How?'

'Press and TV.'

Gawthorpe grunted. 'Maybe that's why. In this job you get so obsessed with what's under the surface, you forget what's above it. Good luck.'

Calder rose. 'I'll need it, I think.'

James Calder was a good agent. His strength lay principally in his steadiness, his willingness to keep going on even when his assignment looked like a brick wall. He also had the enormous advantage of an unmemorable face which people who had met him once rarely remembered if they met him a second time. He was forty-one, and had entered the department by a highly unusual route. Twenty-two years earlier, as a national service conscript, he had found himself working on the periphery of intelligence, in the codes and ciphers department of the Foreign Office. When his army service ended, he had joined the police force in his home city of Bradford, pounded a beat, become a detective constable, and passed ten hard-working but undistinguished years and, to make the performance of his job less frustrating, had learned Urdu. At thirty he realized life was closing in, promotion had not come, and he should do something about it. He volunteered for the Cyprus police and there came into contact with an Intelligence Corps captain running an undercover execution squad whose job was to trick, ambush and kill Eoka terrorists in the Paphos Mountains. Somehow, in the sunshine of Cyprus, Calder's capacities had flowered; not spectacularly, but enough to bring him to the attention of DI6. He had also learned Greek and Turkish with an ease that had greatly surprised him. Calder's patient years spent interrogating Pakistanis in Bradford paid dividends among the Cypriot Turks and Greeks. He was quietly but remarkably efficient. In due course, and to his own great astonishment, he was enlisted. The department, until that time heavily public-school-and-Oxbridge oriented, discovered with pleasure that the quiet policeman from Bradford already had most of the necessary equipment and a flair for languages, too. They filled in the few obvious gaps in his training and found him highly successful across a wide spectrum of activity.

As Calder walked away from Gawthorpe's room he knew that the job he had been handed was the biggest, the most important, and also the most difficult of his life. As he collected his ready-bag from the store his mind was going over and over the information he had been given.

Calder had no doubt that Gawthorpe was right and that something big was on. The pointers were clear, if few in number; certainly something *was* happening in and around Vancouver, something involving the Russians, and involving submarines large and small, something involving the Pacific Conference and Andrei Gromyko himself.

But how, alone in Vancouver, could he hope to discover what it was?

Pushing the questions from his mind, Calder took a taxi to Heathrow airport. Inevitably he would be scalped on the cab fare, but for once he did not allow the thought to trouble him. He switched on the reading light in the back of the cab and began to assimilate his cover story. He was now a new executive on the staff of a British company with large pulp and paper interests in British Columbia, going out to be shown round. It had the huge advantage of simplicity. He then began the process of committing to memory the names on the list Gawthorpe had given to him. That task would, he knew, take several hours, but his memory was excellent.

After Calder had left, Gawthorpe sat quietly for a while. At first he asked himself savagely whether, perhaps, he was not now past it, whether the edge of his efficiency had not been blunted against the wall of facts that daily passed before him. It was, he thought, rather like staring at the horizon from a ship; the horizon changed constantly, but after a while the eyes gave up, changed focus unbidden and could only be refocused by an effort of will. He thought about it for a while, deciding finally that he was neither stale nor bored; he had merely missed noticing one fact that had not, at the time, seemed important. It was not, in any case, as though the department had missed it; naval security knew all about it. What had gone wrong was the bloody cross referencing, the correlation, the old, interminable bloody problem.

Well, the best way of getting back at it was to make sure no detail slipped him now. He rang for his assistant. 'David: I want to talk to the submersible people over here.'

David Norton left him, returned to his own office and rang the Admiralty Duty Officer.

'DI6 here. Who's the expert over here on the *Tyee* class submersible?'

'It's operated by Plaid-Cromwell. If you'll hold on, I'll find out.'

David Norton waited. 'It's a subsidiary company,' the duty officer reported a moment later. 'Managing director's a chap called Lavering. Kenneth Lavering.'

'Address?'

'I'm not sure . . . yes, here we are. Oak Lodge, Horton Lane, Leatherhead.'

'Thanks.' Norton hung up and reached for the Surrey directory. Then he dialled.

'Mr Lavering, please?'

'I'm sorry, my husband isn't home yet.'

'You *are* expecting him?'

'Oh yes. He telephoned.'

'You don't happen to know which train he'll catch?'

'As a matter of fact, yes. The eight-five.'

'Thanks.'

Kenneth Lavering was in his regular first-class corner seat in the Leatherhead train, reading his newspaper, when he felt a tap on his knee. Glancing up in irritation, he saw that the tapper was a fellow member of his golf club.

'It's for you, old boy.'

'What is?' Lavering had been vaguely aware of the station loudspeaker in the background, but had assumed it was making routine announcements.

'The loudspeaker, old boy.'

Damn! Lavering thought. He listened, but the announcement was not repeated. 'Are you sure?'

'Kenneth Lavering, they said, old boy. Stationmaster's office. They said it twice. You been travelling without a ticket?'

'I was travelling hopefully,' Lavering said irritably. He put on his overcoat and bowler, took briefcase and umbrella from the rack, and left the train.

'I'm Kenneth Lavering,' he told the clerk in the station-master's office.

'Oh, yes sir. You're to wait please. They're sending a car.'

'Who is?'

The man looked at him. 'I dunno. Your office, I expect.'

He was kept waiting less than two minutes before a man in a peaked cap with brass crown lapel badges came in. 'Mr Lavering, sir?'

'Yes. Who are you?'

'Foreign Office, sir.'

'Why would the Foreign Office want me?'

'I don't know, sir. It's important, though. Must be.'

Lavering's train left in two minutes. He sighed. 'Very well.'

'This way, sir, if you please.'

The car was parked in the middle of the No Parking zone and a railway policeman stood beside it threateningly. 'Your car, sir?'

'Her Majesty's,' the driver said.

'You do realize,' the policeman began, heavily, but the driver thrust a card under his nose. 'All right, sir. Carry on.'

'You make powerful magic,' Lavering said.

The driver grinned. 'Sometimes.'

A few minutes later the car halted in Parliament Street and Lavering said, 'This isn't the Foreign Office.'

'Annexe,' the driver explained. 'It's Mr Gawthorpe, sir. They'll take you up in the lift.'

And they did, silently and with promptitude. Lavering took one look at Gawthorpe and knew he was in the presence of an important man. He realized he was thinking suddenly about Baxter and wondered why.

'I see you're carrying the *Evening Standard*,' Gawthorpe said. 'Have you seen the back page?'

'No. I'd been reading the financial –'

'If you'd look now, please. Column five, a bit more than halfway down.'

Lavering found the paragraph and read it. Then he looked up at Gawthorpe. He said, 'It's impossible.'

'Why's that, Mr Lavering.'

'Because *Tyee* is virtually unsinkable.'

'Explain please.'

'There are two spheres. The front one is one-inch steel, seven feet in diameter. The back one is a little smaller and filled with oil. With the hatch into the front sphere closed she wouldn't go down unless an explosion destroyed the sphere's integrity.'

'I see.' Gawthorpe was watching Lavering closely. After a moment he said, 'There's something else, I think?'

'I don't know,' Lavering said. 'It's odd, that's all.'

'What is?'

'The pilot. Our own man. The chap who pilots our *Tyee*.'

Gawthorpe waited, listening to the sudden thud of his own heartbeat.

'He's in Germany,' Lavering said.

'Yes? And what's odd about that?'

Lavering told him. When he'd finished, Gawthorpe frowned. 'You should have reported it, you know.'

'I know. But that second cable – '

'Could have been sent,' Gawthorpe said, 'by anybody. By anybody at all.'

It was a small circle at first, and Kenneth Lavering was alone in the middle of it while Gawthorpe and David Norton prowled the perimeter. As the late evening progressed, however, the circle expanded to encompass a variety of people in a variety of places.

The first was the manager of Plaid-Cromwell's pension scheme, who was busily pasting to the wall of his study a figured and extremely expensive wallpaper. No, he didn't have to go back to his office to name Baxter's next of kin, thank you very much. 'It's a brother. Henry, I think. Yes, Henry.'

'Where does he live?'

'Sussex. Or is it Suffolk? One of the two.'

'Perhaps,' Lavering suggested, 'it might be sensible to check.'

'Suffolk,' the pension manager said firmly. 'Sudbury, Suffolk. You'll find I'm right.'

Next, the village policeman at Great Waldingfield, close to

Sudbury, in Suffolk, found himself walking briskly along the mile of unlit road that separated the police house from Henry Baxter's cottage. The cottage was locked and unlit, the garage empty. He reported accordingly. Yes, he knew Baxter's car; a Morris 1300 Estate.

'Which means,' David Norton said, 'that he *may* have had an accident.'

'Or he *may* be out for the evening with Margot Fonteyn. Stop knocking it, David,' Gawthorpe said. 'The bucket's half full, not half empty, and we both know it. The question is, where's his car?'

'If he's abroad he'll need a green card.'

'True. AA and RAC then. Find out if a Morris 1300 Estate, COO 501 G, is out of the country. If so, where.' The car was, in fact, where Henry Baxter had left it, in the vast car park at Colchester railway station. It was blue, and dusty, and if Baxter had deliberately sought a perfect hiding place, he could not have found a better. Over the next forty-eight hours, police forces all over the country were asked to keep a watch for the car, but it was not found.

The circle expanded then to take in the airports. Within an hour, John Baxter's flight to Hamburg was confirmed. That was easy, because Lavering knew both the date and the approximate time. But there was no sign of a Mr and Mrs Henry Baxter on any flight list.

'So Baxter One is in Hamburg,' David Norton said.

'Or Bremerhaven. Or somewhere. What's his address, Lavering?'

'Blackheath, somewhere. South London.'

'Phone?'

Lavering spread his hands. 'Sorry. I expect he's in the book.'

Baxter's flat was first telephoned. There was, of course, no reply.

The next person to be dragged into the circle was the duty Metropolitan magistrate, who was asked to sign a search warrant. The magistrate frowned. 'Of what is he suspected?'

'We don't know, sir.' The Special Branch Chief Inspector,

whose name was Emsley, was properly polite. 'It's a security matter.'

'It always is, if there aren't genuine and justifiable grounds.'

'Yes, sir.'

'I don't see,' the magistrate said angrily, 'why we bother to have this procedure. A magistrate has to sign a search warrant so you people can't break down any old door you fancy. The whole system is for everybody's protection. Then you bypass it with the magic word "security".'

'Yes, sir.' Chief Inspector Emsley had been through this before, with other magistrates. He said, 'If you'd like to telephone the Commander?'

'No.' The magistrate shook his head. 'There isn't anything I can do and I know it. I'm just protesting.'

'Yes, sir.' He watched the magistrate sign the warrant.

'Here you are, then.'

'Thank you, sir.'

The Special Branch Jaguar which drew up outside the block of flats in Vanbrugh Park, Blackheath, contained in addition to Chief Inspector Emsley, a locksmith, a fingerprint man and Emsley's sergeant. Emsley rang the doorbell and when his ring was not answered said shortly, 'Open it. No damage. We may want to leave this place as we found it.'

'Right. Oh hell, it's a deadlock.'

'Can't you do it?'

'Of course I can do it. It just takes longer.'

It took four minutes. Then the four men were in Baxter's flat.

The fingerprint man started in the kitchen, dusting cups and saucers. After a minute or two he emerged. 'Dozens of sets and all the same. Is he single?'

'Yes,' Emsley said. 'Now let's get to work. He spent time in Vancouver, so there's bound to be stuff about it. I want every scrap. For the rest, just anything interesting.'

The flat was small and far from elaborately furnished and the search did not take long. The longest task was the searching of Baxter's books, which included guides to British Columbia and the American states of Washington and Oregon. Nothing of any significance was found. Baxter apparently either did not keep an address book, or carried it with him.

The locksmith was sitting smoking a cigarette when Emsley put the last sofa cushion back in place. 'Nothing?'

'Not a thing,' Emsley said. 'Not unless we start slicing things up, and I doubt it, even then.'

'There's a new set here,' the fingerprints man called suddenly from the bedroom. 'On the electric plug.'

'That,' Emsley said sourly, 'will be the daily help plugging in the Hoover.'

'Maybe. If so, she doesn't wash the dishes.'

'Hmm.' Emsley thought about it for a moment. Baxter was missing; they were looking for clues to his disappearance; but he was not suspected of anything. He said, 'I'll remember it if we need it.'

One other person was almost drawn into the circle that night. He was Igor Kovrenko, a comparatively junior KGB official attached for cover purposes to the Soviet Trade Delegation in Highgate. Kovrenko had been in London for almost two years and had exhibited from the day of his first arrival a marked fondness for the more decadent side of life in a Western capitalist state. Once, and only once, he had been seen in a Soho pub in a breathless conversation with a manifest homosexual. Ever since, the department had been trying to catch him at it again, and had even on occasion tried to tempt him. They had not succeeded. The hope was, naturally, to turn Kovrenko into a double agent, but, to do it, somewhat stronger evidence was needed.

Thinking about Kovrenko, Gawthorpe decided that to try anything now, on the flimsy evidence of one observed conversation, however breathless, was to risk losing an opportunity. His decision was finely balanced because Gawthorpe was becoming surer with every passing hour that the Vancouver business was of extreme importance. Kovrenko might be able to add to their information, but for the time being they would rub along without him. All the same, between ten-thirty and eleven-fifteen, Gawthorpe telephoned several distinguished men at their houses and warned them to be prepared.

Finally, after receiving the report from Chief Inspector Emsley and checking carefully with Kenneth Lavering the full range of potential uses for a *Tyee* submersible, Gawthorpe sent a signal to Elizabeth Donald in Vancouver to be passed on to James Calder when he arrived.

XI

The KGB agent in Vancouver had given tugboat skipper Ed Bonney two days' warning that the contract was now beginning. It was late evening when he stopped his car beside a wharf on the Fraser River and waited for Bonney and his engineer to arrive. Beside the wharf, Bonney's boat, the *Squamish Lady*, lay silent, tied fore and aft. The agent smoked quietly as the rain drummed on the roof of his car.

When a battered Ford turned in to park close by, the agent flashed his lights twice, one long, one short, in the prearranged signal. Moments later, the door of his car opened and Bonney slipped into the passenger seat.

'Ready?' the agent asked.

'Yeah. Yeah, I'm ready. You got the money?'

'Here.' The agent tapped his pocket.

'Let's see it.'

Skipper Bonney counted the used notes carefully and slowly. Then he nodded. 'Seven and a half grand. Okay. How do I know I'll get the other half?'

'How do *I* know you'll do the job?' the agent countered.

'I'll do it.'

'And I'll pay,' the agent said. 'To reassure you, the money is already waiting. It is in an envelope at a Vancouver bank. The envelope is addressed to you, and will be given to you when I release it. Here is a receipt. The bank does not, of course, know the envelope's contents.'

Bonney thought for a moment. 'Okay,' he said at last. 'Where do I go?'

'Directly through the Inside Passage, then into Queen

Charlotte Strait, where you will open this.' He passed the skipper an envelope.

Bonney stared at it disbelievingly, then laughed. 'Sealed orders! You're crazy.'

'In a sense,' the agent said, 'they're a protection.'

'All right.' Bonney nodded slowly.

'They contain,' the agent said, 'details of a rendezvous.'

With a swish of tyres on the wet surface, another car pulled in beside them. 'Here's Hudson,' the skipper said.

The agent remained in his car as Hudson and Bonney boarded *Squamish Lady*. He wound the window down and listened to the throb of the tugboat's diesels, then watched as the lines were cast off and *Squamish Lady* headed out on to the North Arm of Fraser River, among the golden lights reflected from the industrial complex across the water. He got out of his car at last and followed the tug with his eyes until the dark shape passed out of sight. When he could see it no longer, he opened the boot of his car and took from it a five-gallon oil-drum.

The oil-drum he placed in the boot of Hudson's car. Then he took a second and placed it in the boot of Bonney's. He spent the next hour driving the two cars away and parking them in public car parks in the city, returning to the wharf each time by taxi. When the job was done, he drove away in his own car. He felt satisfied. The only risk had been that *Squamish Lady* might return before the drums had been placed, and now that risk was over.

The sealed orders did not, naturally enough, remain sealed for long; nor were they of great importance; their purpose was primarily psychological, to emphasize in Bonney's mind the furtive nature of the enterprise.

Bonney had read them before the tugboat turned north out of the Fraser delta to head out into Georgia Strait, the stretch of water which lies between Vancouver Island and the mainland and is permanently sheltered from the Pacific by the rearing bulk of the island. He snorted, but sailed on and *Squamish Lady* moved steadily up the strait for several hours, approaching the narrows of the Inside Passage. At Mittelnach

Island he kept her first rendezvous, with a white cabin cruiser, from which two men came aboard. Both carried automatic pistols.

Bonney looked at the pistols angrily. 'What the hell goes on?'

Colonel Belyaev looked at him coldly. 'The plan is changed.'

'Then it's off. No go, mister.'

'What you will now do –'

'I said it's no go,' Bonney snarled. 'I didn't dig this thing from –'

Belyaev hit him with surprising speed in the solar plexus then waited impassively while Bonney gasped breath back into his body. He said, 'There are eighty pounds of marijuana resin and ten pounds of heroin in the boot of your car. The car is parked where you will not find it. One call to the police will mean a long prison sentence.'

'You bastard!' Bonney, still wheezing, stared at him incredulously.

Belyaev shrugged. 'Merely, as I said, a change of orders. You will be paid, as arranged, when the task is done.'

Bonney scowled at him, massive hands still clutching at his aching gut. He was astonished by the speed and force of the blow.

'You will now,' Belyaev said, 'take up a towline which will be passed to you from the cabin cruiser. You will then proceed north at precisely seven knots, through the Inside Passage. Understood?'

Bonney thought about it, then nodded slowly. He was in it and had to stay in it, that much was clear. He wondered who these bastards were, Mafia, probably. The thought made him shiver suddenly.

'That's better,' Belyaev said. After a while he added, 'You have no alternative. But if you carry out your orders, you will be paid. So don't worry. Just do as you're told.'

'What am I towing?' Bonney demanded hoarsely.

'Eventually, you will see. But not yet. Seven knots precisely, remember.'

The towline was passed and made fast and *Squamish Lady*

moved forward towards the narrows. Bonney and Hudson kept glancing back. The white cabin cruiser had taken up station half a mile behind. From her lines Bonney guessed she was probably capable of at least twenty-five knots, which meant he certainly couldn't outrun her. He thought about it for a while, concluding eventually that he had one option only: to obey. If these guys were Mafia, obedience was certainly his only course. And he'd get the money in the end. The Mafia paid its debts. *Paid its debts!* Bonney shuddered.

Sixty feet below the surface, John Baxter felt the jerk as the towline tautened. *Tyee* was moving forward again. He looked at the depth gauge; there was sixty feet of water above the sail. He watched the gauge carefully for several minutes in case adjustments of the oil ballast were needed. *Tyee* was rising through the water as the tugboat picked up speed. Fifty feet, forty, thirty. With fifteen feet of water above the rim of the sail, the submersible's upward movement stopped.

After a moment he rose from the couch and glanced at the oxygen pressure. Three hours more before he needed to replace the oxygen bottle from one of the dozen full ones stacked on the floor of the crew sphere. The air scrubbers were working perfectly.

He glanced across at his Russian guard, who lay stretched out on the observer's couch. Like himself, the guard was bored to tears. It was unbelievable, Baxter thought to himself, that a man who'd been kidnapped, who was under threat to himself and to his relatives and was being forced to work against his will, could actually be bored! Nonetheless, he was.

Eight hours ahead of *Squamish Lady*, another tugboat, unencumbered by a tow, steamed steadily onward, emerging from the narrow passage. Her skipper, whose name was O'Hara, had also rendezvoused with the white cruiser, but, unlike Bonney, O'Hara was a realist. Where Bonney had believed he would be paid fifteen thousand dollars plus hire charges for doing very little, O'Hara had believed nothing of the kind.

The pistols had not surprised him, when Belyaev came aboard, nor had the revelation about an oil-drum full of drugs.

He knew he was involved in something highly illegal, and accepted the fact. He asked only one question.

'Do I get the drugs as well as the money?'

Belyaev had smiled at him almost with approval. 'Perhaps. As a bonus.'

Now, as he moved clear of the narrow Goletas Channel and headed out into Queen Charlotte Sound, O'Hara was thinking of two things and two only: fifteen thousand dollars, and a load of drugs that was certainly worth even more. For that kind of dough, O'Hara thought, he'd do like the man said. If there were risks, he'd take them. He wanted that bonus. O'Hara put on all speed, setting course for the southern tip of the Queen Charlotte Islands, a hundred and forty miles away.

Seven thousand miles from Vancouver, in London, the inquiry circle widened to take in Janice Caulfield. In the Fulham flat she shared with seven other girls, she got out of bed, waited her turn for the bathroom, showered, then dressed slowly, wishing it were yesterday again. Yesterday had been her day off, and she had enjoyed it, arriving home in the early hours a little the worse for drink, but extremely happy. Harry had taken her to the theatre, then to supper, then to a nightclub. Furthermore. Harry was nice. Harry was also, if not rich, plainly well-heeled, And she rather thought Harry was falling in love with her. She wished, as she put on the blue uniform and neat hat, that she was seeing Harry again today. Instead, she would be spending the day, as usual, in the terminal, being pleasant to people who were not always pleasant in return. And when you had, as Janice Caulfield had this morning, a perceptible hangover from last night's fun and games, the prospect was not exciting.

She worked until 11 a.m. at her BEA desk, doling out tickets and information with a smile that was more mechanical than usual. Her mouth tasted furry from too many cigarettes and too much champagne the night before, and she was glad when coffee time came. Janice headed for the coffee shop and sipped gratefully at a cup of black coffee until a couple of other girls joined her and then she boasted quietly, for a while, about Harry.

'Lucky old you,' one of the other girls said. 'It was a foul day here.'

'Why?'

'Three lots of police inquiries. Three, would you believe.' The girl lowered her voice. 'Can you remember this, miss? Can you remember that, miss? God, but they went on!'

The others laughed at her imitation, and Janice asked, 'What happened?'

'Two hits, one miss, love. One pair was drugs. I know that because I've seen the Drug Squad men before. One of them's rather nice. I quite fancy him. Didn't like the other, though. He was creepy.'

'What did he want?'

'Tickets for somebody called Baxter. Henry Baxter. Not to mention Mrs Henry.'

'I think *I* remember that,' Janice said. 'Last week sometime. Only it wasn't . . .' She paused, trying to recall what had happened.

'Well you'd better tell them.'

'I'll finish this first.' Janice sipped the coffee. 'I've earned it.' What was it that she'd noticed? Something about the names. Baxter was one: the other was . . . what was it, Bexton, Boxton, something like that. She'd noticed it because the envelope and the tickets weren't the same, but were so alike. That's right, she thought. The tickets were for Mr and Mrs H. Bexton, but they were being collected by someone called Baxter. She couldn't quite recall where the tickets were *for*, but it was somewhere in the sun, she thought: Italy or Spain, somewhere like that.

She finished her coffee and sighed. 'Better go see the Gestapo.'

Half an hour later, Gawthorpe said, half-admiringly. 'Crafty sods! The crafty, bloody sods! You see, don't you? Air tickets are usually written out by hand, right?'

David Norton nodded.

'So do me a favour. Write Bexton and Baxter, in small lettering. Go on, do it.'

Norton complied and Gawthorpe examined the sheet of

paper. 'You're *trying* to distinguish between them, David, and there's precious little difference.'

'I get it,' Norton said. 'At least, I think I do. The tickets are booked for Mr and Mrs H. Bexton and they'll be picked up by Mr Baxter who's going to use them. Yes ?'

'Go on,' Gawthorpe said.

'When Baxter gets them, he glances at the tickets and sees his name. It *may* look a bit odd but he's not going to query it, because he'll be fairly used to his name being spelled wrongly. Most people are. I am. Half the time my name appears as Morton.'

Gawthorpe nodded. 'I'm anything from Gawthorne to Gaythorpe. I've even been Hawthorne in my time. So they go to Mallorca, the Baxters. But the name on the passenger list is Bexton!'

'Very neat.' Norton shook his head.

'They go by air. To Mallorca. They may be on holiday, but I know in my water they're not. Then they're reported injured in a car crash in Hamburg and there's a cable from a doctor who isn't there, at least if Lavering got it right. Also there's no car crash in the area involving British visitors. But by that time John Baxter is over there sending a cable from Bremerhaven asking for leave.'

'And asking for leave because the Henry Baxters are at death's door.'

Gawthorpe said, 'It's fixed.'

'I agree.'

'What's more, it's cleverly fixed. That kind of thing takes organization. I want it cleared up. Let's see, for a start, if we *can* trace the Henry Baxters in Mallorca. Do the Spanish police keep records ?'

'It's one advantage of totalitarian systems,' Norton said. 'They do.'

'Right. Meanwhile, I'll get the Mets to chase up the German police.'

Norton wondered, as he tried to get through by telephone to the British consul's office in Palma, Mallorca, why Gawthorpe chose to get involved himself, and so often, in the actual doing of comparatively small and routine jobs, like asking the Metropolitan Police to use their good offices with the Hamburg police. He was, after all, head of the entire Soviet operation, espionage and counter-espionage, yet sometimes he behaved like the office boy. Norton was neither experienced enough, nor sufficiently perceptive, to see through the confidence and attack of Gawthorpe to the constant fear beneath: the fear that some vital detail was sliding by unnoticed in the vast flow of information.

Through the porthole of the radio room, Radio Operator Nikita Ivanov could see land. It was low on the horizon in the grey autumn light, but it was land beyond doubt. As he looked across the Pacific swell towards it, trying to measure distance with his eyes, his stomach cramped in despair. There wasn't a hope of swimming it; not the slightest, faintest trace of hope. They must be ten miles offshore! All the same, he continued to stare, knowing that it must be Canada, that in Canada he could ask for asylum. In Canada he would be safe; Canada would not hand him back.

Ivanov felt tears prickling in his eyes as he looked longingly across the water. The land was so near! Yet to plunge into the water would be to die. If he were seen, the ship would stop and pick him up and he would die when it returned to Vladivostok. If by any chance he were not seen, which, in daylight, was unlikely, he would die of cold and exhaustion somewhere between the ship and that low, dark shore.

It was still in sight when his duty period ended. Now his misery increased; another man sat in the radio room. For sixteen more hours Ivanov would go through the hell of wondering if the signal would come, if he would be dragged from his bunk, or the mess room, and flung into the cell up forward by the chain locker. For that would, without a shadow of a doubt, be the end of him.

For an hour after he came off duty, he sat moodily in the mess room, a glass of tea untouched on the table at his side. Then, suddenly, he heard the engines slowing. He rose quickly to go out on deck, but was stopped by the loudspeaker. 'All personnel,' it blared, 'will remain below until further instructions. Lowering party only on deck.' That was that! He was at a porthole, watching as a tug approached, as the deck cargo was lowered over the side in the gathering gloom. It took twenty minutes, and then the ship was under way again. Now he couldn't even see the land.

It occurred to him only later that he could have perhaps swum to the tug and for a moment Nikita Ivanov cursed himself for not thinking of it. But he realized, thinking it over, that it would have been useless. The tug had met the ship, so it was 'friendly'. He would inevitably have been returned aboard.

'Off duty personnel,' the loudspeaker announced, 'may now proceed on deck.' There was very little to see as Ivanov stepped out into the night air. He thought, but wasn't sure, that he caught the faint, brief glow of a shorelight off to the north. The moon was up, water spread in all directions to the horizon, and the land was gone. He mooched round the deck for a few minutes, lamenting the lost opportunity, and was about to return to the mess room when he noticed that not all the deck cargo had gone. Part of it, yes. But the rest was still there.

Which way, then, was the ship heading? He was astonished to find she was moving roughly south-east and that was not, most definitely was *not*, the way back to Vladivostok! And, he thought with mounting excitement, the ship hadn't brought that deck cargo across the Pacific to take it back again, so it must be going somewhere else. South east! Was it possible they were going to approach the Canadian coast again?

He went and lay on his bunk, then got up again and ate, choking down as much food as he could without attracting too much attention. He didn't want food, but food was fuel.

Time went by and the ship moved smoothly on. Once or twice he went on deck again to check her course. It remained steady, roughly south-east. Hope buoyed him up at first, but faded gradually as the ship moved through the broad water. If only he knew where they were! But that knowledge was confined to the bridge; the crew had not been told.

It was late, almost two in the morning, when the steady throb of the engines began to slow. The hope that had flared hours earlier had long died and Ivanov was staring miserably at the ceiling above his bunk. Swiftly, so as not to waken the two other occupants of the cabin, he slid off the bunk. He must get out on deck before the loudspeaker ordered all hands below. From beneath his mattress he took a greasy parcel containing the fat and margarine he had managed to save up during the voyage, and three bars of sugary sweetmeat he'd bought in the canteen. Then he slipped out on deck and moved quietly and in shadow towards the stern.

The moon rode high in the sky, silvering the water, and Ivanov stared anxiously around him. Then his heart jumped as he saw red and green navigation lights. Another vessel! But was there anything else? Above all, was there *land*? Desperately his eyes searched the moonlit ocean. Was there land anywhere? Yes! Yes, there was! Not much land: a small, conical island lay about two miles astern, a dark, triangular shape rising from the water. There were no lights on it. Maybe there were no people either; that was a chance he had to take.

The ship was losing way now; soon she would be stationary in the water. This was the moment, almost certainly the only moment there would ever be. He ripped his sweater over his head, slid off his trousers, and began to rub the fat over his skin. Face, feet, arms, chest, legs; he coated them all, as thickly as he could. Then he stuffed his lighter and the sweetmeats into a plastic bag and tied it round his waist with a piece of string.

There was a line beside the lifebelt. That was why he'd chosen this spot. He waited until he heard the clatter of the winches up forward, then fastened the line to a stanchion and slipped quietly over the side. He was dangerously near the propellers, but with the way off the ship they would be turning slowly, if at all. He went down the line quickly, too quickly, burning his right hand on it. Moments later, with the night air chill on his body, he was only a few feet above the water, which looked dark, hungry and very cold. He didn't want to immerse his body in that water; didn't want to commit himself to that lonely, two-mile swim which, in all probability, would be beyond his strength. For all he knew he would be swimming against a tide or a current.

Then the loudspeaker brayed on deck. 'Personnel below!'

Ivanov took a deep breath and lowered himself into the water, which promptly drove the breath out again as his body protested involuntarily. He still held the end of the rope. Looking up at the high, curved wall of the stern, he ached to climb back up, but already he was two metres at least away from the steel plating. It took an effort of will to release his grip on the rope, but he made himself do it, and, turning, struck out gently for the dark shape of the island.

His first fear was of being spotted, but the minutes went by and his distance from the ship increased and the only sounds were from the water and, dimly, from the winches. Damn! He'd left his clothes on deck! When they were found it would be known he'd deserted; perhaps a search would begin. If he'd dropped his clothes in the sea, as he'd intended, the rope hanging from the stern would be suspicious but not con- clusive. whereas his clothes were stamped with his number. Damn! Damn! Damn!

He kept glancing over his shoulder. No sign of pursuit, no boat being lowered, no silhouetted head at the stern, searching the sea. And now he'd swum four hundred, even five hundred metres. But it was cold. He could feel the cold penetrating the inadequate coating of grease, getting to his fingers and his legs, draining the warmth from his body.

Nikita Ivanov swam on. He swam strongly, too, for swim- ming came naturally to him and his body was powerful and fit. The ship receded farther, but for some reason the island seemed to come no nearer; it remained, black and infinitely desirable, as far away as ever. Gradually, as he swam, his strength ebbed. His flesh seemed to be melting, leaving only his bones to hold the chill that was creeping over him. But his mind was clear and it continued issuing its simple order to his unwilling limbs. Swim! it said. One, two, three, four; one, two, three, four; one, two, three, four. How far had he come? He glanced back again. The ship must surely be a mile away now. Was the island nearer? It was so difficult to tell! He thought of the deep ocean beneath him and wondered whether,

117

in a few minutes, in half an hour, he would be sinking down into it to be eaten by fish, to vanish for ever. The island was nearer, he was sure of it now, and the thought renewed his waning strength a little. He forced his legs to kick, his arms to reach, and decided he would not look at the island until he had done a thousand strokes. He began to count and realized that the act of counting required additional effort, so he stopped. But he did not look up for several minutes, and, when he did, he was sure it was nearer. Yes, it was! He could see its shape much more clearly.

But his strength was going. For the moment his will remained, but his arms and legs felt cold and rubbery, not quite controllable, and the chill was deep in his chest. One, two, three, four. Now, again, one, two, three, four. Don't look up. Don't think about distance. Don't think about anything but keeping going. Minutes went by and he raised his head again. The island was closer, definitely closer. If he could *only* swim on for just a little while longer!

He was less than a quarter of a mile away when the calf muscles of his right leg knotted in cramp. He grunted at the sudden agony and tried to straighten the leg; to pull with his foot against the tug of the muscular spasm, but it didn't work and the thigh muscles too began to squirm and knot. He stretched the leg as hard as he could, trying to straighten the muscles, and slid beneath the water, choking. His arms forced him to the surface again and he kicked determinedly with his right leg, keeping his toes raised, thrusting his heel as hard as he could away from him. Gradually the cramps lessened but he knew the leg would no longer function in a swimming stroke. Awkwardly, the leg stiff behind him, he forced himself forward using arms and one leg only. It made him lopsided, The forward drive was less effective, his progress painfully slow. But he made progress, laboriously winning fifty, a hundred, two hundred metres.

Then the cramp struck again, in both legs now; appalling and excruciating pain twisted him and he cried out at the sudden agony. Two hundred metres left. Two hundred! And he was going to die. He was no longer in control of his body

118

and again he sank beneath the surface. But this time he sank only a few feet and then his knees scraped against rock. He was in the shallows! If he could only . . . Adrenalin, driven by his excitement, poured into his bloodstream and he fought his way to the surface again, striking with his arms, trying to ignore the crippling agony in his legs. He won a few more feet and sank again, but this time only a foot or two. He found his body was resting on a rock and managed to turn so that he was sitting on it. In that position his head was, most of the time, above water. Holding on, straightening his legs with pain and difficulty, he fought the cramps. Cold and weariness fed them, and only his mind could resist, but behind him the peak of the island jutted encouragingly into the night sky. After a while the cramps were quiescent; the ache was still there and the spasms would return soon, but his legs were straight. Carefully he pulled himself upright and stood swaying on the rock. All his muscles were trembling, his body shivered in the night breeze, his teeth chattered not just noisily but painfully, as though they might shatter under the clicking impacts. For a minute or two Nikita Ivanov breathed deeply, as slowly as he could. The breaths were in fact neither deep nor slow, but great whooshing gasps punctuated by shudders. Then, forcing himself to push, he fell forward into the water and struck out weakly for the shore.

When finally he crawled exhausted beyond the water's edge, he lay for a long time on the cold rocks, uncaring that his skin was scraped away in many places. But then his tired mind grasped the fact that he was getting even colder; he had to find shelter or he would die of exposure. Ivanov forced himself to stand and stumbled across the rocks.

He moved through a nightmare, scarcely conscious, falling and bruising himself endlessly as his feet slipped on the wet rock. At times he had difficulty in remembering what he was looking for, but he found something finally: an old box that had been washed ashore and lay, dried by the wind, above the tide line. He picked it up and began to look for a cave, a shelter away from the rocks. That search, too, took forever. He wanted only to drop where he was, to let unconsciousness wash over him and escape the cold and the weariness of his battered body. Then he found the cave. There were feathers in it and he collected them and finally made his numb hands strike flame in his lighter and the feathers burned. So did slivers of dried wood as he tore them off with his teeth. Then he had a fire. A small fire, but a fire. He had to stumble out again to find more driftwood. He was terrified his fire would go out while he was away, but it didn't and the wood burned. He huddled over it, feeling the warmth creep slowly back into his body. He remembered his sweet bars and ate one, and as the sugar entered his bloodstream felt a little stronger. Finally, he fell asleep.

He awoke before daylight with the fire dead and his body cold again and racked with shuddering spasms. He forced himself out of the cave. As dawn came he was staggering along the shore, naked but for his cotton pants, still looking for wood. Enough perhaps, to keep a fire going all day, and there might be more. But inside him there was only despair, for he had found nothing else. There were no people, no houses, no food. On this rocky outcrop there was nothing to help him. Another island was visible, several miles away, far beyond his ability to swim. Nikita Ivanov knew now that death was inevitable. He had escaped it in Vladivostok, escaped it on his long swim; but death had not been beaten, merely held at bay. Here it had waited triumphantly to welcome him.

Later in the morning he saw a tug close to shore on the other side of the island. For a moment Ivanov thought he was saved. But then he saw what was attached to the tug. The barge had been part of the deck cargo of his ship. Death had not relented.

XII

They had taken his watch. All John Baxter knew, when he surfaced in *Tyee II*, was that it was night; judging by the position of the moon it was the middle of the night. He was ordered to go aboard the tug, given a hot drink and some food, and told to sleep. He was dog-tired from his long tow in the submersible and dropped off almost immediately, guiltily aware, as he felt sleep blanketing him, that boredom and acceptance of his circumstances were inducing in him a weird kind of lethargy.

When he felt a hand on his shoulder he awakened reluctantly, trying to shrug the hand away, but the hand was persistent and he finally sat up, blinking, his eyes focusing reluctantly on the leader of the Russian group. Arkady Semichastny's right hand was still on his shoulder; his left hand held a mug which steamed invitingly.

'Come. It is time.'

'For what?'

'We are at the site. It is time to dive.'

Baxter took the mug and sipped at it. Lemon tea. At this time of day, lemon tea. All the same, it was hot and refreshing. He clambered off the bunk, put on his trousers, shoes and sweater and splashed his face with cold water from the wash-hand basin.

Then he went on deck, shivering a little in the morning chill, and looked round the seascape. An island lay a mile or so away, rocky and deserted, a harsh, dark, triangular shape that made a wedge in the sky. Another island was faintly visible to the east, small and indistinct and probably no more hospitable. Apart from that, nothing. The white cruiser had gone; no shipping was to be seen anywhere on the wide sweep of the ocean. There was just the tug on which he stood, a barge which had mysteriously appeared during the night, and on the barge two familiar objects: a lifting crane and the bulbous, orange shape of *Tyee II*.

On the deck beside him stood several members of the Russian party, three of them in frogman's suits. In the wheel-house stood a stranger, a dark, burly man who stared morosely ahead. Was *he* Russian, too? Baxter doubted it. His eye fell on a lifebelt with the name *Squamish Lady* in black on the white-painted cork and he doubted it more; this man was almost certainly Canadian, a licensed tugboat skipper. For a moment Baxter wondered whether the skipper might be an ally, but logic drove the thought from his mind. The man was clearly unhappy about something, but his mere presence, unguarded, in the wheelhouse, indicated clearly enough that he was part of the operation, whether willingly or not. Probably not. But in that case there must be some powerful hold on the skipper, as there was on Baxter himself.

'Come,' Semichastny said, moving aft to where a rubber dinghy was being inflated. Within a few moments Baxter, Semichastny and the man known as William Adams, who spoke in a strong mid-western drawl, were in the dinghy, crossing to the barge.

Adams went immediately to the crane, while Baxter followed Semichastny into the crew sphere of *Tyee II*. Through the open hatch he heard the cough, then the roar, of the crane's engine and a few moments later Adams's head appeared, framed in the open hatch. 'Ready?'

'Are you?' Semichastny asked.

Baxter nodded. 'She's okay.'

'Then secure the hatch.'

He stood on the step, reached up to hinge the hatch downward, then screwed the pressure ring tight. As he was doing it, he heard the clank of the crane's hook as Adams attached it to the submersible.

'You do know,' Baxter said, 'that you forgot to steal the communication packages.'

Semichastny settled himself on the observer's couch and stared back at him. 'They are not necessary.'

'No? We can't talk to the surface once we're down. It's useful sometimes. Also a hell of a lot safer. And the tug won't know where we are.'

'If you are thinking as I imagine,' the Russian said, 'let me tell you that we shall be accompanied by frogmen and they have limpet mines. If you attempt to escape, I shall, of course, prevent it. If you overpower me and try to get away, you will be blown to pieces. Stop speculating. You have work to do.'

Baxter said, 'Those limpet mines. They'd blow you to bits, too.'

'I know.'

Baxter looked into his eyes. Was there a flicker there? Was

the man afraid? No, he was not. Well, confidence was a weakness, too, if it could be exploited.

The *Tyee II* submersible gave a little jerk as the crane lifted her off the barge's deck and Baxter sprawled quickly on to the pilot's couch, watching the deckboards sliding away and the ocean appearing. *Tyee II* swung slowly back and forth for a moment on the end of the crane's cable, and then the sea rose towards the glass ports.

'Straight down?' Baxter asked.

'To the bottom.'

'Right.' He operated the oil pump, shifting oil ballast from the canvas bags into the sphere and watched the depth gauge as *Tyee II* slid slowly down through the water.

'Lights, please.'

He switched them on, pivoting the 1,000-watt quartz-iodine beams downward. The ocean floor was suddenly in view: basically rock, but with the mud of ages filling the gaps and interstices.

'That place looks suitable. Forward a little.'

Baxter saw the flat surface of the rock a few yards ahead and manoeuvred *Tyee II* on to it. The sub grounded almost imperceptibly. 'What now?'

'We wait.'

Half an hour later a frogman swam into view, a light line trailing behind him.

'Follow him,' Semichastny ordered.

Baxter lifted *Tyee II* delicately off the rock, fed battery power to the electric motors, and followed the frogman through the gloomy water. Very little light penetrated to this depth, but there was enough to turn the jet black of the deeps to the dark grey of this spot.

The frogman was hauling himself along the line, kicking as he went, and Baxter slid slowly after him, the quartz-iodine beams knifing a golden channel ahead. Suddenly, in the twin beams, he saw the structure. It was shaped like a right-angled triangle with the right angle at its base. The vertical side was roughly half the length of the base, and the rocket ramp was at an angle of about forty degrees.

He heard Semichastny sigh, then say, 'First, we look. Closer. I wish to see the top of the ramp.'

Baxter let *Tyee II* rise through the water and turned her until the end of the launching ramp lay squarely in the lights, then nosed forward, stopping ten feet away. From there the ends of the tubes were almost invisible beneath the encrusting marine life. Barnacles and limpets clung to the flat ends of the cylinders. He said, 'If they were fired, wouldn't those things damage the rocket?'

'The end sections fracture under gas pressure and swing out. No. They are all right. Now I wish to see the base of the ramp.'

Baxter moved *Tyee II* round the big, girdered structure, while Semichastny inspected the retaining chains that anchored it to its concrete blocks. He could hear Semichastny's breathing above the noise of the air scrubbers.

'All right,' the Russian said softly. 'Now the next.'

The second concrete block came into view, and a length of chain lay on it, the end severed.

'Now the next,' Semichastny's voice was tense.

The third chain lay straight, but the fourth had kinked round a link close to the structure's foot.

'Closer, please.'

From five feet away Baxter could see the kink clearly. The distorted link was badly buckled. He heard Semichastny whistle beneath his breath.

'Not so good, eh?'

'A matter of days. Hours even.'

'So what would happen?'

'Diagonal rocking. It would move. Soon it would be destroyed. We begin the removal now.'

'Okay.'

The three frogmen waited beside the top of the ramp. Close by, suspended on a line from the surface and weighted heavily against its own buoyancy, hung the first of the special casings Semichastny had had prepared in Vladivostok.

Baxter knew the task. It had been demonstrated to him in Moscow. As one of the frogmen hinged back the rocket's housing, exposing the shining stainless-steel cylinder beneath, he nosed forward until *Tyee II* sat directly above. Beneath him a frogman would be attaching a line to the handling ring on the casing. Soon the frogman appeared in his observation port, carrying the line, and looped it round the jaws of the torpedo grab on *Tyee II*'s nose.

'Slowly,' Semichastny said, warningly. Baxter said nothing; he was allowing oil to flow out of the bags in a tiny trickle, increasing buoyancy as slowly as possible. A slight downward movement of *Tyee II*'s nose told him the line had tautened. He waited until the frogmen signalled that the line was also vertical, then increased buoyancy again.

Oil was pouring through, now. All the little submersible's lifting capacity would be needed to hoist the rocket from its housing. He waited, watching the oil ballast gauge until the oil sphere was empty, then began to pump air into the midships water ballast tank. He was damn near at maximum buoyancy now and the steel line outside the port was taut as piano wire. Wasn't she going to lift? But she did. The little sub gave a small shudder and began to inch upward. The frogman's arm was raised, ready to signal a halt if necessary, but it remained raised as *Tyee II* floated higher. Baxter checked his depth, waiting until he had risen twenty feet. It was time to turn.

As the sub's nose came round, he saw the three frogmen at the casing. Weights held it down and had been carefully adjusted so that it floated level. At either end of the casing, slings passed beneath it, held wide by twelve foot separating poles. Carefully, Baxter nosed *Tyee II* forward, the frogman at his window signalling minute changes of course. A thumb up. That meant the tail of the rocket was safely in the casing. Left a bit. A bit more. Now the rocket was aligned. Baxter moved oil and allowed Tyee *II* to sink slowly deeper. There was a scrape on the sub's fibreglass hull as one of the lines caught it, but then the frogman's thumb was in the air again and Baxter was decreasing buoyancy fast. When it was stabilized, he edged forward, away from the slings, and turned the sub round. Directly ahead the huge stainless-steel cylinder gleamed inside the casing, the separator bars were removed and the casing slid up towards the surface.

Beside him, Semichastny let out a sigh of relief. Baxter glanced at him and saw the Russian was shiny with sweat; he was in a similar state himself.

'Five more,' Semichastny said. 'You did that well.'

Baxter scowled at him. 'I doubt if it will do me any good. Or my brother. Or his wife.'

'No.' Semichastny sat up and was leaning towards him earnestly. 'We have explained. You will be released. Perhaps not immediately, but you will.'

'Thanks,' Baxter said. 'I'd like to believe it.'

'Believe it, Mr Baxter.'

'All right.' But he didn't. He thought Semichastny was naïve if *he* believed it. Belyaev had said the same thing, and while Baxter had no doubt Semichastny believed his own words, he was equally in no doubt that Belyaev didn't.

'Five more and your task will be over,' Semichastny said.

The British consul in Palma, Mallorca, had had a long day. The previous evening, after David Norton had finally succeeded in getting through on the telephone, the consul had gone directly to the police, who had chosen to be less than helpful.

'Not until morning,' he was told.

The mañana syndrome, he thought savagely. It was dying; many Spaniards liked to believe it was dead. But it popped up endlessly and always at the inconvenient moment. He pleaded, he insisted, and he got nowhere. The officer to whom he spoke was lethargic from a good dinner and a warm evening and somebody else could help the consul tomorrow.

Next morning there was co-operation. A Henry Baxter was at a hotel at the northern tip of the island and the consul spent the day driving up there to meet him, only to find that although the man's name was indeed Henry Baxter, he came from the Lake District and was seventy-eight years old.

So the consul was driven back to Palma. No señor. No other Henry Baxter.

126

The consul said, 'He may have left or he may not. Could you check again?'

Sighs and shaking of heads were followed by a reluctant check. He wondered momentarily whether the Bexton trick had been used again, but realized it wasn't possible. The police worked from passports.

'Please look again,' he said, wearily.

The third time, with exclamations of surprise, Henry Baxter was found. The hotel was five miles from Palma. The consul thought about his long drive and about the previous evening's lack of assistance, then he remembered his manners, thanked the police and left.

He drove up into the hills behind the town, entered the Hotel Son Vida and went directly to the bar for a temper-cooling pastis. When he'd drunk it, he went to the desk.

'Mr Henry Baxter, please.'

'Señor Baxter? He is gone.'

'When?'

The clerk told him.

The consul said, 'Do you know where?'

'No, señor.'

'It's important.' The consul handed over five hundred pesetas. 'I'd like to know how he left.'

'How?' The clerk frowned, pocketing the money.

'By taxi, car, what?'

'Ah! Wait please.'

It was a good hotel and, once the consul's purpose was understood, the answers came quickly. He heard about a youth in sailing clothes who had come to see the Baxters and who, while they were upstairs, had arranged for their luggage to be packed. The youth, it seemed, had also collected the luggage later. In a Seat car.

'Do you know where he was from?'

Nobody knew with certainty, but the page thought he'd come from a yacht in the bay. He had no idea which one.

The consul then talked to the fishermen on the beach. 'Ah, but so many yachts come and go, señor.' Nobody remembered anything.

At last, from his office, the consul called London and spoke to David Norton. The information he gave was accurate, but sparse. There was a record of the Baxters' arrival in Mallorca, but none of the departure. They had left their hotel. They could be still on the island, or not. It was possible they had gone aboard a yacht.

A little later in the evening, an Assistant Commissioner of the Metropolitan Police came on the telephone at DI6 headquarters in Parliament Street. He spoke to Gawthorpe.

'Any luck?'

The Assistant Commissioner said, 'Hamburg police would have preferred to know why. They don't like inquiries in the dark.'

'I don't blame them,' Gawthorpe said. 'But did they discover anything?'

'Well, on the question of an accident, they checked hospitals and police reports within fifty miles of Hamburg. At my request that was.'

'Thanks.' Gawthorpe winked at David Norton, who wondered why.

'There's no Baxter. No Bexton, either.'

'I see. What about John Baxter?'

'He was met by somebody at Hamburg airport. They put out a passenger announcement on the speaker.'

'Who met him?'

'Unknown. Hamburg police talked to the girl on duty. She's not sure she remembers, but she thinks the two men shook hands and left together.'

'No name?'

'No.'

'Or description? Surely she can remember what the bloke looked like!'

'She can't. Hat, glasses and raincoat. That's all.'

'Bloody hell!'

'I'm sorry. They've done their best. And there's one other thing.'

'Yes?' Why couldn't he just tell the tale without all these promptings?

'As a favour to *me*,' the Assistant Commissioner said, 'they circulated a photograph of Baxter I wired across.'

Gawthorpe held his breath. He wanted to crawl down the phone and strangle this pompous fool. 'And?' he said.

'A copper on the docks thinks he saw him.'

'Go on.' It was like mining for information. He wondered who in DI6 had given grief to the A/C.

'A man boarded a Russian ship in the docks. The dockside copper thought he looked like Baxter. He's not sure. He was some distance away.'

'Who was with Baxter?'

'That's the point,' the Assistant Commissioner said. 'He was alone. Got out of a car and walked up the gangplank.'

Gawthorpe said slowly, 'Are you sure?'

'It's Hamburg who say it.'

With deliberate smarminess, Gawthorpe thanked him.

'John Bloody Baxter boarded a ship,' he told Norton.

'In Hamburg?'

Gawthorpe nodded. 'A Russian ship. And he was alone.'

David Norton whistled. 'Was he? Do you think he's – ?'

'Gone over? The thought had never entered my head till this minute.'

'And now?'

Gawthorpe said, 'It seems wrong, somehow. But it *is* a possibility.' His fingers drummed on the desk. 'David, if they want him for what he can do – which means piloting that submersible, why an obvious defection?'

'Do you think they meant it to be obvious?'

'I don't know. There was certainly a trail to follow. They must have known it would be followed sooner or later.'

'Not *so* soon, surely.'

'All right. What does it mean?'

Norton said, 'Henry Baxter goes first. He and his wife. They go to Mallorca, then on to a yacht. *Possibly* on to a yacht. Then John Baxter gets that cable. And if Lavering is right, Baxter was badly affected by news of the crash. Maybe it was a summons and he's a good actor. I don't know. Then he's met on arrival and goes aboard a Russian ship. Alone. The "alone" bit means one of two things: he walked aboard because he had to, or he walked aboard because he wanted to. The disappearance of the Henry Baxters suggests to me that he *had* to. They were threatening him.'

'All right.' Gawthorpe nodded. 'Essentially, I agree. But we have to look at the other side. If he went because he *wanted* to, he's been in a position to feed them information. I admit it's difficult to see where Henry and his wife come into that thesis, but it isn't completely impossible that Henry simply went to Mallorca for a holiday and went aboard somebody's yacht. I'll tell you this, David. I think they've got a hold on him and Henry *is* the hold. He was lured over. That's what *I* think, but we've got to take a fine-toothed comb to it. And quick about it, because that *Tyee* submersible vanished in Canada and I'm reasonably certain they've taken him there.'

'So what do we do?'

'Another go at Baxter's flat. And a go at Henry's place, too. If Baxter has been playing games, there must be some trace somewhere. Go to Blackheath with them, David. Make sure.'

'You don't think Henry's in on it?'

'No, I don't. But I'm going to be certain.'

This time they took Baxter's flat to pieces. Pictures were removed from frames, the bath panelling was taken away, upholstery was unfastened, curtain linings were separated, an electric fire was unscrewed from a wall.

There was nothing.

'It's clean,' Chief Inspector Emsley said. 'There's only that business of the fingerprints.'

'What fingerprints?' Norton demanded.

'When we came before we dusted the place. There was a set of dabs on the electric plug in the bedroom. Probably the charlady's.'

'Probably. Show me.' Norton followed him into the bedroom.

'Over there.'

'Not much, is it? But if it's the charlady, why weren't her

prints elsewhere? Look, we're going to have to take the floor-boards up. We may as well start here.'

'All right, sir.' Emsley bent to pull back the carpet, found the access board and lifted it. He shone his torch inside. 'Nothing here.'

'No? Then the charlady it probably is. I suppose there is a Hoover in the place?'

Emsley blinked up at him. 'No, I don't think there is. I'll check.'

'Stay there. I'll look.' There was a cupboard in the hall and Norton was making towards it when Emsley called to him. He returned to the bedroom. 'What is it?'

'Paper. Under here. I can't see it but I can touch it.'

'Well get it out!'

'Half a minute.' Emsley put on a glove and reached into the hole. A moment later, he straightened and his hand appeared holding a large envelope carefully by the corner.

In Vancouver, Calder had had a fruitless day. On landing at Sea Island, he'd telephoned Elizabeth Donald and a quiet Scottish voice had passed him the news that not only had the *Tyee* submersible vanished but a *Tyee* pilot had vanished, too. She told him about the submarine approaches to Queen Charlotte Sound and the nature of the approaching Soviet cruiser. Also, they had learned the name of the cruiser – the *Suvarov*.

It was, Calder thought, a fair assumption that if the sub had been stolen, the pilot was being used to operate it. He was, he thought sourly, better informed but no wiser. He stared at a map of British Columbia, wondering what the hell was going on. Queen Charlotte Strait began almost three hundred miles from Vancouver. The land around it was wilderness, the water area was enormous. Both mainland and island were honey-combed with fiords. The province was enormous and, apart from a few population centres in the South, very sparsely populated indeed.

What could the Russians be after? Laying mines? Possibly, but it was very doubtful. Rockets then? Hardly, with ICBMs able to reach any target from home soil and nuclear subs at sea. They could be trying to plug in to the defence network, or after samples from the SOSUS/CAESAR system. Calder knew the boosters and hydrophones were brand-new technology and therefore highly desirable hardware, but they were far out in the ocean. There was no need to come close inshore after them. For a start, they probably didn't lie close inshore, and secondly they could be sought, in safety, elsewhere.

Still, he had to begin somewhere. He began with a former Sub-Lieutenant in the Royal Naval Volunteer Reserve who had been demobilized a quarter of a century earlier and was now a reporter on the *Vancouver Sun*.

Jim Burnell was at his office. Sure he could come out, but what was the story? Calder was intriguingly discreet and Burnell came to meet him in the bar of an hotel.

'Okay, so what's the story?'

Calder said quietly, 'I must point out formally that you are still bound by the Official Secrets Act 1911.'

'Bullshit!'

'I'm afraid it isn't. You remain in the naval reserve and you remain bound.'

'I'm Canadian.'

'You're a British citizen, Mr Burnell.'

'Who the hell are you, anyway?'

'I represent the British Government.'

'So what the hell are you doing here, in Vancouver? What goes on?'

Calder said, 'You hold Her Majesty's Commission. You are presumably, still interested, however casually, in naval matters.'

'Are you some kind of spy?' Burnell laughed. 'Jesus Christ! A British spy in Vancouver! There's nothing to spy *on*!'

'It would be technically possible, Mr Burnell, to recall you to the colours. You understand that?'

'I'm fifty.'

'Technically possible all the same.'

'Not with the stink I could make, it isn't. This is Canada. A free Press and a free country.'

'Also extradition. Under the Official Secrets Act.'

Burnell stared. 'You're crazy.'

'Not crazy. Nor am I threatening. I'm pointing out that I am entitled to ask your assistance and that you are bound to give it.'

Burnell was silent for a few moments. Then he said, 'Just supposing all this is true. Supposing. What do you want?'

'To pick your brains. Newspaper people are well informed. They notice things other people miss.'

'A bit vague, isn't it?' Burnell grinned suddenly. 'Christ, I thought I must have stolen the secret plans or something.'

Calder knew how stupid he must appear. It didn't worry him. He said, 'There's a lot of water, a lot of shipping. Things happen. Odd things. Local stories that don't go much farther. That's what I want to know about.'

'Okay. I don't mind that. Where do I start?'

'I know,' Calder said, 'that the Canadian Navy's based at Esquimault. I know there's a torpedo range in Jervis Inlet and I know there's a disused ammunition dumping ground in Georgia Strait.'

'That's all there is. The rest is civilian. This is lumber country, mostly water-borne. There was a collision a couple of years back between a ferry boat and a Russian ship.'

'What kind of Russian ship?'

'I forget. We get a lot of them here. Grain ships mostly. There's a wad of cuttings in the office morgue.'

'Go on. What else?'

'Well, there's been trouble between Russian fishing boats and ours. It's gone on for years. It'll go on for ever. Factory ships ploughing in among the little boats. Happens everywhere, the way I understand it. Scotland, Japan, you name it.'

'Anything else?'

'Don't think so. There used to be some lumber piracy, but it's been stopped.'

'Piracy?'

'They fixed it. Oh, maybe five years back. Not much nowadays.'

Calder nodded. 'And that's it?'

'There's the submersibles. Two companies building them. One sank the other day.'

'I know.'

The two men sat silently for a moment or two. Then Calder said, 'If anything occurs to you . . .'

'Yes?'

'Ring this number. Ask for Elizabeth Donald and pass on the information. It will reach me.'

Burnell looked at the piece of paper. 'Who is she?'

'Don't try to find out. Don't behave like a newspaper man either.'

'I'm tempted.'

'Resist it. Let your life stay comfortable.'

But Jim Burnell did not resist it. Or not entirely. When his day's work ended, at four o'clock, he strolled from the big editorial room into the morgue and began to ask for cuttings: the file on lumber piracy, on the fish war, on the submersible. Just for the hell of it, he'd look through them.

The girl librarian brought them to his table. 'That's all?'

'I think so.'

'You don't want them copied.'

'No. Why?'

'Why? Everybody wants them copied. That one specially.'

'The submersible? I'm not surprised. It sank.'

'Yeah,' the girl said. 'I just seem to have been making copies for weeks.'

'Weeks? Before she sank?' Burnell asked, wondering why he was pursuing it.

'Oh, sure. Before, during and after.'

'Who was the before?'

'I don't know. Some guy from a magazine.'

'Which magazine?'

She didn't remember that. She remembered the man, though. Smallish, trace of an accent. Very polite.

It was, Burnell thought, so small an event as to be insignificant. But he smelled a story in Calder, who wasn't in Vancouver for nothing. If there was a story, he wanted it, which meant maintaining contact. He went back to his desk in the newsroom, tucked the phone between his shoulder and his ear and dialled a number. 'Elizabeth Donald?'

'Speaking.' A Scottish voice.

'I have a message for Calder. It may be nothing, but . . .' He gave her the details.

'Thank you. I'll pass it on.'

The phone went dead before he could say, as he'd intended, 'Let me know if it's any use.'

XIII

It was during the retrieval of the second of the six rockets that John Baxter began, surreptitiously, the long business of making *Tyee II* inoperable. For days he had tried to work out some means of saving not only himself but Henry and Jane, too, and he had come, finally, to a conclusion. It had long been clear to him that his only chance lay in achieving a hold over the Russian group that would outweigh the double hold they had over him. Equally clearly, this could only be done by getting hold of one of the rockets. If he could only do *that*, he could dictate terms. The question was: how to do it? Effectively he was the prisoner of the frogmen while he was under water. They carried limpet mines; they need only attach one of them to *Tyee II* and he was finished. Furthermore, he had been warned that Semichastny's presence aboard *Tyee II* wouldn't stop them. What would stop them was the presence of the Sword missile trailing on a cable actually attached to the submersible.

So he calculated the equation that presented itself to him. First, he must take Semichastny unawares. Second, he must do it while the missile was suspended beneath *Tyee II*, being transferred from the ramp to the casing. Third, he must do it while the frogmen were physically tired, because although the little sub could make five knots flat out, she wouldn't be able to do so with the rocket dragging behind. He needed to get clean away first time. If he failed, the three frogmen could conceivably swim with him, or hang on to the skid. Unless he actually lost them, it wouldn't work.

Stage one, then, was weary frogmen. If they reacted slowly when he made his move, his thin chance would improve. He had thought hard about the method. Now he began to act.

Beneath the pilot's couch lay a six-inch, handled wheel. He had to turn the wheel, and keep on turning it, and he could only do so by reaching beneath the couch. The foam-rubber cushion on which he lay face down rested loosely on its metal frame and he managed to move it to one side and slide his right arm through to grip the wheel. At first it wouldn't move and he had to manufacture an excuse to crawl under the couch for a moment and so get both hands to it for one good heave to start it off. After that, using his right arm in the odd moments when it was not needed to operate *Tyee II*'s controls, he turned the wheel, inch by careful inch. He had no way of knowing how many turns would be required and could only keep moving that wheel, a little at a time. Fortunately it became easier, and he felt grateful to the maintenance men at Martec who had not forgotten proper lubrication. The wheel was there only for emergency purposes and to the best of Baxter's knowledge had never been used on any of the three *Tyee* class subs Martec had made.

He had to stop during the tricky manoeuvring of the second rocket from ramp to casing, but when it was safely housed and being lifted to the surface by the crane, he managed several turns.

'Now,' he heard Semichastny say, 'we go up.'

'Why?'

'The frogmen must rest.'

'Okay.' Baxter increased buoyancy and *Tyee II* floated easily upward. Beneath the couch, his hand was busy at the wheel. How far to go now?

The water had cleared and Baxter trimmed the sub tail down so he could look upward towards the silver undersurface. He said, 'When we're on top, you'll have to open the hatch and guide me.'

'Yes.' Semichastny looked at him thoughtfully. 'I am aware of it.' Was Baxter being too co-operative? He had to co-operate of course; it was a question of degree, of willingness.

Semichastny could think of no way in which Baxter could sabotage the operation. Not, at any rate, if he wanted to survive it.

'On surface,' Baxter said.

'Very well.' The Russian climbed off his couch, reached up to unscrew the compression ring, and flipped the hatch back. 'We are fifty metres from the barge. Due east.'

'Okay.' Baxter turned the sub and motored forward. With Semichastny's head out of the hatch he could wind away at the wheel without fear of being seen. 'Call the distance.'

'Twenty metres. Slow.'

'Slowing.' Baxter eased off power and gave the wheel several rapid turns. Surely, by now, the screw thread must have unwound.

'Coming alongside.'

'Right. Fend her off.' He could see only Semichastny's boot and trousers; the rest of the Russian's body was through the hatch. Baxter wound hard at the wheel and was finally rewarded. Suddenly, *Tyee II* gave a violent upward lurch.

He heard Semichastny's boots scraping on the footholds as the Russian was thrown off balance. 'What was that?' There was alarm in his voice.

'Dunno.' Baxter switched off the engines and the master circuit and climbed off his own couch stiffly.

An hour later, when *Tyee II* had been hoisted out of the water and was standing on the barge, he said, 'I don't know how the bloody thing came loose. It mustn't have been secured properly, that's all.'

Belyaev looked at him with cold anger. 'You cannot dive without the weight?'

Baxter said, 'I can dive. But I don't have the same control. that ton of lead gives balance as well as weight. I couldn't promise accurate handling.' He bent and looked at the underside of *Tyee II* 'You see where it should be positioned. There's a steel socket in the weight. That screw winds into it. It keeps the balance of the sub forward.'

'In other words, you cannot operate?'

'Not without the weight.'

'You need not think,' Belyaev said, 'that this act of sabotage will halt the operation. Nor that it will be unpunished.'

They returned him to the tug and locked him in the cabin.

Up above, all six of the frogmen stood on deck. The three who had already put in two hours' work were weary from the effort and the ascent, when they'd had to stage for twenty minutes to avoid the bends from too sudden a reduction of water pressure on their bodies.

Semichastny said, 'It shouldn't be too difficult to find. We know it lies within fifty metres or so of the ramp. When you have found it, attach the buoyed line and we will raise it on the crane.'

'Do not,' Belyaev added, 'return to the surface until it is found.' They watched the six frogmen enter the water and disappear. Then Semichastny said, 'We shall have to signal.'

'You realize,' Belyaev snapped, 'that this was done while *you* were guarding him. He did it under your eyes. It was unpardonable carelessness, comrade.'

'Unpardonable?'

'Criminal carelessness then.' Belyaev shrugged. 'It will, in any case, be fully reported.'

'As you please. We must still signal.'

Belyaev watched him go into the radio shack. The operation was not irretrievable; the frogmen *should* find the weight; but this incompetent civilian had come close to wrecking everything. He remembered his final conversation with General Zarubin before they left for Canada. Zarubin had said, 'This operation must succeed and must succeed in such a way as to be a KGB achievement.'

'It is not,' Colonel Belyaev had pointed out, 'in KGB hands.' Zarubin had simply looked at him blandly. 'When a man's usefulness ends, he becomes a liability. This is not a philosophical point. It is an instruction.'

When a man is a trained observer and has spent forty years observing, it is hardly a fluke when he sees something. All the same, it was a fluke; a fluke, however, which came out of a habit pattern forty years old.

Bill Harrison was close to seventy and his sight was failing. When he had retired, four years earlier, from service at the War Office Wireless Station, he had intended to remain in Loughborough, in England, because his roots were there. But then, within a month of retiring, his wife had been killed crossing the road. Even so, he would not have moved. His friends were in Loughborough and he enjoyed meeting them; he was welcome, too, at the station. He was beginning to settle again, when his daughter flew over on a visit, watched him put aside the newspaper unread and marched him off to see an oculist. Bill Harrison knew what the verdict would be; his sight was failing and failing fast. He resisted, for a while, his daughter's insistence that he go to Canada to live with her and her family, but then his sight became a great deal worse and he capitulated.

When the house was sold, he sold most of his possessions, too. All the same, he arrived in Bella Bella on the coast of British Columbia accompanied by several large crates. They contained his radio equipment; radio had been his life. He had started with the Marconi company, transferred to the War Office on the outbreak of war, and afterwards had remained, as a highly skilled intercept operator. For five and a half years he listened in to the Germans. After that, it was the Russians. The function of the intercept operation was to locate and remain in contact with the other side's formations. Each side played the game and each was aware that the other was playing it, so call signs and transmission frequencies were varied daily, sometimes more often. The signal coming from one call sign on one frequency today would not be there tomorrow. If that call sign or frequency *were* used tomorrow, it would be used by another unit. So elaborate direction-finding equipment was deployed round the world. Computers calculated systems out of apparently random patterns, and made predictions: listen here, listen there. The good operator had an important place within the intercept pattern, because he could become familiar with another man's Morse sending; a good operator could say, 'I've heard that man before.'

Nobody, nowadays, told Bill Harrison where to listen, but

he searched the air waves all the same, for hours each day, listening to radio operators tapping keys, smiling to himself when he identified an individual hand.

They'd said, when he retired, 'Let us know if you hear anything interesting.' But that had been when he was living in England. He wondered, now, whether it still applied. For several days he had 'listened out' for a Russian ship with three operators aboard. He wasn't quite sure *how* he knew it was Russian, but he had no doubt it was. Something in the way the bug key was used said 'Russian'; it was like an accent.

He'd picked it up weakly at first, and at night, with the signal bouncing off the Heaviside layer, defeating the earth's curvature. Gradually, it had become stronger, then weakened, but he'd picked it up during the daytime, so it was coming nearer. A single D/F bearing wasn't much use, but he'd taken it all the same, and he knew the ship had come across the Pacific from Asia, then moved down the BC coast. From time to time he'd had to chase them round the dial as frequencies and call signs changed, and there wasn't in any case, a lot of traffic, but he'd known the signals when he found them.

He'd found them again half an hour ago. Two-way: signal and response. And Bill Harrison was intrigued because the call had been inexpert, in slowish, laboured Morse, and the answer had been equally clumsy: a bug key expert trying to send slowly. He'd listened for a moment, then switched on the tape out of habit and used the D/F to find the caller.

He couldn't be sure, of course, but he reckoned the two signals were four or five degrees apart. Judging by signal strengths, a hundred miles, maybe. And *that* was funny. Because one of them, the caller, was close to the Canadian coast. Maybe it was a fishing boat and a factory ship, but the two hadn't been in contact before, he'd swear.

The question was, should he do anything about it. If so, what? He sat, thinking about it; thinking, too, of the time thirty years earlier, when such a random intercept had pinpointed a U-boat and her tanker in mid-Atlantic and the navy had got the pair of them.

Was he being senile and melodramatic? No, he decided. He

was experienced and realistic. Evidence, then? Very little except instinct. But he'd always been paid to use his instinct, hadn't he? They'd thought it valuable for long enough. He felt for the telephone on his bench. What about the cost? A pound a minute – his pension didn't run to Transatlantic phone calls. All the same . . .

'Can I,' he asked the operator, 'make a call to England and have them pay the other end?'

The operator sensed his age and was sympathetic. 'Let's find out, shall we? Who do you want?'

Bill Harrison gave her the name. He wasn't even sure the old chief officer would still be there; he too must be close to retirement. He heard the call routed through Montreal, the dial spinning. Then, 'Ministry of Defence.' The operators conferred, his call was accepted.

'Chief officer, please.'

'I remember you, Mr Harrison. One moment.'

He was through. He apologized, at first, then realized that a pound a minute was a lot of money for an apology. He explained.

'You taped it, you say?'

'Yes.'

'Play the tape. We'll record it.'

He watched the tape turning, calling himself a bloody old fool several times, waited until it had finished. 'Get that?'

'Got it, Bill. What's your number?'

'Bella Bella 87516.'

'Bella Bella. You describing yourself, Bill?'

'It's a place,' he said.

'Okay. We'll be back if necessary. Will you listen out?'

'Of course.'

Seven thousand miles away in Loughborough, the chief officer picked up the green telephone and asked to speak to Signals Intelligence HQ near Bristol. When he reached the man he wanted, he said, 'Scramble, please.' The thing had come over an open circuit, but it would be bad luck if the other side had got it. From now on, they certainly wouldn't.

'What's he like?' the Foreign Office SigInt officer asked.

'Elderly.'

'Nuts?'

'Bill Harrison? He once got a U-boat. No, he's not nuts. Bloody good operator, in fact.'

'U-boats were before my time. Still, let's have it.'

In the underground SigInt headquarters, the message was received and typed out. First step was simple translation. No good, it was enciphered. Numerals in five-figure groups. But probably a simple cipher, almost certainly not computer-generated between two vessels at sea. The SigInt computer attacked it, picking at similarities in combination, juxtaposing groups, whirring through the incidence of letters in Cyryllic. The computer could make many thousands of calculations a second. The simple cipher lasted three minutes. Translated into English it read:

Sword to Belt: DELAY TECHNICAL FAILURE.

Belt to Sword: STATE DURATION.

Sword to Belt: UNKNOWN. POSSIBLE SEVERAL HOURS.

Belt to Sword: REPORT EIGHTEEN HUNDRED. RELAYING SCABBARD.

'Who the hell,' the SigInt officer wondered aloud, 'are Sword, Belt and Scabbard?'

Gawthorpe asked himself the same question a few minutes later, when David Norton placed a copy of the signal on his desk. The call was out for anything odd, anything at all, about British Columbia, and the message had been relayed direct from Bristol by teleprinter to Parliament Street.

'Have they got a D/F bearing?' he demanded.

'One.'

'Fat lot of use. We'd better watch this six o'clock schedule like hawks. I want at least two, and preferably three, bearings for triangulation. You'll have to fix it, David. Ships at sea, War Office stations, anybody with D/F equipment, I want them listening out at eighteen hundred.'

In his hotel room in Vancouver, James Calder picked up the

telephone and dialled. When Elizabeth Donald answered, her voice reminded him again of a Scottish actress he'd seen in a dozen films, but couldn't put a name to. Always wore plain dresses with high lace collars and played disapproving school-mistresses. He wondered how Elizabeth Donald could conceivably be working for Gawthorpe.

'Any news?'

'We've been listening to the radio. Very interesting. There should be more on the six o'clock bulletin.'

He wondered what they'd got. 'I've been working hard, but I don't seem to make much forward progress. Some confirmation, nothing else.'

'We'll perhaps have something later. Why don't you ring me after six. I've scones to bake.'

Calder hung up. Scones to bake indeed! These deliberately tangential conversations with their laboured domestic references were irritatingly unreal. Indeed at the moment everything was unreal. He'd spent an hour at the *Vancouver Sun* office library, chatting up the girl who remembered the cuttings being copied and pretending to be a private detective looking for a missing person, but he was aware he hadn't done it very well; the girl had been puzzled and unresponsive. Later he'd gone to Martec and posed as a BBC producer to talk about the possibility of hiring a *Tyee* submersible to search for the legendary sea monster of Loch Morar. Plainly, the Martec people had not believed *Tyee II* had sunk; they were angry about it, and rather noncommittal.

Altogether, it had been a depressing day. Until he spoke to Elizabeth Donald, Calder had been growing more and more certain that there was no way ahead. Certainly the Russians were up to something, but whatever it was, they'd covered their tracks with such skill that he was completely blocked.

But now something had been heard. Intercept had picked something up and were hoping for more. Well, it was encouraging, but he wouldn't want to build hopes on it. He walked to the window and stared out over the dark, empty water of English Bay where, in a few days, the Russian cruiser

Suvarov would drop her hook. Why the hell were they sending her?

He settled down to wait for the phone call. Without more information, there was nothing he could do.

Gawthorpe had made a decision. He made it regretfully, almost certain it was a wrong decision and a waste of a potentially very useful situation. He gave instructions that Igor Kovrenko, the junior KGB man attached to the Soviet Trade Delegation, should be 'lifted'. Having made the decision and given the instructions, he continued to brood guiltily about it. Kovrenko might or might not be queer; if he wasn't, and if he had to be released afterwards, the operation would give away the lift technique which, so far as Gawthorpe knew, was still unknown to the other side, or to the Americans for that matter. Also, it would probably deprive the department of the chance of having a double agent within the KGB.

The lift occurred as Kovrenko parked his car near the Trade Delegation headquarters on Highgate Hill. Another car slid in alongside it and as Kovrenko stepped out of one car he was invited to step into the other. The invitation was backed by a gun which could fire a cloud of instantly fatal hydrocyanic gas and its potential needed no explanation; the gun was of Russian origin and Kovrenko recognized it immediately, with widening eyes.

Within half an hour, he was in a soundproof room in the basement of DI6's Parliament Street building, with his jacket off, his sleeves rolled up, and a cocktail of drugs being injected into his arm. Ten minutes later he was sitting on a small podium in the middle of the room in an armchair, bemusedly facing the five men whom he had watched filing into the room.

The argument then began. That was what puzzled Kovrenko. He had expected interrogation, even torture. But this was argument. He listened with surprise as it developed. The five men were talking about Marx, about Lenin, and they'd got it all wrong. He found himself wanting to join in, to correct their misapprehensions. The argument became rowdier, but remained good humoured, and Kovrenko, listening, could see how confused they all were. They must be blockheads! Every argument that was advanced he could easily contradict, which was surprising, because some of the arguments were quite ingenious. He seemed to have an unusual clarity of mind. Probably the injection had done that. He wondered why they'd given him the injection when all they wanted to do was talk among themselves. There was no interrogation here, and the British were such fools! He was KGB, didn't they realize that? They'd pay for this. How they'd pay! He felt suddenly infinitely superior to these fools and his superiority gave him the right to intervene. He'd smash their puerile arguments right now, demonstrate their stupidity.

He shouted suddenly, 'Listen to me, you idiots!' Naturally, they did. Instantly all five faces were turned towards him inquiringly and he felt like Socrates as he began to dispense his wisdom.

In two corners of the room, small television cameras were hidden, relaying the pictures into Gawthorpe's office. One was focused on Kovrenko, the other moved from face to face among the five other occupants of the room.

He wondered how long Kovrenko would last; how complete his break would be. He watched almost dispassionately, disliking the technique he had invented, but sure of its power. Professor De Sales was talking to Kovrenko now, setting his logician's traps and springing them gently, never conceding a point of any kind. De Sales wanted his knighthood, which was why he allowed himself to be used in this way by the department.

An hour passed. Another injection was given. The argument went on. Now Dr Cruxton was mincing Kovrenko's arguments and Kovrenko was growing more confused, shouting more loudly, asserting every point he made with maniacal intensity. In his blood several drugs were circulating: sodium pentothal, the truth drug; a minute quantity of hallucinogenic STP; and the other one, Gawthorpe had forgotten its name, which made him so aggressive.

It was such a simple method. You simply gave a man the urge to talk and bent his mind a little, then confronted him with several minds of far, far greater capacity than his own. You let him advance his argument, then destroyed it. When he switched his argument, you destroyed that, too. It was brainwashing in a particularly pure form. Over a few hours, every belief a man had was smashed by the remorseless hammers of superior intellect. The normal brainwashing technique took months; this method, depending on the capacities of the subject, a few hours. At the end he would not know what he could believe with safety; there would be no corner of his mind that had not been scoured out by destructive argument.

After two hours, Kovrenko was going. He was bathed in sweat, weary from the mental beating, but the drugs kept his brain hyperactive, and now he was given benzedrine, too, to stimulate it more. Gawthorpe watched, feeling slightly sick. There was a kind of sadism in the way the five academics went about their task, a trace of obscene delight in their own unassailable superiority. He particularly disliked the languid Dr Cruxton, Fellow of All Souls', who sat coiled in his chair like some kind of elegant lizard, flicking out his tongue from time to time to snuff out a belief.

The argument now was about subversion and espionage, and Kovrenko was retreating almost hysterically from the battering ram of the five minds. Gawthorpe watched the hysteria mounting, saw the pressure building inside Kovrenko like steam. The KGB man's face was twisted in despair as he fought to escape from the corner in which he had been finally trapped. The corner of his own enormous, irredeemable evil, evil that was driving him inexorably to madness. He was, after all, Cruxton said viperously, mad already. It had been demonstrated by his own admissions, A and B, by his arguments X and Y. Hadn't it? Hadn't it? Hadn't it?

They pushed him and battered him. They tore at his scruples, his beliefs, his personality, his biological make-up. And, thought Gawthorpe sourly, they loved it. He could tell how they loved it from the way they looked at the broken Kovrenko as he sagged in the armchair after his mind exploded.

Gawthorpe thanked the five academics as they filed out of the room, each with his dusting of smugness, and sent them off to lunch. Then he went in to talk to Kovrenko himself. In twenty minutes he had all the information Kovrenko had about the Russian operation. It was pitifully little and nothing was really new. KGB London, Kovrenko told him confusedly, had made the arrangements for the two Baxters. John Baxter had been taken to Moscow. Henry and Jane were on a Soviet ship in the Mediterranean. Kovrenko confirmed what Gawthorpe suspected, but he had no idea what had been the purpose of the operation. Gawthorpe looked down at the slumped figure with pity. He'd have to decide what to do with the Russian once he'd been pumped clean of any general information he might have.

They were no further forward, and he could see no way of moving forward now, unless that six o'clock schedule was picked up. Everything depended on that blasted schedule!

XIV

The six frogmen had begun their search close to the Sword missile launching ramp. They were systematic about it, swimming in widening circles from the base of the ramp, their hand lamps lighting up the stones and mud of the ocean bottom as they moved steadily along. But it was not easy to be systematic; the ramp had been sited on an island area of flat rock and the farther they moved away from it, the more difficult the search became. There were fissures in the rock, and as they investigated them, clouds of mud were stirred, disseminating widely around them in the moving water. After a while they felt as though they were swimming through ochre clouds and had to stay very close to the ocean bottom to see anything at all. It also became increasingly difficult to be sure of direction and the search that had begun so systematically became blundering and awkward. The frogmen found themselves bumping into one another, barking their hands and bodies on the rocks.

But, inevitably, in time, they found the weight. It was of lead, roughly oblong, shaped to fit snugly against the curvature of *Tyee II*'s underhull, and in falling a corner of the soft lead had struck a rock and splayed out. The line was attached, the buoy inflated and sent to the surface. Soon afterwards a steel cable was lowered, the ton of lead was attached to it and it was hauled off to the surface.

Three of the frogmen promptly departed on their upward staging. It would be some time before they surfaced, after staging halts. The remaining three found their way back to the ramp and waited.

As the weight rose dripping from the water, John Baxter looked with satisfaction at the distorted corner. The thing would have to be cut and reshaped before it could be replaced; the frogmen were still under water, using their energy; and the lifting of the weight from the deck of the barge to fit beneath *Tyee II* wouldn't be easy. Not without jacks. He'd be interested to see how they set about it.

In fact it took more than an hour's sweaty work with wedges and levers, gradually raising the weight upward, before *Tyee II* could be lifted by the crane, lowered gently over it and ma-noeuvred awkwardly until screw and socket came together. Belyaev himself, in shirt sleeves, perspiring freely and ex-tremely irritated, climbed into *Tyee II* to wind the handle and drive the screw home. Baxter could imagine how ferociously he was tightening it. Three of the frogmen had appeared while the job was going on; they looked drawn and weary. And the other three, waiting below, would not, Baxter thought, be exactly happy.

Belyaev clambered out of *Tyee II*'s hatch and jumped down to the deck. When he spoke, his voice was low and threatening.

'No more mistakes,' he said. 'Remember that. The punish-ment for error will be of extreme severity.'

Baxter nodded. 'It wasn't my fau – ' His protest died away as it occurred to him that Belyaev might be addressing Semi-chastny, too. He glanced at the leader of the Russians and knew it was true. Semichastny said sharply, 'That's enough!' But he was pale and less than wholly confident.

With a new oxygen cylinder fitted *Tyee II* dived again. Short of sabotaging the submersible's electrical system, which would almost certainly entomb them both, there was little else Baxter could do. But he did what he could, slowing every movement of the sub, dragging things out, as first one rocket, then a second, was taken from the ramp housing and raised to the surface.

Two more to go, and the second crew of frogmen came down. Baxter watched them through the observation port, thinking they must be worn out. They'd a total of four hours per man underwater so far and the better part of three more ahead. Well, he'd drag it out till they were exhausted. He swung *Tyee II* round and returned to hover over the ramp, waiting for the housing to be opened and the rocket cable attached. He timed the operation as he waited. They were slower, significantly slower; it took an hour and twenty minutes to complete the transfer.

Then number six. He could feel his own weariness increasing. His shoulders ached from the long hours on the pilot's couch, his eyes were sandy from staring into the glare of the quartz-iodine beams. He concentrated hard. The time was coming; it was more than an hour away, but it was coming. He glanced occasionally at Semichastny on the observer's couch. The Russian lay on his side and he was looking out of the port, but every time Baxter glanced across, he met Semichastny's eyes. The Russian had positioned himself carefully so that any movement Baxter made happened on, not outside, the periphery of his vision.

Number six was slowly attached. Increase buoyancy . . . the long, hard lift. He felt the sub take the strain, waited for that first tiny upward movement. Once the missile was clear, he'd lash out with his foot, trying for Semichastny's gun. If he got it, full ahead with both motors and hope eight horse-power would be enough. He had to risk a glance across the sphere to gauge the distance, a very casual glance. He grunted and moved his head as though to ease his muscles, risking the glance.

And he could have wept! Semichastny's gun was pointing directly at him. The Russian's eyes were bright and alert; they held Baxter's for a moment, and in that moment Baxter knew he had given himself away, knew his own intensity had communicated itself.

'It was the obvious time,' Semichastny said quietly.

Baxter tried to sound innocent. 'For what?'

'Go ahead. Finish.'

Tyee II lifted slowly away from the ramp and Baxter thought ironically that the job *would* have been easier without that extra ton of lead. Possible, too, but the Russians weren't to know that. He watched bitterly as the frogmen swam into view and the signals began. Left a bit, right a bit. Now forward. The tail in place, the lowering. It was easy now, practised, going smoothly. He manoeuvred the sub, following instructions, glancing once at Semichastny, knowing it was useless. The chance he'd planned for had gone. Slowly he began to decrease buoyancy, lowering the rocket into its casing. He'd have to take another chance. Once that last rocket was in position, Semichastny *must* relax for a moment. He wouldn't be human if he didn't let out a sigh of relief when the job was done.

Thumbs up in front of the window. So the rocket was in place. Baxter sensed a movement on the other side of the cabin and saw Semichastny was signalling to the frogman, pointing to the ramp. But the gun hadn't moved and Semichastny was keeping a wary eye on him.

He said wearily, 'What now?'

'I want that fractured chain.'

'Why?'

'To examine it later. I have an interest in the structure of metals. As you have in the possibility of escape.' Semichastny smiled. 'Don't worry. You will be released. Not immediately, perhaps, but later when the danger is over. You have a cutter, I think.'

'I have a cutter.'

The rocket was gone now. In a moment it would be on the surface. Baxter fingered the buttons of the submersible's telechiric arm, ejecting the grip into the tool rack and clicking the electric cutter into place, then he brought *Tyee II* round and headed for the ramp. The idea came as he approached the triangular structure and he saw that it formed a kind of cave.

If he could get into it, *back* into it, the cutter would be a hell of a weapon against the frogmen. But what about Semichastny? How would he . . . ? Suddenly that problem, too, was solved, as Semichastny sat upright. Baxter increased motor speed slightly as he approached and caught the structure a deliberate glancing blow that knocked Semichastny off balance. Wildly, he lashed out with his foot at the Russian's head, and felt his toe connect, heard the grunt of pain. One motor reversed and *Tyee II* was pivoting. Where were the frogmen? Then the beams caught them as the sub came round, two black figures suspended in the yellow glow. Two! Where was the third? A moment later he, too, appeared and signalled his intention of going upward. My God, it had worked! He glanced quickly at Semichastny, who lay still, groaning in pain, on the other couch, and reached across and grabbed the gun, then watched the frogmen again. They were almost beyond the yellow beams now, moving slowly upward. Until they were out of sight, he wouldn't move; he'd spend a couple of stationary minutes pretending to examine the structure. As the second hand of his watch made its fourth, slow circuit, Semichastny began to sit up, holding his head. He opened his eyes and saw the gun.

'Yes,' Baxter said. 'It's over. They've gone. The frogmen have gone.'

'Gone?' Baxter saw his eyes widen.

He said, 'One mistake, that's all. This time you've made it. We stay down and move away, then later we surface. We'll get ashore –'

He didn't live to finish the sentence. The first explosion smashed the steel ramp down on the submersible; the second cracked the inch-steel of the sphere like an eggshell and the unbelievable pressure of the water smashed the breath instantly from both bodies and poured into their lungs.

Three hundred yards away, the explosions jolted the swimming frogmen. On the surface, it was felt through the plates of the tug. Then the surge of gas bubbles. Belyaev pursed his lips. His orders had been carried out successfully.

Elizabeth Donald and Gawthorpe had worked fast. A P&O

liner in Vancouver harbour had its instructions, as had another British ship three hundred miles out in the Pacific on its way from Sydney to Seattle. Bill Harrison was also sitting in his radio shack at Bella Bella, so three radio operators were now waiting for the six o'clock schedule. All would tape the signal, if it came, but the content of the signal scarcely mattered. What did matter was that three D/F bearings would be taken, and three D/F bearings would pinpoint the signal's source.

In Bella Bella, Bill Harrison checked again that he had the frequency right. Beside him his daughter stood counting off the seconds as the clock ticked towards six o'clock. He had the tape spool turning, ready for the moment when the signal began.

'Two minutes.'

Harrison nodded. There was silence in the shack, apart from the soft hum of the equipment.

'One minute.'

He waited.

'Six o'clock.'

Still nothing. The seconds ticked by. Damn it, had he missed it? Were they on another frequency by previous arrangement?

'Six one.'

He could feel disappointment cold inside him. All that trouble and no bloody signal.

Abruptly he heard the Morse. His hand flashed out to fine the tuning, then he was busy on the D/F, knowing he probably had only seconds. The Morse beeped on as he worked frantically. He knew it would stop in a few seconds; you could always tell – it was as detectable as the approaching end of a conversation.

It was over. He said, 'Read that bearing for me.'

His daughter bent over the dial and read off the figure with practised ease. She'd been doing it all her life.

Harrison picked up the mike and added the bearing figure to the tape recording, then switched off and rewound it. At ten past six the telephone rang on the bench beside him and he played over the recording to WOWS, Loughborough. Like Harrison's earlier recording, it was passed to the cipher-breakers at Bristol. But this time the computer was not needed: after the previous break the cipher system and keys had been printed out. Within minutes of receipt the five-figure numeral groups had been deciphered and translated and were being teleprinted to DI6.

Gawthorpe looked at the message. On the other side of the room, David Norton bent over a table on which Admiralty Chart No. 3993, Canada West Coast, was spread. He was drawing in the bearing line from Bella Bella.

The signal read:

Sword to Belt: SWORD DRAWN. TWO PARTY LOST.
Belt to Sword: QUESTION OPERATION SECURE.
Sword to Belt: AFFIRMATIVE PROCEEDING.
Belt to Sword: CEASE CONTACT. INFORMING SCABBARD.

Gawthorpe said, 'Success attends their bloody efforts, David. No further contact. So we've got to get it right this time. I hope the Merchant Service gentlemen got those bearings.'

'It's not a long message,' David Norton said. 'They didn't have a lot of time.'

'We got one. We should have them all.'

They waited for the signals. The P&O liner came through first. Then the merchant ship. Gawthorpe rose and watched as Norton drew them in with the parallel rule. The three bearing lines did not intersect on a point; they formed a small triangle, a few miles west of the northern tip of Vancouver Island.

'Let me see,' Gawthorpe said, bending to examine the chart. Then he said, 'That's funny.'

'What is ?'

'The triangle. The island just outside it is called Triangle Island. Harrison's original bearing hit it.'

Norton asked, 'Do we tell the Canadians ?'

'There's not much to tell yet, is there, lad ? No, we tell Jim Calder. Then we'll see.'

At seven o'clock local time, Calder telephoned Elizabeth

Donald from a public telephone in a drugstore on Robson Street. He was given the result of the D/F operation and instructed to act appropriately, which meant: go there. He telephoned the president of Canadian operations of the British pulp and paper combine by whom he was theoretically employed, requested the use of an aeroplane, then took a taxi to the seaplane park on Burrard Inlet. By the time he arrived, a single-engined Piper floatplane had been prepared for him by a plane rental company. He showed his pilot's licence.

'Where you going?' he was asked.

'To the north of the island.'

'Okay. There's a survival pack aboard. A dinghy, too. Inflatable. You'll find the air cylinder is also aboard.'

He signed, and was rowed out on to the dark water. A few minutes later, with the Continental engine roaring, the mooring was slipped and he turned into the wind and, on maximum boost, began his take-off run. He climbed out over West Vancouver, leaving the sea of city lights behind him, and rose steadily through the darkness over Georgia Strait. At five thousand feet he settled back and crossed Vancouver Island south of the high ground, then turned on a heading west of north up the island's Pacific coast. The single-engine Piper, with the drag of the float rig holding her back, was not fast; his indicated air speed was one-forty knots. The flight to Triangle Island would take roughly two hours in all. In his mind he went over the facts again. Harrison's original bearing had touched Triangle Island. The three later bearings triangulated a spot several miles east of the island. It might be meaningless: radio bearings taken rapidly on signals of brief duration were notoriously inaccurate. Or, it might indicate movement. The job the Russians were doing was over, or part of it was, and the signal from Belt had instructed Sword to proceed. And the *Kresta II* cruiser was coming in to Vancouver in a day or two. So logic suggested that they would be moving into the funnel mouth of Queen Charlotte Strait and then down through the Inside Passage towards Vancouver.

Below him lay the Pacific. To starboard was the fiord-indented coastline of Vancouver Island. Calder decided he would find Triangle first, then fly towards the funnel mouth. In the darkness it was long odds against seeing anything at all, but he had to try. He eased down to two thousand feet soon after he passed over a prominent peninsula, kept careful watch to starboard until he saw the Cape Scott light, then swung almost due west over the rocky chain of the Scott Islands. Triangle Island was the end of the chain and he had no difficulty in spotting the conical hill which gave the island its name. He flew round it twice, looking carefully at the bare, dark slopes, seeing nothing that could conceivably be significant. Then he circled higher, searching the sea for lights. There were a few over to the east, and he turned the Piper in their direction, flying towards the narrowing entrance to Queen Charlotte Strait. He passed over them low: boats of one kind and another, some small, presumably fishing boats, one gigantic lumber barge that dwarfed the tiny tug towing it, and away to north and east the bright lights of a big coastal ferry, bound, presumably, for the upper coastal region.

How in hell, Calder asked himself savagely, can I hope to make sense of this? Somewhere down there were Russians. They might be on one of the fishing boats, or on a tug. They could even be on that ferry hurrying north. They might be anywhere between Triangle Island and Vancouver, three hundred miles or so away, and he had no idea how they were travelling, how fast they were going or where to begin to find out. It was even possible they were flying, as he was, in which case they had almost certainly gone for good.

He glanced at the petrol gauge, saw the tank was roughly half empty, and decided to drop down to the seaplane station at Port Hardy, refuel and report.

As the hired white motor cruiser moved into Queen Charlotte Strait, Colonel Belyaev heard the aircraft and began to search the night sky for its winking lights; finding them, he watched the lights swing across the sky, passing over him and going on over the tugboat ahead to turn finally south-east. Was the plane innocent? There was no way of knowing. It was significant that it had come from the area they had left four hours before and that it had flown over both vessels, but Belyaev knew of the air-sea rescue unit at Holberg, not far away, and thought it more likely the plane was searching for some fishing boat than that it was searching for him. No, he thought, they weren't searching for him. They didn't even know he was there. How could they? And if they did, if the slightest hint had slipped out, nobody would ever guess either what he was doing, or how the Swords were being transported. Semichastny, he thought with a mixture of contempt and admiration, had been too soft, a fool in many ways, but his transportation idea had been brilliant.

Twenty miles away, another pair of eyes had also watched the aeroplane. They had watched it circle twice round Triangle Island, but they had watched helplessly. Nikita Ivanov was, by now, almost too weak to move, but hearing the engine he had dragged his body to the mouth of the cave and seen the aircraft's navigation lights. Then, hopelessly, he had dragged himself back, to lie huddled on the damp floor, weakly piling the feathers he had collected over his shivering body, in the hope that they would insulate him a little against the deepening chill that was slowly spreading over him. The last of his food had gone early the day before, and that had been only a few pieces of one of the sweet bars he'd brought from the ship. For thirty-six hours he had eaten nothing except a couple of gritty, rubbery shellfish he'd managed to smash off a rock with a stone, and they had given him an ache in his stomach that had seemed likely to kill him. He'd taken water from a rock pool that morning, but nothing since because the effort of climbing was beyond him now. The effort required even to breathe was increasing, and Ivanov knew why. Exposure was inducing pneumonia and soon it would all be over. He would die here alone, on this bleak outcrop in the ocean. He almost now wished he had allowed himself to be arrested and sent back to Vladivostock. He would have died there, too, but at least he'd have been fed, and died warm.

During the afternoon he'd almost decided to try to attract the attention of the tug working a mile offshore, but he'd thought about it too long and it had gone away. He wondered what had happened to the little orange submarine that had been going up and down and had finally not come up again.

Now Ivanov looked at the wood fire glowing a few feet away and reached out to add to it the last of the wood he'd collected. For a few more hours it would give out a little heat, but the draught that blew through the cave would carry most of the warmth away, and after that there would be no more fire because he would not have the strength to search for wood, even if there was any more, and in any case he had lost his lighter somewhere during the search.

Ivanov lay for a while, staring at the rock-framed patch of sky at the cave mouth, certain that it would be the last thing that he would ever see. When his eyes closed they wouldn't open again. He strove to keep them open as long as he could, but they grew heavier and he drifted into something that was half sleep, half coma.

XV

Calder had spent the night at Port Hardy. He'd gone ashore to telephone Elizabeth Donald, had had some food, then returned to the moored floatplane and spent the night curled uncomfortably in a sleeping bag on the two rear seats. Before first light he was ashore again. He got coffee from a machine, ate a bar of chocolate and again phoned Elizabeth Donald, but she had had no further news.

Now, having taxied the Piper to the filling stage and tanked her up, he took off into the grey dawn wondering what it was he was seeking. He knew three things: he knew where the Russians had been; he knew where they were probably going; and he knew their probable route. He was angry that, when he knew so much, his task remained impossible because he had no idea what he was looking for.

He decided to start again at the beginning. Triangle Island had yielded nothing in the dark; it was unlikely to yield more by daylight, but that island was all he had. He circled Triangle once, at five hundred feet, but there was nothing to be seen on the cone-shaped hill that had not been there for a million years. He came lower and altered the trim: using more flap and letting the propeller-wash blast at the flaps so that his stalling speed was reduced. It was tricky and dangerous; at a mere hundred feet a sudden clout of wind from behind the hill could smack the Piper floatplane down like a fly. But still there was nothing; nothing but rock and shore and the cone climbing steeply. Or was there? A puff of something blew suddenly from among the rocks and he swung his head to stare, but the movement had gone. Smoke? Surely not. He noted the position carefully and came round again, flying as close as he dared. No, there was nothing, though he glimpsed what might be the entrance to a cave. As he came round a third time, he saw something glinting by the cave, if it *was* a cave. What had glinted? Water, probably. Just a flicker of reflected sunlight from a tiny patch of water among the rocks.

He dismissed it and began to turn, but the sight of the line of the Scott Islands stretching away towards the tip of Vancouver Island reminded him of the immensity of the area he must search for something he couldn't begin to identify. He brought the plane round, circling Triangle Island again. That little glitter, that tiny puff of something, were literally all he had. He caught the glitter again and realized it was the only one. If there were other small pools of trapped water, they failed to shine.

Could he even get down? From the air he could see the reefs, submerged ledges stretching out from the island to east and west for the better part of a mile. The wind, what there was of it, was from the south-west so a landing had to be on the north-eastern side. Well, the Pacific was living up to its name and there seemed to be a tiny beach of sorts tucked into the island's precipitous sides. He came round, turned into the wind, and landed cautiously on the slight swell, then jumped down to the float and let the anchor go, waiting till it held. Now he brought out the dinghy, inflated it, paddled ashore and began to climb, working across the slope.

He approached the cave from above and saw, looking down,

the source of the glint: a plastic bag. His teeth grated in exasperation. A bloody plastic bag! Wait a minute, though, how had it got there? He scrambled closer, found the mouth of the cave and peered in. . . .

The man was as cold as stone and at first Calder thought he was dead, but the faint hiss of breath among the fluid in his lungs showed he was just alive. As Calder bent over him, he watched the wind puff ashes from what had been a fire and scatter them through the cave mouth. That was what he'd seen; that and the plastic bag. Awkwardly he lifted the cold flesh and buttoned his donkey-jacket round the man's shoulders and chest, then he straightened and looked down. The man was almost certainly dying: respiration so shallow as to be almost nonexistent, flesh chilled, legs blue below the knees, arms the same from elbow to fingertips, lips blue, too, but face chalk white. The man needed warmth, food and antibiotics. He needed them quickly and even then it was doubtful if he'd live.

Calder scrambled back round the hillside and paddled out to the floatplane. What was in the survival pack? He tore it open. A small stove-cum-cooker and two cylinders of liquefied butane, food in compressed bars. Brandy. Condensed milk. He rowed ashore again, returned to the cave and wrapped the man in the quilted sleeping bag, then got the stove going. After that he tried to dribble brandy into the man's mouth and was rewarded by a ghastly, heaving cough. The eyes remained shut.

He worked for an hour, massaging the cold limbs, the chest, the back, trying to restore circulation. The stove's warmth was largely dissipated in the air current that flowed through the cave, and Calder was sure very little of it reached the man who lay so still on the damp floor.

He propped the man's back against the cave wall so that he was in a sitting position and began again to spoon warm condensed milk into him. Then a little more brandy. Calder doubted if it would be possible to get him out to the floatplane alone; it meant manhandling him into the dinghy and then literally lifting him up. It just wasn't on! The dinghy would wobble and tip them both into the water and this guy wouldn't stand immersion.

His arms and hands aching from the effort of an hour's massage, Calder sat back on his haunches, staring at him, sure that the answers he wanted lay with this man who sagged limply against the cave wall. If he could only be made to *talk*! Oxygen might help. My God, there was oxygen in the plane! He made the cumbersome trip again, scrambling quickly, glancing at the Piper's radio and thinking about, then dismissing, the idea of an SOS. It might bring the Canadians running, but then this guy would be whisked away out of his reach.

Returning, he clamped on the mask and gave artificial respiration, seeking to force oxygen deep into the fluid-filled lungs. Time dragged by and his arms ached with weariness, but he persisted. After another half-hour, the eyelids flickered. More food, more of the condensed milk that was now turning to caramel in the heat. That didn't matter; it was just milk and sugar; pure energy. The man's eyes opened glassily and Calder slapped the cold cheeks crisply, hearing the teeth click. Recognition came dimly. He moved the little stove between the man's knees, saw the eyes wander to it and the arms twitch weakly. Was he winning? The man's breathing was awful.

Time moved on, and Calder glanced at his watch. Three hours, now. He'd been working for three hours and, apart from the evidence of the open eyes, there was nothing to show. He gave oxygen again, waiting afterward, hoping the thin warmth and the food would begin to dispel the hypothermia. If he could get the man to hospital, he would, but that was not the priority.

Soon after one o'clock, the man began to cough weakly, and fluid spilled from his mouth. Between coughs, Calder still fed him, adding chips of chocolate to the condensed milk. The eyes were no longer so vacant, the heartbeat a little stronger. But still the breathing was appalling. Somehow the man must be got off this damned island before pneumonia killed him; Calder knew instinctively that if the man remained here death would come before speech. And the man must speak.

Finally, he worked out how to do it. He used the dinghy as a stretcher and tied the man to it, dragging him round the hill-side, then floating him out to the plane. Calder climbed aboard first and began to try to lift him aboard. It was killing work, hauling on the dinghy's painter while the man lay slumped in the dinghy, in danger every second of falling into the sea. In the end, though, he made it and wrestled to separate the partially deflated dinghy from the man. When he'd got the dinghy stowed and the man strapped into the passenger seat, he began to think where he could go. Vancouver was out; Vancouver meant hospitals and Canadian officials. He got out a map. There were hospitals enough, but the same problem would exist any-where.

Mentally, Calder ran through the list of names he'd been given before he left London. There must be a doctor. He re-cited the list to himself, parrot fashion, till the doctor's name came out: ex-Surgeon Commander Forres McQueen, RN, Kitimat, BC. Where on earth was Kitimat? He found it on the map, finally, way up the coast, but at least there was a seaplane landing. Distance around two-fifty miles. Well, it was closer than Vancouver, even if it was in the opposite direction.

He got away just in time; the Pacific swell was beginning to increase and he'd been lucky that the ocean had remained as calm as it had; now the take-off was distinctly tricky. He made take-off speed bumping disconcertingly but as he pulled the pole back the floats lifted cleanly. He swung north, turned the cabin heater high and concentrated on flying, glancing only occasionally at his passenger. There was no need to look; he could hear the rasping breath constantly, despite the engine's roar.

From Kitimat Calder telephoned Elizabeth Donald three times daily and she, in turn, relayed the reports to London. Each message was the same: 'Still unconscious. No other lead.'

Gawthorpe scowled at the latest one. He knew Calder was right, but fretted at the delay. It was now more than two days since Calder had found the man on Triangle Island.

He said, 'We're no forrarder. Not an inch.'

'At least it doesn't look as though the man will die. So the doc says.' This was Norton.

'Maybe. It's an extended bloody stupor though. Damn it, that Russian group could have got to New Zealand and back by now. They may have returned to Russia. Anything.'

Norton said quietly, 'The *Suvarov* arrives tonight with Gromyko. Presumably . . .'

'Presumably! You mean they're presumably heading for it. Presumably *Suvarov* is Scabbard. We don't know that, David! All we *know* is that they *were* at the island. But Calder missed them there. Not his fault, but he missed them all the same. They're slipping away, I can feel it in my water. I'll tell you what I'm going to do.'

Norton waited.

'I'm going over there myself.'

'Will "C" permit it?' The Head of DI6 had to approve all foreign travel by senior department personnel, even on holiday.

Gawthorpe dragged his fingers wearily across his lined forehead. 'He will if he wants to keep his teeth.'

Norton smiled. 'They're false. Sometimes you can hear them click.'

'All right, I'll break his plate. Wish me luck.'

Norton waited. 'C' wouldn't permit it. A few minutes later, Gawthorpe stamped angrily into the room. 'The bastard. Says he won't let me within a thousand miles of a Russian cruiser.'

'Neither would I.'

Gawthorpe looked at him, the anger evaporating swiftly. 'No,' he said. 'And I wouldn't either. But I wish that bugger in Kitimat would either die or mend. I can't stand the strain much longer.'

Belyaev had put the two days to good use. The missiles must travel slowly, but even three knots maintained twenty-four hours a day ate up distance steadily, and the boat was now almost at the far end of the narrow Johnstone Strait, tightest reach of the Inside Passage. He could see it now, a mile or so ahead, chugging securely on about its business.

Nor had the aircraft made a reappearance. There'd been

plenty of aircraft of one kind and another, but none on search patterns, none coming low to examine the steady two-way stream of waterborne traffic.

It was far too soon to be pleased about the operation, but, even assessed coldly, it had gone well so far.

There was no reason on earth why anybody should be suspicious of the tug; neither of the pleasure cruisers had attracted the slightest attention. Why should they? His group was merely a party of holidaymakers, properly equipped with papers, backgrounds and sporting equipment. And, if the worst came, there was the other tug in reserve. Belyaev sipped a steaming cup of lemon tea and stared round him at the water and the steep-to sides of the narrow channel, wary always but neither seeing nor sensing anything that could threaten them. Two hours earlier he'd sent Adams in the second cruiser to Kelsey Bay to telephone Vancouver, a routine call to the KGB man at the Sylvia Hotel, in case there was information to be passed or some change of plan. He expected neither; the plan was unlikely to be modified now, short of some kind of disaster to the *Kresta II*.

Half an hour later, he saw Adams's boat coming up astern, drew towards the bank and waited. After a while it came alongside, and the deck thudded as Adams jumped aboard.

'Well?'

Adams said, 'There's one thing. A sailor deserted from Belt.'

'Deserted?'

'Went over the side. He was wanted on a criminal charge at Pacific fleet HQ in Vladivostok.'

'When?' Belyaev snapped. 'Precisely when?'

'About the time they made the second drop. Belt says they never came closer than three miles to the shore, and that was off Triangle Island. Even if he got there, he's five miles from the next island and they're all uninhabited.'

'Did he have a boat? Radio? Equipment of any kind?'

'All his possessions were intact. No boat is missing. There was just a rope over the side and his clothes.'

'What was the criminal charge?'

163

'He killed a man.'

Belyaev thought for a moment. He said, 'Then he had a choice. Be shot, or drown. Do they know if he was a strong swimmer?'

'Fleet records say yes.'

Belyaev said: 'You will return immediately. Go ashore on Triangle Island and all the others of the group. If you find him, kill him.'

'I understand.'

Belyaev watched Adams move off in the cruiser, engines roaring, picking up speed as she swung north. Mentally he measured three miles. It was a long swim, even for a strong swimmer, but the man might have made it. If he had reached Triangle Island, what about the next stage? That was an even longer swim and the water was cold. Without proper equipment survival was very doubtful. He wondered how much the man knew, or could guess. Almost nothing, probably. He'd know about the deck cargo; nothing else. Only Belt's captain knew the nature of the operation and he was in radio contact with Tolstikov. Belyaev reviewed the situation soberly and began to believe that very little had changed. Almost certainly, the deserting sailor had drowned, or would drown. Even if he did not, he had no information that could damage the operation. Except his knowledge of the deck cargo.

Belyaev frowned, trying to put himself in the position of some Canadian policeman hearing the sailor's story. Much would depend on the policeman, of course. It was conceivable that . . .

His frown became a scowl. On second thoughts, he decided, the sailor *could* be a danger.

XVI

'This man has the constitution,' Commander Forres McQueen said, admiringly, in the soft accent of Inverness, 'of a crocodile. I doubt if you could kill him with a hammer.'

Calder looked down at the sleeping man. 'When he's talked,

you can bottle him for your specimen room, doctor. What I want to know is how soon he'll waken.'

'Waken naturally? A few hours.'

'Unnaturally, then?' It was nearly noon on the third day after their arrival in Kitimat, and they were in a spare bedroom in the commander's home. 'I need to get going.'

McQueen pursed his lips. 'I don't approve.'

'It won't kill him, will it?'

'No, Mr Calder, it won't. He's through it now. Out the other side.

'Then waken him.'

'It'll be an instruction from Her Majesty's Government, I suppose!'

'Put it that way if you like. Then leave me alone with him!'

'I'll have no violence, Mr Calder. Not in my home and certainly not with a sick patient.'

Calder said, 'Let's hope it won't come to that. Waken him and leave us, please.'

'All right.' McQueen left the room, returned with a bottle of smelling salts and began to move it close to the patient's nose. Calder watched the irritant at work, the twitch, the cough, the gradual awakening, the puzzlement in the eyes. The man blinked several times and began to cough.

'Goodbye, doctor.'

McQueen stared at him angrily.

'I said, goodbye.'

'All right.' The doctor left the room, leaving the door carefully ajar. Calder went and closed it.

The blue eyes looked up at him, wide with incomprehension. Calder said, 'Who are you?' He tried it in English first, then Russian.

The Russian words brought a response. A weak, rusty voice answered him. 'Nikita Ivanov.'

'You *are* Russian?'

'Yes.'

'From a ship?'

'Da.'

'Speak English?'

'Nyet.'

There wasn't much strength in him. 'What,' Calder asked, 'were you doing on the island?'

The man blinked. 'This is Canada, please?'

'It's Canada.'

'I stay here, please.'

'That depends,' Calder lied, 'on what you can tell me.'

'I tell you everything.'

'You'd better. Otherwise we hand you back.' He saw the flicker of horror in Ivanov's eyes. 'What were you doing on the island?'

'I leave my ship. Swim to the island.'

'Deserter?'

'Da.'

'What ship?'

'*Konstantin Budenny.*'

'That's her name?'

'Da.'

'From what port?'

'Vladivostok.'

'Bound for where?'

Weakly Ivanov shook his head. 'I do not know. I think she returns to Vladivostok.'

'So why did she come here? What cargo?'

'Deck cargo only.'

'Nothing in her holds?'

'Nyet.'

'On the ship. What was your job?'

'Radio. Radio operator.'

'Does the name Sword mean anything to you?'

'Nyet.'

Calder stared down at him. 'Damn. Belt, then, or Scabbard?'

'Belt is a code name.'

'For the *Konstantin Budenny*?'

'Da.'

'And Scabbard?'

Ivanov shrugged slightly. His eyes were frightened and his voice weakening; Calder made himself relax and gave an en-

166

couraging grin. 'You nearly died. You know that? You're okay now, though. Or will be. There aren't many more questions, then you can go back to sleep.'

Ivanov gave a tiny nod. 'You will not send me back? Please not. I tell you everything.'

Calder smiled. 'I don't suppose you'll be sent back. That deck cargo. What was it?'

Ivanov blinked, remembering. 'A crane. A big mobile crane.'

For the submersible. Of course! 'Go on,' Calder said encouragingly.

'A floating barge. Big. Twenty metres.'

Also for the submersible. They got as far as the sub and stopped every time. What the hell was the sub *doing*? Calder said, 'Is that all?'

Ivanov frowned. 'There were trees.'

It was Calder's turn to blink. 'Trees?'

'Yes, trees. Cut trees.' Ivanov was exhausted, sagging towards sleep.

'Without roots or branches? Logs?'

'Da.' The eyelids were closing, the word barely audible.

Calder thought, damn you doctor, where *are* your smelling salts? McQueen had taken them. He would! What's more, he wouldn't part with them again. Calder lit a cigarette, placed it between the Russian's lips and saw the smoke do its work. Ivanov coughed hard and his eyes watered, but at least he was awake again. Calder said, 'The logs, what were they for?' he had to wait for the spasm of coughing to end.

'They make a raft. I saw. From the island.'

'You watched from the island, did you? What did you see?'

'A little submarine. Orange.'

'It dived, did it?'

'Da. Three, four times. Then it not come up.'

'Not come up? Did it bring anything up?'

'Da. Logs.' Ivanov's voice was very weak now; his eyes no longer focused; he was slipping into sleep.

Calder slapped his cheek roughly and the Russian sailor's eyes flew open, showing hurt and fear. 'Were the logs taken away?'

Ivanov nodded, swallowing.

'By what?'

'A boat. A tug.'

'Can you remember anything about it? The tug, I mean?'

The Russian could manage only a whisper. 'Da. Small. The funnel was yellow.'

Calder hurried to the telephone. As he picked it up, he heard the doctor enter Ivanov's room. Before he'd dialled half the number, McQueen was at his elbow, angry as hell. 'You hit him!'

'He's asleep, doctor. It's over.'

'But you hit him!'

'I'll be gone in a few minutes.' Calder had forgotten what he'd dialled. He started again. 'Keep him here. Don't let anybody know.'

'I'll have to –'

'You *have* to do nothing. Hello?'

Elizabeth Donald was on the line.

Calder said, 'They were raising something. They're using a log raft to carry it. That's right, a log raft. It's towed by a tug with a yellow funnel. That's right. I'm going to look for it. Leaving now. The man's what we thought he was. Jumped ship. He'll stay here, with McQueen, until you make arrangements. I'll call when I can.'

He filled the Piper's petrol tanks and flew south, down the indented coastline. Behind him the high, white smoke plumes from the enormous aluminium smelter at Kitimat faded gradually in the distance and he was back in the ancient wilderness of wide water, fiords and mountains. The Piper wasn't fast and there was a headwind to slow him even more, but after two hours he was approaching Queen Charlotte Strait. Away to starboard there was a thin haze over the water and he could see the cone of Triangle Island rearing through it in the distance. No point in going back there now. The Russians would be far away, with their yellow-funnelled tug and their logs.

Logs! below him were millions of them. He'd flown over three huge log rafts already, one of them at least half a mile long, on their way down from the forests of the Queen Charlotte Islands to mills down the coast. Calder's lips compressed as he thought about the problem. Logs were buoyant. A big log could, he knew, take the weight of several men and barely float an inch or two lower in the water. If the Russians were quietly making off with some undersea installation, the logs would both carry the weight easily and be totally unremarkable in a land where the movement of lumber was the principal industry. He wondered, briefly and half-admiringly, what ingenious KGB man had dreamed up the idea of using logs. But there were two other and more important questions: firstly, what was *in* the logs; secondly, where, among the uncountable numbers of felled trees on the waterways of British Columbia, the logs he wanted were to be found?

He'd asked just one question before leaving Kitimat. How fast did a log tow move? Commander McQueen simply hadn't known, but the Esso men at the fuel depot had given him an answer. Two or three knots. Calder knew time was getting tight. The logs had been on their way a full seventy-two hours. If they moved twenty-four hours a day, they'd done somewhere between a hundred and fifty and two hundred and thirty miles, which brought them too close to Vancouver for comfort.

And there were, he thought sourly, a couple of other nasty complications. The light wouldn't last more than an hour and a half; the autumn day was drawing in. Also fuel. He'd enough to last till the light went, but not much more. Four and a half hours at maximum continuous was about the limit of the Piper's endurance.

He came low, throttling back to slow the speed, and began to look carefully at every boat and ship he passed. There wasn't much hope this far north, but he looked all the same. There were logs everywhere; big barges, rafts large and small, feeding the province's giant lumber, pulp and paper industry. Now the waterway was narrowing, as Queen Charlotte Strait funnelled into Johnstone Strait, and he flew over it low, zig-zagging over every vessel, searching for a small tugboat with a yellow funnel. Damn it, how small was small? How yellow was yellow? Was it all yellow, or just in a band? He should have asked that, even at the price of another clout. There was yellow there, below him now, and he swung round to look at the vessel again, only to find it was yellow and white and not a tug at all but some kind of small coaster.

He wound slowly down Johnstone Strait past Kelsey Bay, where lights already shone from houses and street lamps, heading on through the even narrower waters of Discovery Passage. No yellow-funnelled tugboats here, either. To his left lay a mass of islands and inlets and he thought savagely that an entire fleet could hide successfully in these waters, let alone one small tug towing a few logs.

Now lights were appearing on the shipping below and the narrows were widening. Discovery Passage was turning into the big Strait of Georgia which reached down, more than a hundred miles long and almost thirty wide, nearly as far as Seattle. The strait seemed almost to be carpeted with logs. Where the hell did a man start to look for just a few.

Circling, turning, banking, dipping low to fly over every possible vessel, he moved slowly southward. Light was going fast, the gloom would soon be dusk, then night, and he'd be finished. It was already like looking for the needle; once darkness closed down, it would be like searching the hay with the barn door closed and no flashlight.

He swung again, away from Vancouver Island, back towards the mainland. There was a big island in the middle of the strait and he glanced at his map to identify it. Texada Island. He flew round its northern tip and saw a big log tow below. Was this the timber route? It seemed probable. The water would be more sheltered in the lee of the island. Right then, he'd search here first. It would be a good idea, in any case, to head away from the air base at Comox on Vancouver Island; they'd be boggling at their radar screens over there, wondering whether they were watching an aircraft or a demented wasp; and he'd no flight plan filed.

On through the strait, then looking down he could see that the weather was roughening; there was white now on the darkening water. He switched on the cabin light to glance at the map and cursed himself, as he switched it off again, for partially destroying his night vision. The haloes persisted, it seemed, for minutes. He was somewhere off Jervis Inlet now, a bare sixty miles from Vancouver, blind as a bloody bat, and still no sign of yellow-funnel.

Texada Island was sliding back into the growing darkness and the water was roughening more as he skimmed over it at no more than two hundred feet. What now? Follow the coast, or try to search the other side of Georgia Strait? A moment's thought and he decided to follow the coast, to hunt the quick route.

A couple of minutes later, he saw that a raft beneath him was turning slowly, like a long sausage, heading for the coast. Why? Was it too rough now for towing? He wished he knew something about the logging business. Where was the raft going? Not far away were lights, but what lights? What was the place? He flew towards them, coming low over a small bay in which several log rafts lay motionless on the water. Then, quite suddenly, he saw something else and swung violently to starboard to have another look. Below him lay a little raft of logs, almost invisible now in the darkness, with a small tugboat towing them towards the big rafts moored in the bay. But it was too dark to see the funnel properly. The colour was pale, certainly, but was it yellow? Dare he fly over it low? He decided he had no option. Calder brought the Piper round again, dropping under a hundred feet in the darkness and shuddering a little at his own foolishness, then he slid across the water towards her. Was that bloody funnel yellow? He was over her in a flash, then climbed away, trying to decide what his next move should be.

Colonel Belyaev had heard the aircraft two minutes earlier, and came up to the cruiser's narrow, pitching deck. For a while he had difficulty in finding it; then, as his night vision improved he saw its lights and watched as it flew low over the water towards Trail Bay. It passed quite close to the cruiser, and he could just discern the silhouette against the starlit sky. A seaplane. The other aircraft, four days ago, had been a seaplane too. Now the plane was coming round low, its lights quick across the sky, and flying directly over the tugboat.

Belyaev swore softly as the seaplane lifted, climbing off to the north. It could be nothing, a crazy pilot buzzing boats for fun, but he was not prepared to give the benefit of any doubt. Anything not absolutely loyal *must* be regarded as hostile. He could remember General Serov's words at a staff course he'd attended fifteen years earlier. Treat it as hostile; it probably was.

On the walkie-talkie handset he gave his orders to O'Hara, the tugboat skipper, then ordered increased speed from the cruiser, and moved ahead to come parallel to the tug, a couple of hundred metres away. Maybe the operation was blown. Maybe it was not. In either case, appropriate remedial action had been taken. There were other ways of moving the Sword missiles than towing them openly straight down the middle of the waterway.

The cruiser waited until the tugboat had entered the shelter of Trail Bay, then followed her in. As the way came off, the cruiser slowed, too. In her cabin two men had struggled into rubber suits and now waited quietly. Belyaev gave his order and they moved into the cruiser's stern well and slid quietly, two dark shadows, into the water. One man carried an inflated bag of tools.

When the swimmers reached the tug, she had already slipped the towline and they dived and found it and struggled to the surface, then waited as the tug manoeuvred away, avoiding entanglement with its screws.

Leaving them there in the water, the tug turned slowly and began to move out of the bay on to the broad, roughening seascape of Georgia Strait.

It was night in Vancouver; morning in London. The news from Calder reached Gawthorpe via Elizabeth Donald, as he breakfasted early in his office, and he read and reread the typed message without enthusiasm. From this moment, without doubt, the matter would pass beyond his control, moving inevitably from the relatively simple status of counter-espionage investigation into the far more difficult status of political pressure factor. Any action taken now must be taken only with express approval from above.

Finishing his coffee, he buzzed 'C's' secretary on the inter-
com. 'Is he in yet?'

'No, Mr Gawthorpe.'

'When he arrives, I want to see him.'

'Urgently?'

'At once. Tell him the thing's going political.'

He then signalled Elizabeth Donald in Vancouver: 'No
further action without authority London. Repeat no un-
approved action. Instruct accordingly.'

It was just before 10 a.m. when 'C' arrived and Gawthorpe
went immediately to his office to report. 'C' listened without
comment, then dialled the Principal Secretary on his private
line. A few minutes later the two men were striding briskly
into Whitehall on their way to the office of Her Majesty's
Secretary of State for Foreign Affairs.

Twice before, Gawthorpe had been in the big, panelled
office, with the portrait of Palmerston on its wall, and it always
seemed to have a run-down air. There had been a time, once,
when the occupant of this room had been one of the most
powerful men on earth; now it was a bit like being in the
boss's office with the factory running down.

It remained, however, a citadel of good manners. The
Foreign Secretary rose as they entered and came round his
desk to shake hands before returning to his chair to sit, pale
and dark-suited, beneath the Palmerston portrait. The room
was almost gloomy, Gawthorpe thought; the only flash of
colour lay in the red-and-gold striped silk of the Marylebone
Cricket Club tie beneath the Minister's skeletal face.

Gawthorpe asked the awkward question. 'You'll have read
the briefing, Minister?' Reports of DI6 operations went to
both Foreign Secretary and Prime Minister's office each day,
along with hundredweights of other assorted paperwork.
Theoretically, everything was read; in practice, it was easy for
a paper to be skimmed over, even missed in the late-night or
early morning cramming.

The corners of the Foreign Secretary's wide mouth widened
a little. 'I'm familiar with it, Mr Gawthorpe. Tell me about
the development.'

Gawthorpe said, 'We now know, sir, that there is quite certainly a Russian party operating in British Columbia. The DI6 operative has now managed to interrogate the man he found on the island and he *is* Russian. He has also described what he saw. Briefly, it is this. The *Tyee* submersible stolen in Vancouver made a series of dives off Triangle Island, apparently raising something from the ocean bed – '

'You said "something",' the Foreign Secretary interrupted gently. 'Do you know what it is ?'

'No, sir. We do know, however, how that "something" is being transported. At any rate, we're fairly sure we know. Logs of wood are being used.'

'How do you know ?'

'The Russian saw them, sir. They were carried across the Pacific from Vladivostok in the ship from which he deserted. He also saw them at the dive site while the submersible was at work. We believe now that they are being used to transport the object or objects raised from the ocean bed down the passage between Vancouver Island and the mainland coast of British Columbia.'

'Believe ?'

Gawthorpe nodded. 'I'm sorry. It's no stronger than that, but the signs point that way. The logs are being used, we must assume, because logs are part of everyday life in British Columbia, and therefore unremarkable. As a means of transport they are perfect because they will attract no suspicion at all.'

'But why, Mr Gawthorpe, do you assume they are moving in that direction. Why not out to sea ?'

'For two reasons, Minister. First, the construction of a log raft is not really suitable for ocean water. Secondly, there is the presence of the *Kresta II* class cruiser, the *Suvarov*. It arrives tonight in Vancouver Harbour.'

'I shall be dining aboard her, I understand, four days from now.' The Foreign Secretary's teeth showed in a brief smile. 'Perhaps I should request a tour of the ship. You think, do you, that whatever it is the Russians have raised is to be taken aboard the ship ?'

'Yes, sir, I do.'

The Foreign Secretary leaned forward, elbows on the desk. 'And what does DI6 think this object is?'

'C' said crisply, 'We do not know. There are several possibilities. One is that at some point a Soviet submarine was lost there and that the objects may be either equipment or armaments from her. Or they may have been stealing equipment from the SOSUS/CAESAR or Suspended Army System listening networks. Or there may be a seabed torpedo installation. Whatever it may be, it is clearly of great importance to them.'

'Why did they not destroy it where it was?'

'That,' Gawthorpe said, 'is the question. Either they can't, or they daren't.'

'Which presupposes either armaments or stolen American or Canadian equipment?'

'C' said, 'The Soviet equivalent to the Polaris missile is almost certainly too big to be handled like this. The *Tyee* submersible does not have sufficient lifting power to handle it. I incline to think they're helping themselves to American equipment. The underwater listening network is a tremendous irritant to them and in that area of technology the Russians lag three or possibly four years behind the U.S.'

'I see.' The Foreign Secretary gave a thin smile. 'Well, the buck stops here, gentlemen. Now, I will tell you what must be done, and why. I'm sorry, but you must suspend your own operation.'

'I've already sent orders to the department operative, Minister,' Gawthorpe said.

'So the reason is obvious to you. All the same, I will state it so that there can be no misunderstanding. The talks which I, Mr Gromyko, Mr Kissinger of the U.S. and many others will be attending, are of considerable importance in themselves. But beyond that, the new warming of relations between Russia and the West is still fragile and it is important that the Soviet Union should not be embarrassed internationally through any small stupidity, either of their own or ours.

'And there are other matters, not all on the Vancouver

agenda, but still important. The Russians have again had a bad wheat harvest and are buying from Canada. For purely humanitarian reasons – and I prefer to believe, gentlemen, that the improvement of humanity's lot is the prime purpose of politics, domestic or international – we wish to see the Canadian wheat go to Russia. Historically speaking, Russia is most dangerous when she is hungry. In addition to the wheat deal, there is fish . . .'

Fish? Gawthorpe frowned. *Fish!* He lowered his eyes deliberately to hide it but the pause continued and when he looked up again, he found the Foreign Secretary regarding him with perhaps a trace of amusement.

'Yes, fish, Mr Gawthorpe. We wish to continue fishing the White Sea and the Russians may well continue to permit it, even after the coming revision of territorial waters. Iceland now has at least one Communist minister, but remains a member of NATO and the most important source of fish in Northern Europe. That area is very tricky indeed. Also on the matter of fish, Canada and the Soviet Union have reached some measure of agreement about the operation of the Soviet fishing fleet off her coasts. That agreement is important, too. International peace, if you will forgive this ancient analogy, is a very slow jigsaw puzzle. I grant you that the puzzle can never be complete, but the object is to put as many pieces in place as we can and to keep them there as long as possible. It has taken a dozen years to recover fully from the idiocies of both sides in the U-2 incident. There must be nothing like it again.'

'That is entirely clear, Minister,' 'C' said.

'Not to me,' Gawthorpe said quickly. 'Forgive me, sir. It's a matter now of interpretation.'

'Go on.'

Gawthorpe ignored 'C's' warning glance. 'Your instruction is that we let them get away with it, whatever it is ? And that we don't inform Canada ?'

'On no account do you inform the Canadian government. As host nation they would unfortunately be unable to turn a blind eye if they knew, however much they might wish to. The thing is on their soil, in their territorial waters. As to letting the

Russians "get away" with it, gentlemen, I must repeat what I have said. They must not be publicly embarrassed. Like you, I would like to know precisely what it is they are carrying. So, I am sure, would the Ministry of Defence. But *not* at the expense of the current diplomatic situation.'

As they walked back along Whitehall, 'C' gave a small sigh. 'On my head be it. As usual.'

'We'll just have to keep a crafty eye on the *Suvarov*,' Gawthorpe said.

'Distant and crafty, Gawthorpe. No Commander Crabbes. Are you certain your instructions will get to Calder?'

'Elizabeth Donald's his contact. The signal's gone to her. He ought to get it.'

'He'd better.'

Neither could know why the order to suspend failed to reach James Calder.

XVII

As his Piper floatplane banked and climbed away from Trail Bay, Calder reached for the BC airways map and switched on the map light. His problem was now to get down and the water in Georgia Strait was far too rough for him even to contemplate a landing there. What he needed was sheltered water, close by, and having glanced at the map he stared out at the moonlit land below for confirmation. It was, he thought, time for a bit of luck. Behind Trail Bay ran a long arm of water named Sechelt Inlet and at its southern end was a seaplane landing. A neck of land no more than half a mile wide separated the end of the inlet from Trail Bay itself.

He flew north climbing, for about ten miles, under no doubt that the tugboat had seen him and hoping by flying so directly away, to damp down any anxiety his flight might have aroused on the boat. It was not much of a hope; he knew he must have alerted them; all the same it was good psychology to depart in a straight line before swinging east over Sechelt Peninsula. Clearing the mountains he lost height quickly and turned down the long silver streak of Sechelt Inlet to a landing at the southern end, where he taxied in, close to shore, and moored the Piper. When the boat came out he gave instructions that the petrol tank be filled, then set off to walk across the narrow land-neck towards Trail Bay. At the top of the slight rise he stopped and looked at the moonlit seascape, trying to orient himself to this ground-level view of what he'd seen from above. After a while he succeeded in picking out the big raft he'd seen earlier. Where then was the little one, and the tug with the yellow funnel? It had been ahead about a couple of miles, so it must now be in the bay. He stared at the long rafts that carpeted the bay, searching for it, and then saw something that made his stomach contract in disappointment. A boat was leaving the bay, moving quickly through the water, too quickly to be towing logs. Calder could not see the funnel. He could see, in fact, little more than a dark shape with white phosphorescence at bow and stern. There were several other tugs at anchor in the bay, but only one was moving. He knew with sickening certainty what had happened: the tug had slipped its towline and dumped the little log raft here, among the big ones.

Damn! It would be impossible to find it. Assorted log rafts lay scattered like great leaves on the surface; logs in thousands, perhaps hundreds of thousands. And somewhere among them lay the Russian raft. But where?

All right, then. Think. He could at least get a hint from the direction of the tugboat. He watched it, drawing a mental line back from its position. That gave him an area, but it was a depressingly large area: something more than a square half-mile, crowded with floating logs. Well, there was only one way to get among them, and that was on the water.

He returned to the floatplane mooring, deflated the rubber dinghy and began to carry it along the little road towards Trail Bay. It was a good deal heavier than he'd imagined and, burdened with the oars too, he had a load that was both weighty and awkward. He made slow and uncomfortable progress until a pick-up truck stopped and an amiable driver asked if he'd like a lift. He accepted gratefully, volunteered no explanation though one was clearly expected, and got out a couple of minutes later quite close to the water's edge. He waited in the gloom until the van's tail lights vanished, then used the air bottle to inflate the dingy and pushed it out on to the water.

As he rowed, he watched the shore. Somebody would have seen him, but nobody seemed interested enough to be looking and the dinghy would, in any case, be disappearing from view. Two hundred yards from the shore, he approached the first of the log rafts; the long logs which formed the side retaining barrier stretched away on either side. He began to paddle round it, working gradually towards the point from which he thought the towboat must have begun its departure.

Beside him, logs lifted and fell with the water, crunching and grating against each other, filling the night air with a steady, low rasping sound. He rounded the raft and rowed on. Now there was another raft, even bigger. All the rafts seemed enormous; nowhere did there seem to be one that did not contain thousands of logs. He moved from one to another, trying to keep his bearings, but finding it increasingly difficult as the water forces bent the stationary rafts out of the cigar-shaped configuration they assumed while towing.

After two hours, and despite the exertion of rowing, Calder was beginning to feel chilled. Though the night was not particularly cold, the steady breeze from the south-west which roughened the water of Georgia Strait was penetrating his clothes; it had a rawness that stiffened his hands and numbed his feet. He was in the right area now; had been so for an hour, but progress was slow. Sometimes he had to row almost half a mile to round a raft in order to make a hundred yards of direct forward progress.

It was after ten o'clock when he found the logs and even then he wasn't sure, at first. By that time Calder had looked at so many logs, all so much alike, that the task was beginning to seem impossible. The thing that attracted his attention first was the sheer size of the logs. Several had a diameter of more than four feet. Then he noticed that a ruler-straight crack ran almost vertically down the butt end of a massive log that lay more than half-submerged in the water. Nor did the log bear, as did all the others he'd seen in the last couple of hours, the distinctive mark of some company's stamp of ownership.

Taking the dinghy closer, Calder examined the crack and decided it wasn't a crack at all but a lengthways saw-cut. As he looked along the log, it seemed the cut ran the entire length of it. It must have been sawn in half and put together lengthways! Excited now, Calder examined the logs on either side. Neither had been similarly cut. He pulled himself along the edge pole to the next big tree trunk, and found the same pattern: one large log, cut lengthways, and flanked on either side by uncut smaller logs. Then he saw a steel binding line glinting in the moonlight and discovered the logs were bound together in threes; in each, case, one big and two smaller, and the big one cut in half. Six times, there was the same pattern: eighteen logs altogether, plus the four which made a framework round them.

Turning in his seat, Calder looked around. Had he been seen? It seemed unlikely. The few tugboats in the bay still lay at anchor, riding lights on. It would be difficult to get at whatever was inside the logs, but he'd have a try. Then he froze as a flicker of light caught his eye. He had to stare at its source for a moment before he realized what had happened. A towboat away to his left no longer showed riding lights; she showed navigation lights now, she was under way. As if to confirm the thought, the logs rasped warningly beside him. What was going on? He stood shakily upright in the dinghy, staring across the horizontal forest on the water surface, towards the tugboat. As he watched, the towline rose and fell, smacking the sea as it took up tension, slowly dragging its big raft into line. Again the logs rasped beside him, shifting in the water. Calder maintained a precarious balance, feeling like a bareback rider as the dinghy rocked beneath him. Quite suddenly, he knew what was happening. The little raft the Russians had brought into the bay was now attached to the big commercial raft, getting a free and unobtrusive tow. And the sea must be calmer, so the tug was able to move on.

There was a decision to make, and Calder made it quickly.

Either he let the logs slide away into the darkness and himself returned to the aircraft; or he too took a free and unobtrusive ride. He grabbed the side retaining log and hauled himself aboard, taking the dinghy's painter with him and knotting it to one of the binding lines. Beneath his feet the logs bobbed a little, threatening at any second to throw him off balance, and he squatted, searching for a firm surface, wondering whether his hasty decision had been the right one. There was still time to return to the dinghy and row back, but the chance would not last long. The alternative, remaining aboard the floating raft, became more dangerous the more he thought about it. Quite apart from the possibility that some unpredictable movement of the logs would trap and crush a hand or a foot, there was the fact that he had neither food nor water, and had had nothing since leaving Kitimat ten hours or so earlier.

Swiftly Calder began to work out times and distances. The raft was about thirty miles from Vancouver. At three knots, nine hours or so; at two knots, nearer thirteen. And he was cold. God, but he was cold! He looked back longingly to the small ring of lights at Sechelt, wishing he could return instead of remaining aboard, but his original decision had been confirmed in his mind. If he left the logs now, they might never be found again. He must stay with them and suffer.

The first thing was some kind of shelter. Rising unsteadily, he dragged the dinghy aboard, laid it across the logs and sat on the inflated rubber cushion. No good. It was more comfortable, but also more exposed; he would have to improve its position somehow. He tried lying inside it, but the bottom of the dinghy had no soft air cushion and the moving logs beneath were hard and excruciatingly uncomfortable. He began to explore the make-up of the raft, crawling awkwardly along its unpredictably undulating surface. The construction was simple enough: a square framework of four logs fastened with steel ties at the corners. Within the framework the eighteen logs floated in bundles of three. And on top, presumably to stop them bobbing clear of the frame, a couple of thinner logs were strapped across the raft. Simple but strong, and there was some shelter behind the strapped transverse logs. With the dinghy propped half-sideways against the after one, Calder found he had at least a little protection from sea and wind.

The midnight message to London from Elizabeth Donald in Vancouver was bald and unhelpful: 'NO CONTACT CALDER STOP NO KNOWLEDGE WHERE-ABOUTS.'

Gawthorpe regarded it with distaste, well aware of what it meant. He said, 'If he *could* make contact, he would. We know that. So?'

David Norton frowned worriedly. 'So he can't. Two reasons I can think of. First, he's injured or dead. Secondly, he's in some place where contact is impossible.'

'All right, David, but the bloody man has an aeroplane. Wherever he lands there are phones.'

'So either the plane is down somewhere, or he's abandoned it in favour of something else.'

'That's it: it must be. So he'll have to be told.'

'The Foreign Secretary?'

'Himself. He leaves this morning.'

The Foreign Secretary, tweed-suited, ready to go, sat beneath the Palmerston portrait, pale and coldly angry, his thin lips tight in a flat line of disapproval. Mentally, Gawthorpe withdrew his earlier thoughts about the powerless state of current Foreign Secretaries. Enough power remained to break him and the department, enough authority to bring sweat bursting through on his back, his forehead and his hands.

'From what you know of the man . . . er, Calder, what is your opinion?' The bony fingers were tented, the grey eyes hard.

Gawthorpe said, 'Either he is dead or he is, for some reason, unable to make contact.'

'Of course. But which?'

'We must assume he's unable to make contact, sir. If he's dead there *is* no problem.'

'Go on.'

'If Calder is alive, sir, I can say only that he doesn't give up easily.'

'Very well. We assume the worst possible circumstances.

They, as I see it, are as follows: he retains freedom of action and is close to, or in touch with, the Russian party. In this he is performing his assignment, following his orders?'

Gawthorpe nodded.

'A great deal depends, therefore, on the assignment he was given. What was it?'

'To find out what was going on.'

'If that is all,' the Foreign Secretary said, 'he will presumably not interfere.'

Gawthorpe said miserably, 'The standing instruction to agents operating alone is to seek advantage, sir. He may have seen an opportunity.'

There was a pause and Gawthorpe glanced upward at Lord Palmerston. On the whole, he thought, he'd rather have faced his lordship.

'Listen to me,' the Foreign Secretary said crisply. 'I leave London Airport at nine. You will accompany me in the official delegation. When we arrive in Vancouver, Calder will be found. And halted. Is that clear?'

'Sir, I'm forbidden to leave the count – '

'For the moment, Mr Gawthorpe, that instruction no longer applies.'

'Yes, sir.'

An hour or so before Gawthorpe's uncomfortable interview, Colonel Belyaev had stood on the deck of his hired, white cabin cruiser, looking carefully at the sea around him through high-quality Barr and Stroud night lenses. The lenses showed him nothing to cause the slightest concern, yet he *was* concerned. Belyaev, experienced at recognizing the nervous symptoms generated by pressure, had no difficulty in recognizing them in himself.

He felt exposed. His mind knew the feeling was ridiculous; his eyes took in the details of a night seascape that was quiet and peaceful; the evidence of the success of his Trail Bay ploy was evident. Belyaev, like the other members of his party, wore Canadian-made recreation clothes, woollen plaids and dark trousers as anonymous here as fur hats in Leningrad, yet he had an odd sensation of being fifty feet high and spotlit. It was the aircraft that had done it, of course; the aircraft that had flown over them twice, days apart and only briefly, but *twice*. Since the plane had turned north and disappeared out of sight, there had been time for things to happen, if anything had been going to happen. But nothing had. No patrol boat had come close to sniff either at the raft or at his cruiser; no other aircraft had come low over them; the reserve tug moved comfortably on, two miles away, awaiting instructions to close in, and the tug that might perhaps have been identified was far away now, heading up the island to draw off any pursuit there might be.

The method was working; no doubt about that. All that was wrong lay in his own nerves and Belyaev was aware that he could control them if he wished to do so. It was always possible, and sometimes necessary in the KGB, to drop a shutter over a portion of the mind and exclude uncomfortable thought processes. Yet he was reluctant to do so: somewhere among those strange, nervous brain processes lay the source of instinct and he knew the value of the human instinct, knew that it often presented truth in some incomprehensible way. Often people knew they were being watched, even though the watcher was out of sight. There was no explanation of this knowledge; somehow such people could sense the watching eyes. Was something of the sort happening now? Or was it merely nerves? Belyaev shivered slightly, swore to himself, and went below to put on a heavy jacket, then returned to the deck and sat on the wheelhouse roof, continuing his survey of Georgia Strait.

He was following directly in the wake of the big log raft. A mile or so ahead, the twin white lights at the raft's after end remained steady as it moved down the strait. Belyaev could not distinguish the outline of his own small raft, but he knew it was there; had it floated clear, the cruiser would have come upon it as it lay loose in the water. His mind turned over the question of timing. The raft of Sword missiles must be released during the night, but that was the only parameter. His intention had been to release it and pick it up soon after it was safely clear of Trail Bay, but he had not done so. If the operation *were* now under observation, then the little raft was safer tacked on to the big one than it would be proceeding separately. Safer because its presence was unsuspected. And it could remain where it was, making the necessary speed and progress, for so long as darkness lasted.

Belyaev made a conscious decision to trust the jangle of his own nervous system until solid evidence made change necessary. While things were going well, he would leave well alone and merely observe.

For more than a week the operation had been going smoothly, and now it was near its end. Only two things marred it: the sailor missing from Belt and that damned aircraft. And neither was of measurable importance.

He continued his watch, enduring the sense of exposure, counting the passing miles as the little raft moved on ahead.

XVIII

Crouched uncomfortably in the tilted dinghy, Calder had no warm topcoat to protect him from the chill night winds. The sudden squall which had earlier driven the rafts to shelter in Trail Bay had eased, and the water was comparatively smooth. Calder felt as though it was flowing over him, though on top of the logs he was a good eighteen inches clear of the surface. His body was empty of fuel because he had neither eaten nor drunk for sixteen or eighteen hours; he was tired as well as cold, and bitterly aware that many more hours of increasing hunger, thirst and cold lay ahead of him. Hours in which he could do nothing but endure.

But was that so? Was there really *nothing* he could do? Sooner or later the Russians must detach the little raft, mustn't they? All right then, could he beat them to it? And if he could, what then? Land lay a couple of miles away and the Russians were probably quite close by, in some innocuous vessel. Several sets of navigation lights were visible, some bound up the strait, some down.

Calder rose stiffly from his shelter and edged forward along the rough bark on hands and knees to examine the towline. He found it was Y-shaped. The two wire ropes which made up the jaws of the Y were shackled to either end of the cross log which made the raft's nose. Twenty feet ahead they came together, making a single line to the after end of the big log raft. Kneeling, he examined the shackles, and swore quietly to himself. He'd hoped for a spring fastening; instead he found the shackles were held by bolts. No hope there; without a spanner he couldn't unfasten them, and without a hacksaw he couldn't attack the lines themselves.

He looked grimly across the thirty feet of water separating the two rafts, not wanting to make the attempt to cross. All the same, he ought to gain at least two advantages if he crossed: the first was a chance at the other end of the line; more importantly, he wouldn't be on the little raft when the Russians arrived to collect it.

Quickly he scrambled back to the dinghy, tied the painter to a side pole and climbed awkwardly into it. He looked at the oars. They wouldn't be needed; not, at least, if all went well. But if it didn't, if he were to lose his hold, he'd need the oars to reach the shore. He wedged them into the bottom of the dinghy and tried to move forward along the side pole. It didn't work. The drag of the sea and the slipperiness of the wood combined to defeat him. If only he had a rope! But he hadn't; there was only the thin eight-foot painter. All the same, it gave him an idea. He looped a running knot round the side pole, then lay on his side in the dinghy, gripping the pole with one arm, sliding the noose forward with the other. As the noose tightened, he moved the dinghy forward eighteen inches. Now again. It was slow, laborious and brutally demanding, but he moved the dinghy forward, foot by foot, to the front corner of the raft, then sat up, panting from the effort. The next bit was the really nasty one. The logs might appear to be moving only slowly, but speed was a relative thing. Steamrollers, Calder thought sourly, were also slow, and moved just about as inexorably. If the dinghy banged hard enough and awkwardly enough against the front of the raft, then man and boat would vanish beneath it. It would be like being keel-hauled as the rough bark scraped over him. He looked at the taut wire slanting forward from the raft corner, and swallowed. He'd have to try to use his body to brace the dinghy clear, then pull them both sufficiently swiftly along the line to clear that dangerous, advancing front log. He sat still for a moment, gathering his strength, then held the tow wire one-handed while he unfastened the painter with the other and paused again, unwilling to make the move. Already the strain of holding the dinghy was making his arm muscles ache; he'd have to go soon. Calder took a deep breath, leaned out, advancing his hand along the line, and began to heave himself desperately, hand over hand, along it. At the second tug, the buoyant dinghy swung treacherously beneath him and he was left hanging from the towline by his hands, his feet hooked behind the rubber sidewall, as the dinghy moved towards the raft. He thought for a second his back would break; every muscle ached with the sudden, desperate tension as he tried to flex his knees and drag the dinghy back toward him. One more forward reach, one more! And one more after that. And another! God, he was clear, pulling the dinghy forward until he could tumble into it.

He rested briefly, hanging on to the towline, then began to pull himself forward again towards the join of the Y, passing it, then dragging at the main stem of the line until he arrived, sweating with the strain, at the rear of the big raft. Hauling the dinghy close, he tied it to the log frame, scrambled aboard and crouched, breathing deeply, waiting for the thump of his heart to subside, before looking at the towline.

The sudden upward bob of a log beneath his feet saved him, pitching him off balance. As he tumbled sideways he heard the sudden slap just behind him and then a solid thump as a knife thudded into the log where he'd been crouching. A knife! If the knife had not embedded itself in the log and taken a moment to pull free, Calder would have died a second or two later. As it was, he barely had time to half-rise to his feet before the next attack, and he hurled himself bruisingly sideways to avoid a vicious, hooking stab. By then he'd caught a glimpse of his attacker, and a strange and frightening sight he made: a frogman, in a black head-to-foot wetsuit, crouched in silhouette against the corner light of the log boom.

There wasn't time to wonder where he'd come from or why he was there; there was scarcely time to retreat out of range of another murderous thrust from that long, diver's knife. Calder scrambled away from him across the treacherous surface, using feet, hands and knees to hold some kind of precarious balance and stay out of range. The frogman seemed curiously clumsy and Calder realized suddenly that his assailant still wore flippers, handicapping movement on the logs. Calder backed away, but the frogman kept coming forward, and beneath them the logs moved slowly in the water, all rising and falling a little, all rough-surfaced, rounded and dangerous. Apart from the soft swish of their passage through the water and the occasional grating of log on log, the only sounds were the slap of rubber-clad feet and the occasional grunt as one man or the other stumbled.

It didn't take Calder long to realize what the frogman was up to. Slowly but inexorably he was being herded towards the corner of the raft where he'd be trapped and easy to finish. He scrambled desperately away to his right, trying to circle, to work his way back to the dinghy, but the ploy was spotted quickly and the frogman moved to head him off. Calder noticed he held the knife the clever way, blade upward, thumb on top of the haft, pointing at the navel and used in swift forward thrusts to arm's length.

He scuttled away across the logs, still circling desperately to his right, feet slithering and scraping on the rough, wet bark, but he knew he would not outdistance the man by going backward; he'd have to turn and run. Calder picked his moment anxiously, waiting until his own footholds seemed firm and the other man's less so. Then he spun quickly and tried to scamper across the logs. He got two steps, then tripped and fell painfully headlong, but the bruises didn't matter; the frogman was coming after him fast and the knife arm was drawn back to strike. The dark figure loomed over him, bending a little to straighten the direction of the thrust, and Calder knew he was beaten. There was nothing he could do. In a moment the knife would be in his body. He kicked out frantically, missing the man by a mile. This time the frogman could afford to be careful, to take proper aim, to strike accurately. Then the log upon which Calder lay moved a little, and he slid down its rounded surface, a few inches nearer, and his attacker paused momentarily to adjust his own balance. In that second, Calder lashed out again, clouting the man's knee with his heel, and he grunted with pain and moved back a step. It was the only chance; Calder knew he'd never have another. He scuttled away rapidly a yard or two, then rose, raced along one long log towards the dinghy, and dived across the few feet which separated it from the raft. The landing was hard and bruising as his left shoulder banged agonizingly against one of the oars, but he was, for a moment at least, out of knife range.

He rose quickly, grabbing one of the oars. Now, if the frog-man came after him, he could defend himself. The rubber-suited figure was already at the edge of the raft, glaring across, still with the advantage. With knife and wetsuit he could enter the water and hole the rubber dinghy and that would be that. Calder stared back at him for a long, silent moment before he realized that he held the oar more or less at the point of balance. He hurled it suddenly, handle first, like a javelin thrower, and the short hardwood pole took the frogman squarely in the gut, jack-knifing him as the breath was driven from his body.

The oar fell with a splash into the water in front of Calder and he grabbed it and hurled the dripping five-pound missile again, this time hitting the side of the neck. The rubber of the wetsuit was no protection; the man went down heavily and the knife flew from his hand, but this time the oar landed on the raft. Calder wrestled to get its partner up from the bottom of the dinghy, then hauled on the painter to draw the little boat closer. The frogman wasn't finished yet; he was hauling himself to his feet, clasping his neck, shaking his head to clear it. But now it was Calder's turn. As the round side of the dinghy nuzzled the end pole, he swung the oar in a wide arc, aiming the flat blade at the frogman's head. If the blow missed, the blade's momentum would carry Calder over the side, but it didn't miss and the oar's long swing stopped suddenly, with a terrible thud, as the blade caught the side of the frogman's head. The frogman first staggered, then began unbelievably to straighten, but whatever flaring impulse had made the brief movement possible died then and he swayed slowly backward, then he fell. Calder winced as the back of the frogman's head smacked against a log, recognizing finality in the chopping sound.

He remained in the dinghy for a minute or two longer, sagging against the rubber, still dazed with shock. Finally he realized he still held the oar, and stowed it, then pulled the dinghy close again and climbed wearily on to the raft, but he was careless and a second later had slipped into the water. His grip remained firm, so the water itself held no danger, but as he dragged himself up on to the raft he was grimly aware that, weary as he was and in soaking clothes, he would be in considerable trouble from exposure. The wind was light but chill and it knifed into him. He bent cautiously to examine the frogman who remained spreadeagled across the logs and something in the limpness, the angles of the limbs, confirmed that the man was dead. In that case, Calder thought grimly, as a shiver caught him, he wouldn't be needing the wetsuit!

Stripping the tight-fitting suit from the body turned out to be a long and exhausting task, and getting into it himself, without benefit of talcum powder, was worse. While he wrestled with the wetsuit, Calder thought about the frogman. The reason for his presence on the raft was obvious enough; at the right moment, his job was to release the towline and let the little raft float free, and he was on the *big* raft so the right end of the line would be released. With the suit finally on, and his body now protected a little, Calder went to look at the towline shackle. This one, also, was bolted. How, then, did friend frogman propose to loosen the bolt? The answer could only be that friend frogman had tools concealed somewhere, and since they hadn't been on his person, they must be somewhere on the raft.

It took minutes to find the toolbag, but it was there: a neat affair that could be inflated and contained not only spanners and hacksaw but a Thermos bottle. Gratefully Calder sipped scalding tea without either milk or sugar, feeling the warmth spreading outward. He looked for food, found none, and accepted that one couldn't have everything.

Sipping a second cupful of tea, he looked back at the way the raft had come. Several sets of navigation lights were visible and he stared at them for a while. After ten minutes or so, the position of the different sets of lights in relation to the raft had changed a little. Two of the vessels were moving quite quickly. But there were two more that seemed to be holding station: one a mile or so directly astern, the second a little farther away to starboard. They could, Calder thought, be other tugboats; that was the only legitimate explanation of a steady three-knot speed. But the explanation didn't seem to fit. Three log tows under way so close together in so small an area of sea was unlikely. They'd give one another a wider berth than that.

After a few minutes' thought he was sure the two boats were part of the log operation, and their presence meant he had no hope of fulfilling his original intention of casting the logs loose and trying to tow them away in the dinghy. It had been a forlorn hope in the first place; now it was impossible to try it.

Then there was the other problem. Sooner or later there'd be a signal intended for the dead frogman: the instruction to release the little raft. He didn't and couldn't know where the signal would come from or what form it would take. What was he to do when the signal came? He finished the tea and sat staring out over the sea, fighting the weariness that was dropping like heavy fog upon his senses, and trying to decide.

As the VC10 howled westward through the upper atmosphere Gawthorpe had long given up his pretence of trying to read. The big quiet jet was in VIP-rig and the Foreign Secretary and three of his senior officials were conferring in the partitioned tail-section cabin. Elsewhere on the plane, members of the British delegation to the Pacific talks were passing the nine hours in their various ways, working on papers, playing bridge, drinking Scotch, reading whodunits. Gawthorpe's unopened briefcase lay on the empty seat beside him; an unread novel rested on it. Gawthorpe himself kept his eyes on the door leading to the flight deck. Before he'd left London there had been time to send off a message to Elizabeth Donald in Vancouver, informing her of his impending arrival and demanding assistance. If she received further information from Calder, it would be radioed to the plane, but though radio messages passed in a steady stream from the flight deck to the VIP cabin, none had arrived for Gawthorpe.

He glanced endlessly at his watch, willing the time to pass with the inevitable result that it dragged leadenly by. Nine hours to Vancouver meant arrival at 11 a.m. local time, and by then Calder would have been chasing those logs for twenty-four hours. Plenty of time for trouble; plenty of time for as resourceful and determined an operative as Calder to shovel any amount of chestnuts into the fire. The alternatives were simple and stark; either Calder was right out of it, because he was injured or dead, or Calder was in up to his neck. Briefly Gawthorpe caught himself hoping the first was true. Dead, Calder was no problem. Alive he was big trouble. He stilled the thought, angry with himself. It was necessary, sometimes, to write off human life, but he had always hated it.

He watched a slim young man with a slimmer gold watch chain and a Balliol tie emerge from the flight-deck door holding paper in a delicate hand and move down the long cabin towards the tail. Still no bloody news and they'd be there in two hours.

'Care for a drink, sir?' The white-jacketed senior flight steward stood in the gangway beside him.

'No.'

'Very good, sir.'

'On second thoughts,' Gawthorpe said, 'I will. I'll have a large Scotch.'

'Water, sir? Soda?'

'Just the Scotch.' He'd avoided drinking since take-off, but the strain was getting to him and when the whisky arrived he poured it down his throat, put his glass on the seat-table and wondered again whether he was over the hill. The need for whisky, the missing of occasional if unimportant details, were bad signs. Intelligence departments should not get themselves into this kind of mess. Success should be clean, failure clear, fail-safe planning constant. And they hadn't been. As a result he was sitting on top of an explosive mess he could do nothing to defuse.

An hour before landing, the signal came from Elizabeth Donald: 'Arrangements made. Car at Sea Island. No further signal.'

Gawthorpe turned and beckoned and David Norton slid into the aisle seat.

'Bad news?'

'Not good. She's organized a boat but there's no word from Calder.'

'There's still time.'

'Don't feed me bloody bromides, David. You know what Calder's like. If he's alive he's after them like an Airedale terrier.'

'Do you think he is?'

Gawthorpe nodded grimly. 'Yes. I do think he is. I can feel it. He may have paralysis of his dialling finger, but I'm damn sure the rest of him's ticking. He's a dangerous man is Jim Calder, right this moment.'

'Then what – ?' David Norton began. But the sentence was cut off as the Foreign Office man in the Balliol tie materialized in the gangway beside him, leaning forward with a kind of deferential arrogance.

'The Foreign Secretary wishes to speak to you, sir.'

Gawthorpe grimaced, rose reluctantly and walked stiffly back towards the tail.

'I am informed there's no news.' The minister's grey eyes looked at Gawthorpe levelly.

'None.'

'What do you propose?'

'I have a boat waiting, sir. I'm going to try to find him. Head him off if I can.'

'How, if you have no idea where he is?'

'I have to assume the Russian group is making for the *Suvarov*, sir. That's where I start.'

Gawthorpe watched the corners of the Foreign Secretary's

mouth deepen in irritation. There was a long, cold pause before
the words came. 'I have very little faith that you can succeed.
If you can, of course, so much the better. But the priorities are
clear. First, the Canadians must in no circumstances know
what is happening. I will not have this conference wrecked.
Your agent Calder is actively endangering it and that cannot be
permitted. I propose to inform Mr Gromyko personally of
what has happened so that his people can take whatever action
is necessary. And you, Gawthorpe, will give them any assistance
within your power. Always assuming – ' the thin voice was
cutting – 'that anything at all now lies within your control. Is
that clear?'

Gawthorpe winced. 'It's clear, sir.'

'Very well.'

A few hours earlier, as the gaping, island-studded mouth of
Howe Sound began to open beside him, Colonel Belyaev had
changed his mind. He'd spent three hours alone on the white
cruiser's deck, three hours of attentive searching of the waters
of Georgia Strait, three hours in which the antennae of his
nervous system had received no impression that was not reassuring. In those three hours he had begun to feel first that
he was perhaps being over-suspicious, later that the operation
was going smoothly and finally he had become certain that the
switch at Trail Bay had shaken off any pursuit. There had been
no aeroplanes, no fussy launches, nothing but the gentle chop
of the sea in the peaceful night.

Only three things now remained to be done; the release of
the little log raft; its pick-up by the tugboat and the final
casting loose close to the *Suvarov*. The release and pick-up
could be done now or later and he had intended to wait until
close to dawn, but the thought now came to him that on the
tugboat towing the big raft up ahead, a new watch well before
dawn might check the raft carefully. It was doubtful whether
they'd notice the few extra logs across almost a mile of sea.
But they might. So sense dictated the switch now. He con-
sidered his decision briefly. There were no obvious snags; in
fact there were no snags at all.

He called below for the walkie-talkie handset and ordered the tugboat whose course paralleled his own a mile and a half away to close up, then went below and switched the navigation lights on and off five times in the prearranged signal to the frogman.

XIX

For Calder, too, the last hours had passed quietly and slowly. He'd been warmer in the wetsuit and an hour-long battle with increasingly heavy eyelids had been won at last by the simple means of dowsing head and neck with cold sea water. He sat quietly on the big raft, waiting for a signal of some kind. For a while, after he'd tipped the frogman's body over the side, he'd been worried that the following boat might have found it, but there had been no halt.

When the signal came, he did not at first recognize it. The flicker of red and green lights could have had any number of causes from a faulty circuit to too much smoke from a funnel. Only when he noticed that the second pair of lights were moving appreciably nearer, did he connect the two things.

Should he reply to the signal? Since the toolbag he'd found contained a torch, it seemed likely. But what should the signal be? He waited. If he failed to reply, another signal would presumably be sent to him. Yes, there it was. He counted five flashes of navigation lights. He flashed the green-shaded torchlight five times, then went to work on the shackle bolt. Unfastening it took less than a minute. All that remained was to tap the bolt free and the little raft would be released and drift clear. He hesitated, knowing what he must do, but reluctant to commit himself finally. The temptation to remain on the big raft and be transported safely away was almost irresistible. But if he did, he would leave his mission incomplete, would be able to report only that the Russians had succeeded in transporting their logs and whatever they contained. He'd been instructed to find out what was going on, and there was only one way of doing it – he must stay with the small raft.

He put the toolbag in the dinghy, pulled the dinghy to the raft's edge and launched it, then tapped the bolt free, leaning away in case the released cable whipped. But it didn't, it merely slid away beneath the water. Calder slid in after it, picked up the dinghy's dangling painter, and swam towards the little raft. He knew he ought to ditch the dinghy, but couldn't bring himself to do it. Instead he towed it to the raft, tied the painter to the after end of the containing frame, and by the time the approaching boat was close enough to see anything, was himself within the frame, in the space between the front pole and the logs themselves. He watched cautiously as the lights became a tugboat, manoeuvring close to the raft. Then a man appeared on her side with a boathook and began to fish for the towline. When it was up and tied, Calder realized suddenly that the man was shouting and that the rubber of his own helmet was deadening the sound. He peeled the helmet back and listened.

'Anybody there? C'mon, for Chrissake! We ain't got all day. C'mon.'

Calder's scalp prickled. The voice was Canadian or American!

'Jesus Christ, move – wherever you are!'

Calder stayed where he was, motionless. Canadians! What the hell were Canadians doing here? He was still wondering when the light snapped on, spotlighting his helmeted head before he had time to duck.

'What the hell you doin'! C'mon!'

It was impossible now to pretend he hadn't heard, to hide, to play possum. Calder shouted, 'Checking the line.'

'Line's okay. Get aboard here!'

He ducked beneath the pole and swam slowly across the intervening water to the little midships ladder, wishing desperately that he had a weapon of some kind, that the knife had not been lost. This was the end of the road. Whether these men were Canadians or Russians, he was finished. If Canadian agents had somehow got in on the act, they'd clap him in irons faster than that just to show how independent they were. If they were Russians, they'd either kill him here or take him aboard the cruiser.

The only hope was that they didn't yet know who he was and the helmet and face-mask concealed his face effectively. Calder slid off the flippers, hooked the loops over his wrist and apprehensively climbed the ladder. There was no helping hand nor, when he arrived on deck, was anybody waiting for him. The engines throbbed as the tugboat got under way and he stood alone and baffled on the deckboards.

After a moment the wheelhouse door opened and a head appeared, framed in the light. 'There's food below if you want it. Help yourself.' Then the door closed again.

After that nobody came near him. An hour later, with food inside him, he thought he'd worked it out. Licences would be required to tow logs so the Russians had hired themselves a duly licensed towboat skipper. But did the skipper know what he was towing or who his masters were? Almost certainly, the answer to the first question was no and to the second, yes. Calder had enough experience of the KGB to know how tightly their operations were buttoned. These Canadians would be under duress of some kind. He was certain by now that they were not Canadian Government agents; the way they left him alone was proof enough of that.

Still in his wetsuit and by now sweating freely, Calder tucked a kitchen knife in his belt and went on deck. The sky was beginning to lighten and low clouds were glowing in the eastern sky. Soon it would be daylight and tugboat and log raft were now well off shore; they'd been moving away from the coast while he was below. Why? For a while he stared ahead, then turned and made his way aft and watched the raft moving gently forward on the end of the towline. Beyond it, perhaps a mile back, a white cabin cruiser seemed to be following and he watched that, too, wondering whether it had been the cruiser's lights, signalling earlier. It seemed likely. Other waterborne traffic was visible here and there, but the cruiser alone was maintaining station.

He heard the click of the wheelhouse door and footsteps on the deckboards and half-turned, fear prickling at his neck, but the man looked unconcerned and was going below.

Calder risked it. 'Where are we?' he called.

The man stopped and pointed. 'Point Atkinson over there,' then went below.

Calder looked at his breathing pack, still on the deck where he'd left it. How far to land? Four miles, perhaps. He was sickeningly aware this weird hiatus couldn't go on. Sooner or later they'd be on to him, and when that happened he'd have to get into the water fast.

Minute by minute, now, the light was improving. Vancouver must lie almost dead ahead but was shrouded still in a heavy morning mist. All the same, Vancouver was clearly where the boat was going. Point Atkinson was a few miles ahead off the port bow. another headland lay to starboard and the towboat was on a heading between them into Burrard Inlet. The Russian ship would be in there. Calder stared ahead, but the ship was still invisible in the mist. He glanced back at the following boat and realized with a sudden start that it was closer, a good deal closer, and moving quickly, directly towards the raft.

Quickly he buckled on his breathing pack, checked the valves, moved to the midships ladder and lowered himself into the water. Then, ducking beneath the surface, he swam in a rapid semicircle that would take him clear of the screws and waited for the raft to pass above him.

Five green flashes had been the wrong signal. There should have been two, followed by two more, but Belyaev knew well enough that signalling with torches was a clumsy business. Probably there had been an accidental touch of the flash button to make up the five flashes. But, looking back on it now, there was something else. The first signal had not drawn a response, and Belyaev had assumed the frogman was either resting or simply looking the other way. The second signal had drawn an inaccurate response. Then the tugboat's spotlight had shone briefly. At the time that, too, had seemed unimportant, a moment's guidance for the frogman.

Now, as he stared at a small dark shape bobbing behind the raft, Belyaev's mind assessed the tiny flaws in the operation. His binoculars brought tug and raft closer, but not close enough for the dark object to be picked out clearly.

He bent, slid the wheelhouse window open and told the man at the wheel, 'Closer to the raft.'

The cruiser picked up speed, closing the gap quickly, and Belyaev kept his binoculars trained on the black object, trying to decide what it was. By the time they'd gone half a mile, he knew. He climbed down from the wheelhouse roof and shouted angrily into the cabin. 'Did you take a rubber boat among those logs?'

'No, sir.'

'Or see one?'

'No.'

'There's one there now.' Belyaev thought for a moment, then said over his shoulder to the man at the wheel, 'Go alongside.'

The man hesitated. 'You said we should stay –'

'Go alongside. Do it!'

Belyaev went back on deck, watching the gap close. As the cruiser passed the raft, slowing to come alongside the tugboat, he counted the log bundles carefully. Still six. That, at least, was something.

Then the cruiser was alongside, a mere ten feet separating the two vessels. He waited and the tugboat skipper came out on deck.

'Where's my man?' Belyaev shouted.

'He's below.'

'Get him.'

The Canadian shrugged and disappeared. When he returned a moment later, his expression had changed. 'He's not there.'

Belyaev felt his guts contract. Something *was* wrong. 'When did you last see him?'

'Half an hour. No more.'

'You're sure he's gone?'

'Sure I'm sure. His aqualung's gone too.'

Quickly Belyaev glanced round him. In any direction it was a long swim to shore and the only other things near at hand were the raft and his own white cruiser.

'Describe him to me,' he yelled.

'Took no notice. Five-ten maybe, brown hair.' The man grinned unhelpfully. 'He was wearing a rubber suit.'

So, Belyaev thought, with mounting horror, another frog-man *had* come on the scene from somewhere. He'd come out of the night, somehow. Belyaev's own man had been a slim, fair, wiry Ukrainian, so there was no possibility of error and even less of accident; the absent aqualung proved that.

Belyaev looked grimly at the raft. The man must be there, not on the raft or he'd be visible, but underneath; there was nowhere else he could be. Who the hell was he? Was he alone? What did he intend to do?

Belyaev went below. 'There's a man under the raft,' he said. 'Find him.' He took the wheel himself and watched the two men struggling into their wetsuits.

'Kill him, sir? Or – '

'If you can get him alive,' Belyaev said harshly, 'do so. Otherwise kill him. But do *not* allow him to escape.'

XX

From beneath the raft, Calder watched the white hull and twin screws of the cabin cruiser sliding past a dozen yards away. Now the two vessels were so close, the connection between them was established. The cruiser must have approached either to offer some support or to investigate. It was time to get away. Well away. But first there was a job to do.

Calder swam quickly to the rear of the raft where, from below, the empty rubber dinghy made a black shape on the silver undersurface. He used the kitchen knife he had stolen to hack a small hold in the rubber sheeting. The base of the dinghy was not air-filled, so the buoyancy would not be affected. Then, cautiously, he reached into the hole and dragged the tool bag down through it into the water. He attached the bag to his belt and remained still in the water, a few feet below the surface, watching the raft disappear.

Inevitably, now, the raft would be searched, above and below the water; he must be far enough away for the trail of bubbles from his breathing apparatus not to be spotted. After a couple of minutes, he turned and swam steadily away two hundred yards or so. Now, unless he was desperately unlucky, he would not be seen. At this distance the bubbles would be dissipated in the general water movement. But he was in a dangerous situation. He no longer knew with any accuracy his position in relation to the raft and if it continued to move away from him he was unlikely to be able to catch up. Which would leave him with a swim of several miles, far beyond his capabilities.

The minutes dragged agonizingly by. Calder had no way of knowing what was going on; all he could do was to keep turning in the water, inspecting the sea area that lay within the limits of his vision. That, at least, remained empty.

But then, through the water, he felt the throb of engines coming closer. Quickly he kicked himself down a few more feet, then stared upward, watching the surface, as the white hull and turning propellers passed almost directly above him. His heart was thumping. There was no way they could have seen him, but the white cruiser was certainly searching. Did that mean the raft had stopped in the water? An idea was germinating in his mind. To use it he'd have to return to the raft, but if he put his head above the surface to locate the raft, he'd be finished.

The vibration from the cruiser's engines had disappeared, but Calder continued to turn slowly, scanning his own patch of water. Minutes passed as he struggled to find an answer to his problem, minutes in which air and strength were used, minutes in which no solution appeared. Then, turning again, his body froze as he glimpsed a thin dark shape almost at the limit of his vision.

A frogman! He turned to race away, but another quick glance stopped him. The shape wasn't a frogman. It wasn't moving; it was too long and too rigid. Instead of swimming away, he came cautiously towards the object, which turned out to be a sixteen-foot log, waterlogged, butt end low in the water, the thinner end just breaking the surface. It was a deadhead, one of the thousands of logs that escape each year from log booms and infest the British Columbia coastal waters. Calder moved into position behind it, watching the log's movement, seeing its tip break the surface in the little wave troughs. Well, it would have to do. He came carefully close to the surface and waited, timing his movement. One glance would be enough.

Gripping the log, he pushed his head above the surface, then ducked under again quickly. Damn! He'd been facing the wrong way. All that turning in the water had disorientated him. Once more, then . . .

The second brief look told him more than he could have hoped for. Tug and raft lay dead in the water two or three hundred yards away and beside them a frogman was climbing over the side of the white cruiser. It seemed the search was over.

Ducking deeper in the water, he began to swim back towards the raft, but a couple of minutes later again he felt engine vibrations through the water. Somebody must have seen him and be coming to investigate. He dived deeper and swam more quickly, hoping they'd find the deadhead.

Two minutes later Colonel Belyaev was leaning over the side of the stopped white cruiser, prodding angrily at the sodden log with a boathook. He had been in no doubt about what he had seen. Twice a black, rubber clad head had bobbed above the surface. It hadn't appeared before and it hadn't appeared since. Now he pushed the deadhead beneath the surface, released the pressure, and watched it come up sluggishly. This was the spot where the head, if it *had* been a head, had appeared. Now there was only this damned log to feed his doubts.

No, he decided. Not doubts. There was too much evidence for doubt. The empty dinghy that had appeared out of nowhere, the disappearing frogman, the seaplane whose shadow on the clouds still haunted him. Whether or not a frogman had been here, on this spot, there was somebody about somewhere. When in doubt, he thought, presume enemy action.

Now, for almost the first time in a lifetime spent within rigid guidelines and privileged situations, Colonel Belyaev was becoming increasingly uncertain what action to take. His schedule was out; the plan demanded release of the log raft close to the *Suvarov* in darkness, preferably in the early hours of the morning, but the change-over at Trail Bay had delayed matters, and the time spent here on a fruitless search had delayed them even more. It was true the delay was not fatal; not necessarily even dangerous. But in Belyaev's experience it was dangerous to depart from plans. Adaptation and re-adaptation led to error.

He gave the deadhead a final disgusted push, straightened, and waved to the tugboat to proceed. Then he went back to the wheel and angrily gunned the white cruiser forward towards the mouth of Burrard Inlet. The question was whether to take the log raft in now or wait through the day until the approach could be made under a decent blanket of darkness. Either way, there were risks. Delivering the logs in daylight meant they would probably be seen; to wait for darkness gave whoever was working against him several hours to sabotage the operation. How much did it matter if the handover were seen? If the logs were taken in from seaward of the *Suvarov* and handled quickly and efficiently by the warship's crew, probably not much. But there was no margin for error.

Belyaev realized suddenly that the cruiser's windscreen was becoming spotted with rain which quickly grew heavier, cutting visibility. He slipped the leather loop over a wheel-spoke, opened a side window, and waited for the city and the warship to appear. The thickening rainladen mist, at least, was a help. Provided it did not thicken too much, the mist would aid a daylight approach to the *Suvarov*.

She'd be visible soon . . . Yes, there she was! He changed course a little towards the dim grey outline of the warship, now so near. In a few hours, a *very* few hours, the operation ought to be over and he could relax.

But as he came closer he saw a sight that tightened his stomach in fury. There was a protective ring round the *Suvarov*, a protective ring that would be impossible to pene-trate: half the boats in Vancouver seemed to be out on the waters of English Bay, circling the warship like minnows round a tethered shark. There were powered boats, fishing boats, even a few larger vessels nosing cautiously closer for a look. If the tugboat tried to tow the log raft through them, she'd have an audience of several hundred, watching every move with interest.

Seething, he moved in among the circling craft. He must let the *Suvarov* know he was there, waiting. Why in hell hadn't this been thought of, he wondered angrily. Sightseers were the one thing they'd left out of their planning. Semichastny, the fool, hadn't thought of them; nor had the Soviet Navy people, who must have known what would happen; they'd sailed into enough foreign ports!

Belyaev circled for an hour in the thickening mist, coming unobtrusively closer to the warship's side until a wave of recognition from her deck confirmed that he had been seen. Meeting the watchkeeper's downward stare, he pointed to the circling armada of boats and shrugged, then turned and moved carefully among the milling craft, back the way he had come. Unless something could be done to clear the boats, it would be necessary to wait until dark.

'Colonel Belyaev is here, Comrade Minister,' Vice-Admiral Tolstikov reported to Gromyko the moment Belyaev's white cruiser was spotted.

'Good.'

'Not good, I'm afraid,' Tolstikov walked to the curtained ports of the captain's cabin. 'We are surrounded by small vessels. Yachts, pleasure boats.'

Gromyko rose and joined him, looking out. 'Can we clear them?'

'No. *We* can not. Probably they will disperse of their own accord when darkness comes. Not before.'

'If I were to make a request . . . ?'

Tolstikov nodded. 'Perhaps, Comrade Minister.'

'Give me a reason for such a request. A reason that will be acceptable.'

Vice-Admiral Tolstikov eyed the milling boats. 'The mist is thickening. There could be collisions.'

Gromyko nodded. 'Get my interpreter. To whom do we make the request?'

'To the harbour authorities, Comrade Minister.'

'Explain,' Gromyko told his interpreter, 'that we have no objection to the actual presence of the boats. If the weather is good tomorrow, we shall have no objection then. We are merely concerned at the possibility of collisions. And be sure to give the harbourmaster my personal invitation to come aboard while we are here.'

Tolstikov smiled. 'The art of diplomacy, Comrade Minister.'

Gromyko did not smile back. 'It fails, Tolstikov. It fails very frequently.

Gawthorpe's Chriscraft came through First Narrows, beneath the Lions' Gate Bridge, to swing round the northern tip of the wooded peninsula of Stanley Park, and head south past the upthrusting Siwash rock into English Bay. At the wheel, David Norton said soberly at the sight of the boats, 'They'll have trouble getting through that lot!'

'Unless they already have,' Gawthorpe said sourly. 'And if they haven't, we've got to help. I never thought I'd see the day.'

'Want to have a look first?'

'We'd better. Don't hit anything.'

Norton took the Chriscraft in a slow circle round the *Suvarov*. The water was alive with craft, but it was soon obvious that no vessel towing logs was among them.

'What now?'

'When they come, it'll have to be from just about due west,' Gawthorpe said. 'Let's go hunting.'

XXI

The muscles of Calder's thighs already ached from the effort of the swim. A long time had passed since his legs had last needed to maintain the scissors motion at such speed and for so long, but it was essential to reach the tugboat before it was fully under way again. He wished he could surface, however briefly, to be sure of his direction, but dared not take the risk. He must be getting close now, surely. Anxiously he scanned the surface. Yes, there was the grey bottom of the tugboat, the screws already turning, chopping bubbles at her stern. He raced for her bow, sinking deeper to allow the tugboat to pass directly overhead. The thrum of the propellers vibrated at him through the water and he watched them go by, feeling the drag. Up a few feet now; there was the towline, ruler straight where it touched the surface; behind it the dark bulk of the raft slid towards him.

Calder pulled the kitchen knife from his belt and waited. It was on the cards that a frogman would be beneath the raft, even though he had seen one man leave the water. The raft was almost on him now and he searched the underside with his eyes, looking among the spaces between the log bundles for a darker shape. There was no one; at least, there was no one he could see. Calder relaxed a little and eased himself up through the water towards the rear of the raft.

Suddenly a hand snaked down savagely from above, ripped the breathing tube from his mouth, and went on to encircle his throat. Before Calder could even begin to defend himself, water flooded his mouth and nostrils. Half-choking, he sensed that his attacker was attempting to get behind him and kicked desperately upward, trying to turn his own body away from whatever weapon the other man might have. There was a clanking thud at his back as something struck the air cylinder, and Calder struggled desperately to free his neck, but couldn't. Opening his eyes, he saw a black-clad figure still above him and kicked again and again, fighting to move upward. Already his lungs seemed balloon tight and with no purchase anywhere in the water, no resistance to lever against, he was helpless. He kicked his body frantically round, bending his head, trying to sink his teeth into that choking arm. Christ! He had a knife; he'd forgotten the knife! He stabbed upward hard and missed, then stabbed again, feeling the blade scrape across something. His flailing left arm suddenly found and gripped a face mask and he wrenched at it frantically. Something slid across his ribs, almost lightly, but the line of its passage turned, a second later, to pain and he knew he'd been cut. The arm – he must get the arm! He turned the knife in his hand and stabbed towards his own throat, feeling the knife-blade strike bone. Instantly the pressure was eased and Calder kicked himself desperately away. Now, at least, he could see the frogman, but his breath was almost gone and the pain of the cut was suddenly intense in the salt water. A stream of bubbles flying past his face told him the breathing apparatus was still working and he jammed the mouthpiece into place. Swallowing the water in his mouth, he could breathe again, and now the fight was more even. The other man was coming for him again, knife held in his right hand, left arm trailing. Calder kicked upwards towards the logs above, turned as his hands touched them and used his feet to push him downward again hard, body rigid, knife pointed directly at the frogman's side. The frogman's knife arm came up quickly to deflect the lunge, and Calder grabbed for the wrist, slicing at the airline. A wrench of the knife-blade and the line streamed bubbles and the man twisted in sudden panic. Calder thrust again and missed. The frogman writhed desperately as Calder lunged a second time and felt the blow hit. Again. And again. Suddenly the frogman was writhing no longer, his body loose in the water, the movements of his limbs dictated only by the water itself. It was over.

Wearily Calder turned to follow the raft that was now gliding away above him. Gripping the binding wire of one of the log bundles, he simply hung on, allowing himself to be dragged unresisting through the water, until the trembling of his body began to ease. He was losing blood, but how badly? There was no way of knowing, and nothing he could do about it. He opened the neck of the toolbag and rummaged one-handed inside it searching for the hacksaw.

Half an hour later, one of the binding wires was severed and he had moved forward and was sawing tiredly at the other. Above him lay one of the huge logs and he was almost sure that, as the wire went, the log would come down on him. Still he sawed on. If he could release one log from the raft . . .

The wire parted nastily, flicking his arm and momentarily

207

paralysing it, and the log rasped down. He watched it dumbly, knowing that if it hit him the blow would almost certainly be the end of it. But it didn't; the log merely floated lower in the water. Was it low enough to pass beneath the back pole of the framework? He moved aft to look and winced in disappointment. The end of the floating log remained butted firmly against the back pole and there was no way Calder could conceivably pull it down far enough to free it.

That left only one other way; to break the framework, setting all the logs free. His strength ebbing fast, Calder worked his way to the rear corner, looked at the steel linkage and felt a surge of relief. If he'd had to use the hacksaw the cut would have taken forever, but the linkage was bolted. He found the spanner in his bag and began to slacken the bolt.

In rapidly thickening fog, Gawthorpe's Chriscraft was going fast, zig-zagging dangerous across the mouth of Burrard Inlet. Gawthorpe stood peering into the enclosing vapour as the wipers swung endlessly across the glass screen. At the wheel David Norton, pale-faced and concentrating hard, had one hand hovering near the throttle levers in case the speeding boat suddenly sighted something dead ahead and had to take rapid action to try to avoid a collision.

'They could sneak the QE Two past in this,' Norton muttered. It's perfect for them.'"

'Let's hope it stays perfect,' Gawthorpe said.

Suddenly, deafeningly, a foghorn boomed and the great grey side of a merchant ship seemed to race towards them out of the mist. Norton's hand flew to shut off power to the port screw and the Chriscraft almost banked away, missing the ship by a mere twenty feet, her deck canting wildly.

'Too fast. We'll hit something,' Norton said.

'Keep going, man.' Gawthorpe's heavy jaw jutted forward. 'We're going to keep looking till we bloody well find them.'

They were making their fourth crossing when Gawthorpe said suddenly, 'What's that?'

Norton squinted in the direction of Gawthorpe's pointing finger. 'Small boat, I think.'

'Let's see.'

The Chriscraft swung rapidly round and surged after it.

'It's just a cabin cruiser,' Norton said as the boat came into view.

'What the hell's he doing out on the water in weather like this?' Gawthorpe demanded.

The Chriscraft tore past it, into the fog.

'I'll tell you what he's doing. He's going fast,' Norton said. 'Too fast in this stuff. Like us.'

'Let's have another look, then.'

When the Chriscraft returned, the cruiser had vanished.

'Changed course,' Gawthorpe said. 'Why would he do that?'

'To avoid maniacs like us, tearing round in the fog,' Norton said tightly. 'I'd do the same myself.' He brought the boat round again and a moment later said suddenly, 'There's his wake. He's bending back again. Do we follow?'

'It's a thin chance. No. Go past him.'

Increasing speed, Norton raced after the cruiser. As it hove out of the fog, they could see a man standing at the stern, watching their approach.

Visibility was no more than a hundred yards now, and decreasing, as the cruiser slid out of sight behind them.

Norton shook his head. 'It's getting hopeless.'

'Sound the hooter. See if we get any foghorns back.'

They hooted and listened, hooted and listened as the Chriscraft raced, almost at random now, over the fog-shrouded water. There was no response.

'If we only had radar,' Norton said.

'We haven't. Let's hope we've got luck instead.'

Twenty minutes later they saw the white cruiser again, coming on it suddenly. 'That bloke,' Norton said, 'seems to be the only one on the water.'

'He bloody well isn't, David. What's walkie-talkie range?'

'Two miles perhaps. Maybe three.'

'He was talking to somebody on a hand set. Come round in a circle and follow his wake.'

Belyaev watched the big power cruiser flash past for the third time, and frowned. The cruiser was quite clearly a pleasure craft, owned no doubt by some wealthy Canadian. But why on earth was it tearing round Georgia Strait so lethally in the thick fog blanket?

He spoke into the handset. 'Any trouble?'

'No. Everything's quiet. Fog's thick.'

The signal strength was increasing and Belyaev knew he was getting close. He cut speed a little. 'Have you got me on radar?' he said into the walkie-talkie.

'Yes. You're a mile to starboard.'

'I'm coming in.' Belyaev spun the wheel, bringing the white cruiser round sharply. 'Guide me closer.'

'Okay. Half a mile. Six hundred yards . . . five hundred. Four. Cut your speed. We're about dead ahead of you.'

Belyaev nosed forward, waiting anxiously for the tugboat to emerge from the murk.

'Two hundred yards,' said the voice in his handset. 'Keep coming.'

The white cruiser's speed was cut right back as Belyaev searched the vapour for the grey shape of the tugboat. He must be very close now . . . Then he saw it, came round and moved alongside the log raft. The raft looked all right. He wondered about the man he'd ordered to remain beneath it.

With the bolt unscrewed almost to the last thread, Calder waited, clinging grimly to the raft and debating with himself when to complete the job. At the rear of the raft he'd been out of sight of the tugboat as he worked, hidden behind the big logs. Now he was ready, and the fog was both a blessing and a curse. If he could once escape into it, he'd take a lot of finding; equally, though, he wouldn't have the faintest idea which way to go. It was a long time since he'd seen Point Atkinson ahead, and though the raft had moved slowly, it must now be either abreast of or past the headland. He was still bleeding from the cut across his ribs and beginning to feel very cold. There wasn't a lot of strength left.

Again he ducked out from his shelter and looked round cautiously. Still nothing visible except the tugboat. Should he go, then? He fingered the bolt hesitantly, then came to a decision. He *must* go now, while strength remained for the sudden frantic effort he needed. Hell! What was that? He saw the white cruiser nose slowly out of the fog and ducked quickly into concealment. A minute or so later, he watched the cruiser's bottom come closer, slow briefly, then move ahead. Damn! He should have been away before she returned. He allowed time for her to move away, before ducking out again. The cruiser was alongside the tug; this was probably his last chance.

Quickly, Calder checked that the dinghy's painter was tied securely to the strapping band of the log. Then, with numb fingers, he unwound the last threads of the bolt and released the coupling. Slowly, pivoting on the remaining fastening, the end pole swung free, opening a gate through which the logs could escape. One by one they began to move backward, but Calder was concerned about only one: the big log which, without its support logs, now floated very low in the water.

With a painful heave, Calder pulled his tired body into the dinghy, then slipped the oars through the rubber rowlocks and began to heave on them. Could he even move the massive log? Or would its weight, huge even in the water, act as an anchor that would hold him, still and exposed?

It *was* moving; slowly and sluggishly, but it was already a yard away from the others. Two yards. He bent his back desperately at the oars. Another foot, another two feet, another yard. Slowly he was easing it away, and the tugboat was gliding ahead into the mist. All he needed was a minute. Just one more minute and the tug would be out of sight in the fog. But they must know, surely! They must *feel* the difference as the raft broke up. Oh God! Another stroke. Another. Heave!

Then he heard the shout. The tug was now little more than a grey outline. A few more seconds and he'd have been clean away. Through the fog he heard the sudden roar of the cruiser's engines, and pulled frantically on the oars, straining for the last few yards that would mean concealment in the shrouding grey vapour . . .

'There!' David Norton said. 'A tug.'

'And it's towing logs,' Gawthorpe's voice was husky with tension and he cleared his throat noisily. 'Go closer.' He climbed quickly on deck, crouching by the side window, seeking clearer vision than the glass screen afforded. The Chriscraft eased through the water towards the shadowy shape ahead, then Gawthorpe said suddenly, 'There are logs all over the water! What the hell's – '

Norton interrupted sharply. 'There's a man in a rubber dinghy. A frogman, for God's sake!'

'Where?'

'Over there.'

Gawthorpe stood straight and saw him. He said with sudden intuition. 'That could be Calder. Come round.'

'Right.' Norton turned the cruiser, heading towards the little dinghy.

'He's towing something,' Gawthorpe half-shouted. And as the Chriscraft went closer, 'It's a log he's pulling!'

'Is it Calder?'

'Hang on a moment.' Gawthorpe looked at the pale face framed in the black of the rubber helmet. 'It's Calder.' His voice rose to a shout. 'Calder! Jim Calder!'

'The raft's broken up!' The shout came from the tugboat.

Colonel Belyaev turned quickly to look back over the stern of the white cruiser, cursed and swung her round, gunning the engines. The broken framework of the boom trailed behind the tug, and beyond it the logs floated loose in the water, almost at the point where sea and fog met and merged. *The missiles were loose !* He brought the cruiser round in as tight a circle as her increasing acceleration would allow and glimpsed another shape low on the water and almost disappearing in the fog; a shape that moved: a man rowing.

Belyaev's mouth flattened angrily. So near, yet now the whole operation was in danger. Ignoring the logs, he pointed the cruiser's bow towards the rower. Whatever else happened, he meant to attend to the man.

Stern down, squatting on the powerful thrust of her diesels, the white cruiser raced towards the rowing man. Then, almost simultaneously, his eyes flickering from one to the other, Belyaev saw two things: the log the man was towing – and another boat, a big boat, the same damned boat that he'd encountered three times earlier.

And it was closer to the dinghy than he was! Belyaev decided instantly that the man was not to be saved. Not now. His eyes measured the distances and the angles as the cruiser raced closer. Only a few feet separated dinghy and log, but he wouldn't hit the log. He'd smash straight into the dinghy and if the impact alone didn't kill the man in it, the propellers would rip him to pieces.

'That boat,' Gawthorpe said in alarm. 'It's going to run him down. Get between them!'

Norton's hand snapped down to the throttle levers.

Calder had stopped rowing. What energy remained had been drained instantly by the despair that flooded over him as he saw the cruiser turn to come after him. He sat still as it roared towards him, knowing no effort of his could take him out of its path; not with tons of log dragging against his strength. They'd get him now, log and all. They'd get away with the whole thing. Leadenly he watched the cruiser rush towards him. Then, suddenly, he knew he wasn't going to be captured. He was going to be killed. The cruiser intended to smash into him at full speed. He tried to rise, to hurl himself over the side into the water, but there was no longer even the strength for that and he sagged back on to the dinghy's seat.

Then, astonishingly, he heard somebody shout his name and something slid between him and the racing cruiser; something big, and only a few yards away. Where had it come from? Where the hell had *that* come from!

Calder watched the side of the big boat lurch suddenly and drunkenly towards him, heeled over by the crashing impact. He thought it was going to roll over on top of him, but the roll stopped short of that. For a second the boat remained still, looming above him, and he glimpsed at a window a face he thought he recognized. It couldn't be. Surely it couldn't . . . He had a momentary impression of sheeting flame, then the deck of the boat seemed to disintegrate and Calder found himself on his back, dazed, in the bottom of the dinghy.

Blinking, he came upright again. He could have been flattened only for seconds, but already the boats were sinking, both of them, the sea sluicing aboard. It was terrifyingly fast: one moment they were still there on the surface, the next there was only the final triumphant whirl of water and a few forlorn bits of debris floating nearby. Calder waited briefly, but nobody surfaced.

He looked around him then. The tugboat was invisible in the fog. He was alone now, with just the dinghy and the log. And the wound, still seeping blood, on his ribcage.

He took up the oars again and began to paddle weakly through the fog. To his surprise, he found a rhythm of a kind and the big log obediently, if very slowly, followed.

The call the British Foreign Secretary paid to the *Suvarov* soon after his arrival in Vancouver, was described to the Press as a courtesy visit. On deck he was greeted by Andrei Gromyko who noted with satisfaction that the small boats were now gone.

In the captain's small cabin, the Foreign Secretary said, 'I heard of your indisposition. I trust it is now cleared up.'

'Thank you,' Gromyko replied. 'It was merely inconvenient.'

'That is good news,' the Foreign Secretary said. 'I was naturally concerned about the conference.'

'I, too.'

'Yes.' The Foreign Secretary paused. 'It seemed, for a while, that the conference might be in danger.'

'From my indisposition? I think not.'

'Not entirely from your indisposition.' The Foreign Secretary met and held Gromyko's eye. 'One always fears embarrassing incidents. You and I have some experience.'

'We have,' Gromyko agreed. His eyes were stony.

'Her Majesty's Government has gone to some lengths to avoid any such problem. Only today I gave the strictest orders.'

'I have issued similar orders myself.'

'Good, good. The conference is, after all, about co-operation. It is not easy always, to persuade all the machinery of state of the need for it. However, there are times when we need to assist one another. Don't you agree?'

'I am pleased to hear your expressions of goodwill.'

'We are, after all, on neutral ground. That makes extreme caution necessary.'

'It does indeed. The Soviet Union appreciates the concern of Her Majesty's Government.'

'Yes.' The Foreign Secretary rose. 'I hope now that we shall all enjoy plain sailing. I am glad to see you fully restored.'

The tide, flowing slowly northward from Juan de Fuca Strait, gave Calder some slight assistance, carrying him gradually towards the northern shore of Burrard Inlet, but he was unaware of the one-and-a-half knot current and was consequently surprised when the deserted sandy beach crunched suddenly against the dinghy's nose in the late afternoon. Wearily he stepped over the side into the shallow water and pulled the dinghy up the beach as far as the short painter would allow. He straightened stiffly, looked at the log as it rolled gently in the shallows, and wondered briefly whether he dare leave it.

Deciding he had no alternative, he walked up the beach, found himself on short springy grass, and looked for some clue as to where he might be. Two hundred yards farther on, a small triangular flag appeared ahead, hanging limply in the fog, and on the flag was a number. He was on one of the greens of a golf course. It was half an hour before he staggered into the clubhouse and asked to use the telephone. The steward's eyes widened at the sight of the haggard, exhausted figure in a wetsuit, but he led him to the telephone, and Calder asked the operator to connect him with Elizabeth Donald's number.

'Calder here,' he said 'I – '

She interrupted him, her tone stiff with reproof. 'You failed to keep contact.'

'It wasn't possible.'

'Your instructions have been changed,' she said. 'Most urgently. You must co-operate with our friends in their undertaking.'

Calder said wearily, 'It's too late. I've got one.'

'A log?'

'Yes.'

'You'll have to wait until I can contact Mr Gawthorpe.'

'In London?'

'Here in Vancouver.'

Calder sighed. He had not been mistaken. 'He's dead.'

There was a stupefied silence for a moment at the other end of the line. Then, 'you're sure?'

'I'm sure. The boat blew up. The log is on a beach near West Vancouver Golf Club. I'm going back to it now. Somebody had better come and get me.' He hung up, turned, thanked the wide-eyed steward again, and staggered off across the course.

At four-thirty, the tugboat slid out of the fog on the seaward side of the *Suvarov* and was spotted instantly by the stern watch. As the tug slid slowly past the warship's rearing side, the towline was slipped and the little raft drifted on a few yards before losing way. The underwater door of a loading bay opened in the cruiser's side and frogmen swam out, attaching lines so the raft could be brought closer. In twelve minutes the logs lay within the *Suvarov*.

'There are,' reported Vice-Admiral Tolstikov, 'only five missiles.'

'The sixth?' Gromyko asked quietly.

'Stolen. And Belyaev is dead. The story is confused, but it seems there was a frogman, also a boat of some kind. The tug heard an explosion.' He stopped suddenly under Gromyko's hard gaze.

'The British,' Gromyko said.

'I'm sorry.'

'The British.'

Tolstikov wanted to ask how he knew, but restrained the question.

'I should like to speak,' Gromyko said quietly, 'to the British Foreign Secretary. By telephone. Arrange it.'

'At once, comrade minister.'

'On second thoughts we shall in any case meet this evening. I shall wait.'

Between five thirty and eight p.m., a number of things happened. A small motor boat took Calder aboard from the beach in West Vancouver, and the log was taken in tow. It passed beneath Lions' Gate Bridge and was taken aboard a British timber ship in the harbour beyond First Narrows, where it was carefully cradled and tarpaulin screens were erected round it. Two undersea-warfare experts from the British conference delegation then arrived to examine it. They cut the binding ties and watched as a winch lifted away the upper half of the log, whistled in surprise at what they found, and reported back hurriedly to the delegation's headquarters at the Hotel Vancouver, where the Foreign Secretary was dressing for dinner. Within an hour, rocket experts from Hawker-Siddeley Dynamics and nuclear engineers from Harwell were being hauled from their beds in London to be flown urgently to Vancouver.

The pre-dinner reception lasted an hour. After a while, the British and Soviet Foreign Ministers were seen to be talking quietly together.

'Our natural concern,' Gromyko said, 'is for the safety of the city.'

'We shall certainly welcome technical assistance.'

'I thought I had understood earlier, that you would be helping *us*.'

The Foreign Secretary blinked mildly. 'Instead we seem to have been helping ourselves.' He turned, taking Gromyko's arm. 'There are, of course, one or two other points to take up later. Matters arising, so to speak. And, of course, the conference is safe. Now, have you met my wife . . . ?'

EPILOGUE

It would be convenient if the end of a sequence of events left no trailing strands. However, that seldom happens. People who were involved have lives to lead and jobs to do; they travel, are promoted and reconsider positions in the light of new situations. Also, sudden death leaves administrative problems in its wake.

'I walked past Oak Cottage today,' remarked Olive Suddards, wife of Police Constable 198 Suddards. 'They're still not back. Funny that is.'

'If there was any news, I'd be told,' her husband said stolidly. He was newly off-duty, eating his evening meal, and worried that a gang of teenage toughs might dislocate a village dance that night.

'You don't think you should find out?' She often had to nag him gently. 'There's the quarterly bills coming in. Telephone and electricity. They'll have to be paid.'

'After supper, then,' P.C. Suddards said. 'Give me half a chance.'

Fifteen hundred miles away, Lieutenant-General Zarubin, who had been several days trying, without evidence, to decide whether the disappearance of Igor Kovrenko from the London Trade Delegation was related to Operation Sword, or was a defection, or was simply a matter of a too-weak personality off on a spree, finally gave reluctant permission for an approach to be made to the British Foreign Office.

At low administrative levels, neither Suddards' nor Zarubin's questions were answerable. The result was that they filtered slowly upward until they reached levels where the names of Baxter and Kovrenko had been mentioned. But problems remained, caused by the deaths of Gawthorpe and Norton. There was no difficulty over Kovrenko's whereabouts; following his breakdown he had been transferred to the special wing of a military hospital in the Eastern Counties and there kept under sedation until further instructions were received from Gawthorpe personally. Kovrenko had not been forgotten. Rather, he had not been remembered.

Henry and Jane Baxter were another matter. In official minds they scarcely existed. Gawthorpe had only *deduced* that they had been used to coerce John Baxter, just as he had only *deduced* that John Baxter had been piloting the *Tyee* submersible. Like Zarubin he had had no evidence that could be called proof.

As a result, both sides were playing blind chess. Additionally, neither conceded precedence to unimportant individuals over affairs of state. It is almost certain that both British and Russians would have shrugged their respective shoulders if an Oxford don had not drunk far too much one night at High Table and mentioned, in support of an argument he was advancing, a brainwashing technique he knew about. A dozen people heard him, and thought little more about it. One, however, was very interested; he was a Marxist academic who had been recruited by Russian Intelligence in the thirties. His report of the conversation reached General Zarubin within thirty-six hours, arriving shortly after a Foreign Office assurance that nothing was known about Kovrenko, but that discreet police inquiries were being made. There was also a gentle Foreign Office request: if the Russians knew anything of the whereabouts of two missing British citizens, Henry and Jane Baxter, man and wife, information would be appreciated by Her Majesty's Government.

'Do they know?' Gromyko asked.

Zarubin shook his head. 'They can't. They may suppose, but that is all.'

'Exchange?'

'And reveal their techniques to us? No.' Zarubin spoke with certainty.

'But if it worked, useful?'

'Certainly.'

Even then the matter might have rested there, with delicate

feelers put out and rejected, if Kenneth Lavering had not privately told the chairman of Plaid-Cromwell Shipping the story of Baxter's disappearance. The chairman was a back-bench Conservative M.P., a director of many companies, and an almost apoplectic believer in the importance of the State supporting the individual instead of the other way around. He raised the matter with the Foreign Secretary personally in the House of Commons smoking room, was politely put off, and promptly and angrily threatened questions in the House, with the attendant publicity. Under his pressure, wheels began to turn.

Accordingly, one afternoon almost two weeks after the events in English Bay, and six days after the close of the Vancouver Conference, a charter flight landed at London (Gatwick) Airport bringing holidaymakers home from the Black Sea resort of Golden Sands. Aboard it were the Baxters, grief-stricken at the knowledge of John's presumed death, news of which had been given to them by a British diplomat when they were put ashore at the port of Constanta. They were taken, immediately on landing, to the Foreign Office, briefly met the Foreign Secretary himself, and left having promised to keep strictly to themselves what they were assured was a matter of profound importance to state security.

At roughly the same time as their plane landed, Igor Kovrenko took off from London (Heathrow) aboard a TU 104 jet of the Soviet state airline, Aeroflot. Ahead of him, he knew, lay debriefing by the First Chief Directorate of the KGB. Other passengers saw how he trembled, but affected not to notice.

Radio Operator Nikita Ivanov, having talked to Calder, was now ready to talk endlessly to anybody who would listen, on condition he was not returned to Russia. He had to be removed from Canada before he talked to, or even met, any Canadian official, however junior. Calder, the knife wound in his ribs stitched and strapped, flew again to Kitimat to collect him. Ivanov began his journey to Britain, cabin class, on the Peninsula and Oriental Steamship Company's liner *Orsova*. He was to be confined to his cabin throughout the voyage, but whenever the closed environment bothered him, he called up a mental picture of the harsh punishment barracks of the Soviet Pacific Fleet. The picture had a remarkably soothing effect upon his mild claustrophobia.

Duncan Kyle

'The outstanding thriller-writer discovery of the seventies.'
Evening News

WHITEOUT! 75p
A CAGE OF ICE 80p
FLIGHT INTO FEAR 80p
TERROR'S CRADLE 80p

Fontana Paperbacks

Fontana Paperbacks

Fontana is a leading paperback publisher of fiction and non-fiction, with authors ranging from Alistair MacLean, Agatha Christie and Desmond Bagley to Solzhenitsyn and Pasternak, from Gerald Durrell and Joy Adamson to the famous Modern Masters series.

In addition to a wide-ranging collection of internationally popular writers of fiction, Fontana also has an outstanding reputation for history, natural history, military history, psychology, psychiatry, politics, economics, religion and the social sciences.

All Fontana books are available at your bookshop or newsagent; or can be ordered direct. Just fill in the form and list the titles you want.

FONTANA BOOKS, Cash Sales Department, G.P.O. Box 29, Douglas, Isle of Man, British Isles. Please send purchase price, plus 8p per book. Customers outside the U.K. send purchase price, plus 10p per book. Cheque, postal or money order. No currency.

NAME (Block letters)

ADDRESS

While every effort is made to keep prices low, it is sometimes necessary to increase prices on short notice. Fontana Books reserve the right to show new retail prices on covers which may differ from those previously advertised in the text or elsewhere.